THE C

The Granite King

MARY WILLIAMS

WILLIAM KIMBER · LONDON

First published in 1982 by
WILLIAM KIMBER & CO. LIMITED
Godolphin House, 22a Queen Anne's Gate,
London SW1H 9AE

© Mary Williams, 1982
ISBN 0-7183-0049-1

Typeset by Scarborough Typesetting Services,
and printed and bound in Great Britain by
Biddles Limited, Guildford and Kings Lynn

To Amy, with love

Prelude

Fog shrouded the Cornish hills and lanes on an autumn night of 1857, when a coach slowly made its way from Penzance towards the opposite coast.

The lane it travelled was narrow and winding, cutting between steeply rising moorland hills for a distance of some miles. In a clear light the valley could be seen to be lush with thick undergrowth and verdure, rhododendrons, willow and twisted sloes − a strange contrast indeed to the barren heights where dolmens and distant mine-stacks stood stark against the sky. But on a night such as this all seemed spectral and unreal − the vehicle an illusion conjured of mist, faint whispering wind, and dripping murmur of leaf and tree. The sounds of hooves and carriage wheels were hollow and muted by the cloying atmosphere. Nothing was visible but the intermittent vague shapes of clawing branches and humped boulders briefly visioned then taken again into the creeping milky waves of thickening vapour.

At a point less than a mile from the gaunt north cliffs the vehicle slowed and turned along a track to the right. Presently all sounds ceased except the clanging of iron gates. A single blurred light wavered fitfully for a moment. There was a confused jumble of voices, a further banging of doors and dumping of luggage on the floor. Just for a moment, as a thin beam of water moonlight pierced the mist, forms could be seen − dark shapes moving towards the shadowed arch of a doorway. Then the fog descended again, obscuring all sign of movement.

A little later the echo of hooves and vehicle receded somewhere to the back of the building.

The great doors closed. All was still.

The de Verries family had come home.

1

From the first moment I saw Garth de Verries, my whole life changed. I became aware suddenly of wild emotions I'd not dreamed I possessed. It was a shock, as though a great gale swept through me, dispelling childhood forever, awakening instead a flood of unknown passions and deep flowering desire.

Even now, I suppose, after such years of doubt, pain, and stormy longing, it would be thought unseemly to admit it. Well brought up young women of the mid-Victorian era were not expected to harbour such violent feelings, least of all express them. Sensual longing, if experienced at all, was supposed to stir only very gently and discreetly under the marriage sheets. A girl of my background was taught to believe that it was her duty to accept the first offer of any suitable male willing to cherish and support her in matrimony, and to submit herself, however painfully, to the physical obligations entailed.

This was the conventional pattern. But my father had been more loving, and I had not been so firmly moulded. Even from childhood secret pictures had stirred my imagination of the kind of man I'd one day want as a husband. He must be strong and handsome, ruthless and overpowering when necessary – wild and warm as Cornish winds with the salt and summer sun in them; all fire and light mingled with brooding darkness and the power to quell my most wilful moods. Yet tender too. Oh yes! – somewhere I dreamed, there must be such a man. And one day, despite my deceptively elusive looks, my slender body and fey, shy heart, I would surely meet him. How, I couldn't guess, because I lived so far away from crowds and cities, with little opportunity of social contact. That area of Cornwall which was my home was remote and rugged bound only by wild moors, gaunt cliffs and ever-changing turbulent seas. There were two villages in our immediate vicinity – Braggas and St Clewes. The latter had an inn, where travellers, pedlars, and occasional visitors stayed for a night or two. I used to imagine sometimes that a stranger might appear there and bump into me perhaps in the village street. I would stumble, he would help me up, and I would see a pair of dark, fiery eyes staring down on me.

That would be it.

But of course matters did not work out that way at all. In fact nothing was to be quite as I pictured it. Not even Garth himself.

When I look back, I wonder frequently, how I got through the great holocaust that was to sweep through my life. If I hadn't been so wilful, or Garth so determined — but that would be another story. The story I'm telling now is what really happened, beginning on a certain night in 1857.

All that evening it had seemed to me the house opposite waited. Perhaps it was partly the weather — the steamy oppressiveness of damp October with everything so still and silent except for the dripping of trees and the flutter of a bird through the bushes. Or maybe it was something to do with Miss Ruana who had lived at Tharne alone — except for a servant or two — following her father's, Sir Bruce Verries's, death earlier that year.

Aunt Adela had been mildly amused at my curiosity. But then Aunt Adela, despite her good humour, had always considered my 'sixth sense' — as she patronisingly regarded it — slightly ridiculous and childish.

Perhaps it was, although there had been times when I had been proved right; but I never boasted of such occasions. My aunt had confidence only in her own powers of prediction, and regarded herself as a kind of matriarchal oracle in our own humble household. Aunt Adela was short, stout, and comfortable looking, with a love of frilly clothes, jewellery and an iron will beneath the benign exterior. She also had a moderate income of her own which had enabled us to live at Carnbrooke following my father's death when I was a child of twelve.

She was my mother's elder sister, and had come to take charge of my father and me when mama died. I had been only two then, so I didn't really remember my mother very clearly, except that she had been fair and pretty and very gentle. Papa had been a doctor, admired and loved by his patients, but generally short of money because the people he visited were mostly poor — tin-miners and their dependents who had difficulty in feeding and clothing their own families, and fishing folk from St Clewes and Braggas who all too often lost their menfolk at sea.

If it had not been for one or two wealthier patients like Miss de Verries and my aunt's financial support we would have been — as Aunt Adela put it — in 'sorry straits', because Papa had never pressed for payment at the cost of hungry families and children needing sustenance. So I had learned early to be grateful to Aunt Adela, and to accept her fussy ways and tastes — the hideous ornate bits and pieces she had insisted on installing at Carnbrooke from her home in London, making the house overcrowded and stuffy, with no room in the drawing room or small parlour as our old servant Mrs Crabbe said, 'to swing a cat round'.

Still, until his death Papa's study and surgery had been as he wished it, his own sacred territory; and as I'd grown older I'd stubbornly but as tactfully as possible removed from my bedroom ornate china vases, unnecessary pieces of lace and an intricate gilt-framed picture of a dying child reaching her arms to heaven where angels beckoned.

It was quite a nice room really, and had been mine since I was a small child. The furniture was of mahogany, with a blue carpet on the floor, and a patchworked quilt on the bed that had been made by my grandmother. There were lace curtains at the windows tied back with blue ribbons, and blinds with cords that fell with a rattle when pulled. They went up in the same way when given a sharp tug, and by the sides of those were heavy brown velvet hangings to close against the draught in winter-time.

As I grew older, I often got up when Aunt Adela had said goodnight to me, and pulled everything open again as quietly as I could. I liked the view outside of high moorland hills silhouetted against the fading sky. On clear nights when the moon shone, the landscape had a mysterious quality — sending queer shadows snaking down the slope from the rugged quoit on the horizon, to the great house of Tharne shrouded in its nest of trees.

When the curtains were drawn I could just glimpse the tips of turrets and towers silvered bright under the stars.

Everything about Tharne Hall had a strange fascination

for me, partly perhaps because old Sir Bruce had been such a hermit, except for his forbidding elderly daughter. Their lives had appeared to me to be veiled in secrets, and I'd wondered how they spent their days behind the vast ivy-covered walls and Gothic windows — what they talked about, if they ever talked at all.

'You must not be inquisitive child', Aunt Adela had said whenever I raised the subject. 'Their lives are their own affair. And remember — curiosity killed the cat.' My aunt was an adept at quickly delivering some glib metaphor in answer to anything she did not know. So I stopped my queries, realising, though, that she was secretly just as curious as I was.

As I stood at the window on that misty evening of 1857 watching the vague dark shape approaching through the fog towards the gates of Tharne, I knew with a quickening of my heart that at last it was happening; the new owner of Tharne and heir to the title, had returned from India to take over his estate.

'His inheritance,' Aunt Adela always called it, generally adding, with a hint of disapproval, 'he's only a nephew, of course, and living all his life in that foreign barbaric place won't be to his advantage, I'm afraid. Still — to give the devil his due' — another of her favourite phrases — 'he has at least good blood in his veins. And of course, being in the Army should have imbued a sense of decorum and discipline at least.'

It was a good thing my aunt seldom noticed my sighs on these occasions. She really could be very boring, and since my governess had left shortly after my sixteenth birthday I had found her company increasing ponderous.

That had been a year ago, and although I had been kept comparatively busy helping Mrs Crabbe with the lighter more 'ladylike' tasks of the household, there had been long periods when I'd felt restless for more exciting occupation. At Aunt Adela's wishes I did a little embroidery — rather badly I'm afraid — and tried my hand at sketching. But I had no talent as an artist, and I could not see the point of trying so poorly to emulate what Nature had already done so well. Sometimes I thought I would have liked to be an actress playing dramatic scenes before enraptured audiences, but a long glance at my reflection in the mirror told me the idea was stupid. There was nothing spectacular or majestic about me. I was not even tall.

Slender and well-shaped, admittedly, but my face was pale and heart-shaped. My eyes, though large and slightly slanted above high cheekbones, were neither blue, green, or brown, but a curious mixture of both. My nose was too tilted to be classical; when I smiled my mouth curved upwards at the corners giving me the appearance of a Puck rather than a Titania. My hair was nondescript. Silky, not really dark or fair − just a kind of light brown that had gold lights in it only when the sun shone.

'I wish I was beautiful like my mother,' I'd said once to Mrs Crabbe.

'You're like yourself,' Mrs Crabbe had said, 'and that's good enough for anyone.'

'No. Not for the stage,' I'd told her.

'What do you mean − the stage?'

'It must be wonderful to be an actress,' I'd answered enviously.

Mrs Crabbe had tut-tutted disapprovingly. 'You just get that right out of your head once and for all, Miss Caroline,' she'd said sharply. 'Young ladies like you weren't meant to go struttin' 'bout a platform wearin' nothing but paint and powder and frilly things not meant to be seen by respectable folk.'

I'd sighed, knowing the first part of what she'd said was true. I wasn't the type. It would be better perhaps to be a writer. Someone like Charlotte Bronte who'd created the wonderful story of *Jane Eyre*. But then I wasn't really clever. From time to time I'd written short tales, and once started a longer book meant to sway future readers by its passion. I'd envisaged a hero as dark and wild as the Heathcliff of Emily Bronte's *Wuthering Heights*. But when I'd re-read my own laborious effort I'd known it was feeble and no good; I had neither the talent or wish to write and study over words for hours on end when there were so many other more compelling things to do, such as walking the moors with the winds blowing wild and salty from the sea, or riding my young mare above the cliffs Zaren way.

Aunt Adela didn't really approve of Flash, but because my father had given her to me the year before he'd died, I'd been allowed to keep her on the proviso that she was trained for use with the governess cart when my aunt required a short jaunt anywhere. The thought of roly-poly Aunt Adela driving herself or being able to manage any horse at all had secretly amused me, and I'd never really believed it would work. It hadn't; after the first experience out alone Aunt Adela had returned seated very upright and very red-faced behind Flash who'd had a certain wicked look in her eyes that told me the governess cart might not be used again.

'In future,' she had said later, 'I shall let Adam drive me as usual in the cab when I want to go anywhere. So much more civilised.'

Adam was our odd-job man who came to work in our garden three mornings of the week. He also had a horse and cab of his own which he used when required for private conveyance. He had worked as a young man at Wheal Daisy tin mine on the de Verries' estate, and when he'd lost a leg in an accident old Sir Bruce had equipped him with the cab and a small pension and cottage in compensation for his injuries.

So Sir Bruce must have had a kindly streak beneath his grim exterior, I thought musingly on that foggy night, watching the lights of Tharne flicker for a time behind the blurred windows. I wondered what the new owner would be like. Would he be as dark and forbidding as his cousin Miss Ruana, or handsome and dashing? Perhaps neither; perhaps he'd be just nondescript and uninteresting, or too proud to notice Aunt Adela and myself.

Presently, when the lights had all disappeared leaving the hall just a hump of misted darkness behind the trees, I went back to bed.

Tomorrow, I thought, I'd keep my eyes on the large gates and take a walk during the afternoon with our spaniel Rufus. I might catch a glimpse of the new owner, or possibly meet him down the lane.

However, a week was to pass before Garth de Verries and I came face to face; and the encounter was quite extraordinary – because although I did not realise it at the time, I fell instantly passionately and wildly in love with him.

He was tall, wearing a black-waisted frock coat, over tightly-fitting black breeches. My first impression of his silhouetted figure against the light was only of darkness and rather forbidding dignity. But when he stepped aside, giving a faint bow, the sun caught the lines of his strongly carved face sideways,

and my heart gave a sudden lurch. His looks were sensational —
resembling a character from a Shakespearean play or some
noble Caesar from the past. His complexion, below the crisp
curls, held the glint of mahogany. He must be foreign I
thought, until I saw his eyes. And then I blinked — at least I
think I did — they were so brilliantly blue; more blue than
Cornish seas under an unclouded summer sky, bolder and more
flashing than the brightest diamonds, penetrating too. In those
few seconds I felt them assessing me with the cold quality of a
connoisseur deliberating whether or not I was a prize worth
bidding for. Of course the suggestion was absurd. He could
have no interest in me, most probably had not known of my
existence until that moment, and there was nothing about me to
stir any curiosity in him. I was just a rather shy looking girl who
happened to be skirting the edge of his wood with a dog at her
heels.

I had always used that particular path when I wanted to cut
towards the low lane above the sea. It was actually on Tharne
land, but old Sir Bruce had never objected. The wood bordering the house hid anyone passing, and except for workers on the
estate I had never encountered anyone else, and that was very
seldom indeed. The moorland there, stretching in a rising line
to a hill tipped with a cromlech and a half circle of standing
stones, was wild and uncultivated. Only a few black-faced
Cornish sheep grazed there. It was considered unsuitable for
horses, and I had been forbidden to ride that particular patch
because of treacherous patches of bog and derelict hidden
mine-shafts near the cliff edge.

During the last few years when I'd felt particularly bored and
frustrated by my life with Aunt Adela I'd disobeyed and ridden
Flash to the stones. I knew the area well. There were land-marks
betraying the dangerous bits, and once at the top I'd felt free,
relaxed. Nothing below but wild country and sea in the
distance, with the air salty, and heather-sweet from the moors.

Occasionally I'd been caught, and punished — my aunt, in
spite of her benign appearance, could be strict when she felt it
necessary. But I'd continued at rare times to visit the Granite
King. That's what it was called — because from certain posi-
tions the ancient carn gave the powerful impression of a
gigantic monarch seated on his stone throne above the moors.

There were the hard rugged features — jutting nose and chin beneath the craggy crown, and tattered locks against the open sky. The gaunt presence dominated the scene, and it was easy to imagine that the standing menhirs had really once been rebellious subjects who'd been turned to stone for their misdeeds. Legend said that on certain nights of the year they came alive again to do homage to their master, and that any who saw them did not live to tell the tale.

'Just a fairy story,' my Aunt Adela had said, adding carefully, 'but better be on the safe side and not take risks.'

I never had — at night. And by day I had felt no fear, only a deep, strange kinship with the rocky territory.

Now suddenly, facing this new owner of Tharne, I felt an intruder on the estate and aware that I was trespassing.

'Good afternoon,' I heard him saying with chilling politeness.

I pulled myself together quickly, though my pulses were still racing.

'Good afternoon. I'm just — I hope you don't mind me walking this way,' I heard myself saying, apologising without meaning to. 'It's a short cut to the sea road — you don't have to go through Braggas—'

I broke off, confused by the disconcerting stare, his obvious disapproval.

'I see.' The grim lips softened a little. I waited. Then he continued, 'It's quite all right, Miss — Dorric is it?'

'Yes. Caroline Dorric.' I wanted to ask him how he knew my name, but I was too slow.

'This once doesn't matter at all,' he said, 'but it's only fair to tell you now that in future I'd prefer you didn't use the path. I intend to have the lands of Tharne properly enclosed as soon as possible, which will include, I'm afraid, the whole of this side of the moor to beyond the hill where the estate ends.'

I stared at him blankly while a rush of indignation mingled with acute disappointment flooded my whole body, sending a wave of crimson to my cheeks.

'Do you mean the Granite King?'

'The Granite King?'

'That — the carn, the quoit,' I told him turning my head momentarily towards the rising moors. 'I've always gone there when I wanted. Sir Bruce didn't mind—'

'But Sir Bruce is no longer here,' he said shortly. 'For many years, obviously, the estate has been neglected. Now I intend things to be different. By the way—' he smiled again, 'my name is Garth, Garth de Verries. I hope we shall be good neighbours.' He held out his hand.

I took it mechanically. The pressure was far warmer than his expression. A wave of excitement surged through me. In those few seconds I experienced emotions quite new and alien to even my wildest imaginings of love and romance. Ungovernable longings possessed me. My pulses leaped. Thighs and breasts quivered from the brief contact. I felt first confusion mingled with shame, then nothing at all but extreme exultation in my own wickedness. For of course Aunt Adela would think me extremely wicked.

'You must control yourself and put such sinful thoughts behind you,' she would say severely. 'At once. Or you will find yourself following in your Aunt Henrietta's footsteps, and look what a plight she got herself into.'

Aunt Henrietta had been a younger sister of my father's who had eloped with a strolling player from a fair and later had a baby. The baby had died, and the player had deserted her. After that, according to dark rumour, she had ended up in that most unmentionable type of place – a brothel. 'There was bad blood in her from some far-off ancestor,' my aunt had told me when I dared question her about my erring relation. 'Never speak of her again, Caroline. You must forget she ever existed, and take her miserable story as nothing more than a warning.'

Well, I thought, as I tore my eyes from Sir Garth de Verries's, I had had my warning. I knew now what it was, and had certainly no intention of forgetting it.

All the same, I decided on my way back home, it was not fair of him to enclose the Granite King. He just had no right to bar me from riding Flash there, even if I took the other route from the opposite end of Braggas. Land like that, couldn't be possessed by anyone – not even a de Verries.

Strangely, when I got back to my home Carnbrooke, Aunt Adela was at the front door waiting for me – just as though she had seen me in conversation with Garth de Verries.

'I wish you wouldn't go rambling off at such inconvenient times, Caroline,' she said, eyeing me shrewdly. 'Mrs Clare called and with it being Mrs Crabbe's afternoon off I had to get her an early cup of tea myself. A nuisance. I believe I did tell you yesterday—'

'I'm sorry,' I said in contrite tones. 'I'd quite forgotten.'

My aunt rustled her frills and lace like a fussy hen fluffing her feathers. 'You should try not to forget, dear,' she reminded me. 'You're hardly a child any more. There are certain things in the village you will be expected to be interested in from now onwards. Mrs Clare is having a sale-of-work in the Church room before Christmas, and is hoping to raise a worthy sum for charity. The vicar had mentioned specifically that you most probably would be pleased to assist—'

'Oh yes?' I spoke hardly realising it. My thoughts were still far away with Garth de Verries.

'Caroline!' The sharp way she uttered my name made me start.

'Yes, Aunt?'

'Where did you go this afternoon? Do you mind telling me. Mrs Clare told me that as she drove up Braggas hill she thought she saw you by the wood.'

'Yes. She did. I was giving Rufus a run.'

'There? But that's on Tharne property.'

'I've always used the path, you know that.'

Aunt Adela's round mouth narrowed.

'I didn't know. But I guessed, in spite of my specific instructions for you not to.' She paused, then added, unable to quell her curiosity, 'Did you meet anyone?'

'Yes, the new owner, Sir — what is it? Garth de Verrics,' I told her feeling an imp of mischief deepen in me. 'He's very — impressive.'

'Impressive? What do you mean? I heard only yesterday he's a strange, rather frightening-looking man, and that the whole household's extremely odd. They have foreign servants, including a female with black hair who is obviously Indian. She wears a sari and the theory in the village is that she — well, I may as well say it — that she's the mistress of either Sir Garth himself or some relation they have living there.'

My heart almost stopped beating.

'I wouldn't have thought so,' I said steadily, knowing all the time that the suggestion could easily be true.

'And why don't you think so?'

I shrugged.

'Oh I don't know. If she's a servant it's not very likely. Anyway you said only yesterday that no one knows anything about the family.'

'That again is suspicious,' my aunt insisted. 'They — whoever they are, and however many of them — have been in residence a whole week now, and no one — *no* one has been able to learn a clue about them. Peculiar, don't you think?'

I shrugged. 'Not really. I expect they've had a lot to do settling in.'

'Hm.' My aunt sounded irritated. 'Well, if they're going to be stand-offish it certainly won't help to make them popular in the district. No man, you know, is an island.' After which characteristic platitude she turned away and left me ruminating half amused, half flattened, by her latest snippets of gossip and the suggestion that Garth de Verries had brought a foreign mistress to Tharne.

I didn't want to believe it; but it would certainly explain why he wished to keep the estate so completely private. His manner to me had been quite polite, of course. But when I thought back I had to admit that except for the brief pressure of his hand he had shewn no personal interest in me whatsoever. His one concern had been in impressing the fact on me that any trespassing where Tharne territory was concerned would not be tolerated.

My first indignation returned. He had a right to his own views and ambitions, and in running the estate as he chose. But he had no right at all to treat me as a rather blundering dull girl just out of school who could be commanded suddenly where and where not to go. My father had told me that the Granite King and the immediate terrain surrounding it had once been common land given by some ancient ruler to the people of Cornwall for perpetuity. He had said that bit by bit the ground had gradually been confiscated by former greedy de Verries who had eventually established the wild acres as their own.

No one had contested the claim, simply because it was of little use to farmers, and gipsies weren't wanted there anyway.

So the years had passed. The moor had gone its own wanton way, a retreat for wild things and a threat to man — a curious contradiction of ugly bog and barren patches interspersed by brilliant splashes of golden gorse and rich purple bell heather — of lumpy boulders, and deep shining pools reflecting storm and sunshine and the flash of wings where herons and gulls flew. A lonely unchallenged haunt of nature with the Granite King reigning supreme — until now, and the arrival of an unknown de Verries from India who meant to fence the area in, and most probably drain the land or make some attempt to bring it under the plough.

The very idea made me wince.

I would fight him, I thought. There must be a way. I had to show how desperately important for me it was, to have free access to those few uncivilized acres of Cornish moor.

How?

I didn't really know. I would certainly not plead. To beg for permission would make any man of Garth de Verries' type only despise me. Somehow I had to make an impression. And, oh dear, I wasn't the impressive type. I went upstairs and studied myself quite objectively and as candidly as possible through the mirror. In the first place my clothes were all wrong. The grey dress I was wearing had no cut, no style. My hair was too severely arranged; my face, without artifice, appeared too demure and pale to attract attention. Aunt Adela, naturally, would object to my using cosmetics, but I know very well she quite frequently brightened her own cheeks and lips with make-up or crushed geranium leaves, applied a regular lotion to her plump face made of strawberry roots, walnut leaves and alum that she first boiled before straining through a linen cloth. The concoction was then bottled and placed on her dressing table as an aid for keeping her complexion clear. To ensure her greying curls were always tidily in place she used a pomade made of hazel-nut oil, meat fat, and beef marrow. Other recipes for enhancing what looks she had, were written down carefully in a small notebook with a metal pencil attached. I had read it several times in secret, and although I should have felt guilty, I had only been amused, and gleaned what useful knowledge I could from the enlightening excerpts.

One afternoon, when Aunt Adela was dozing by the parlour fire, I crept out of the room softly and went upstairs to her bedroom. In the ordinary way I would not have dreamed of such deceit. But it seemed imperative at that moment for a little experimentation with my looks. Her reticule lay by the gilt framed dressing mirror, and beside it several small pots of cream. As I applied a little pink to my high cheek-bones and lips I noticed a switch of false curls lying in a drawer that was slightly open. I giggled, and then suddenly felt ashamed. I took a hurried glance at myself, then replaced the lid on the pot, and returned to my own room.

Studying my reflection there, I was disappointed. The effect of the rouge too quickly applied, was clownish. So I rubbed it off and decided to take a walk − not in the direction of Tharne or the sea, but to the village of Braggas that lay in a dip where the road divided into three − one going straight ahead towards Penzance, another cutting as a rough track to the cliffs, and the third winding in an upward curve to the high moors which led back again along the side of the hill. Eventually after little more than a mile, this route passed behind Carnbrooke before joining the main coast road. It was simple to cut down one of the narrow sheep tracks to our own back door, and I liked the loneliness of the way.

The scene was wild from there rather than beautiful, with several derelict mine-stacks silhouetted dark against the moorland ridge. Once it had been quite a busy district, with great pumping rods moving rhythmically against the sky. There had been the singing of miners and bal maidens, as workers left for home following long hours spent hammering and sorting tin. My father had described the industry of such days graphically, and told me many tragic and sad tales of the slumps following, when whole families took off for America, and others remained to eke out a poor living as best they could.

Braggas now was concerned mostly with farming and fishing. It had a small harbour set between gaunt cliffs reached by a narrow, incredibly steep, cobbled main street. The cottages, most of them specially built for miners, were mainly of clob. There was a Church, Chapel, a shop, and a small Dame's school. Most of the inhabitants were oldish, and although some of the small gardens were bright in summer with flowers, on that particular afternoon as I passed through, it had a dejected air, and I was glad to leave it behind.

The October light was fading. The landscape had a yellow

tinge taking the lean dark shapes of trees and bushes into shadowed uniformity. There was no wind, and occasionally a dead leaf drifted slowly and soundlessly from a branch overhead to the damp earth below. The distant sea merged into the blurred line of cliffs and sky. Every small sound, the sudden scurrying of wild feet or rustle of wings from the undergrowth, was intensified. So it was not surprising that the thud of hooves from the moor above startled me. I looked up to the left, sharply. A horseman was cantering down a narrow path to the track where I walked. I rubbed my eyes, trying to get the picture into focus. The rider was visible only as a dark form, erect and somehow intimidating. But the horse was startling; a magnificent white animal that appeared at first to be conjured of light, and mist, and air — the type of charger remembered from fairy-tale illustrations in my childhood books.

I stopped walking, quite taken aback. A minute later the figure reined, paused a moment, then swung himself from the saddle.

In a few quick strides he was towering above me.

'Good evening, Miss Dorric,' he said. 'I thought we might meet here.'

Drawing myself to my full height, and lifting one foot slightly at the heel to give an impression of further inches, I managed to say more calmly than I felt, 'Good afternoon, Sir – Sir—'

'Garth,' he interposed quickly. 'Just Garth.'

'Oh.'

We both waited, then I added quickly, 'Why did you expect to see me? Have you been watching?'

I sensed rather than saw the slight smile touching his mouth.

'Whenever I could. After one first encounter I rather thought we'd meet again – much sooner, especially with your admitted passion for riding my lands—'

His arrogance irritated me.

'If you mean the Granite King, I'd rather not talk about it. Anyway the moors here are quite pleasant, and I—'

'Exactly. That's what I told myself. If Miss Dorric is forbidden Tharne, I thought, then she will go another way. Quite logical, don't you think?'

I frowned.

'How did you know I was out?'

'I enquired from the old man in your garden,' came the cool reply. 'At first he thought I was referring to – your aunt is it? But I soon clarified things, and when I explained he was quite helpful. "You mean Miss Caroline," he said. "The young lady. Oh she's gone to Braggas for something or other. Walking. Mebbe she'll come back the other way round moor." So it was quite simple really.'

By the time he'd finished speaking, my equilibrium had returned and with it, deepening curiosity.

'Yes, well—' I lifted my chin an inch or two higher. 'I must be getting back to the house. Aunt Adela always starts fussing when I'm late. But why did you want to see me, Sir Garth? Is there anything you want to know? About the district, or the people round here?'

He shook his head.

'I've made it my business already to learn what concerns me. And I'm really not very interested in the villagers or their affairs—'

'What a pity,' I interrupted rashly. 'Oh – I'm sorry. It's not my business to tell you what to do. But Cornish people make good friends and bad enemies – my father always said so, and it's true—'

'I'm sure it is. However, as I don't intend to get involved in any way, that's neither here nor there. I simply wanted a chance to explain what I meant when we were chatting the other day.'

'You mean about the Granite King?'

'About Tharne territory,' he said pointedly. 'If you thought me sharp, or overbearing, I'm sorry. I have a reason for my attitude. Really quite a simple one. We have – I have – an invalid in the house, a friend. He's recovering from a very serious illness, and needs extreme care and solitude. It's important he should have every chance to recuperate in complete peace. Any invasion by strangers whether on horseback or on foot could be disastrous.'

An invasion, I thought indignantly, how ridiculous to describe me in such terms!

He paused, and when I said nothing, asked sharply, 'Do you understand?'

I shook my head. 'Not really.'

He made a quick movement of exasperation, jerking the

horse's bridle so the animal reared once, then snorted and settled at a word of command.

'No. Why should you?'

I felt his blue eyes turned hard on my face which was starting to burn, despite the chill of the thin rising mist. 'I could hardly have expected it,' he continued. 'You're young, with no experience of such things. Illness and death haven't touched you, have they?' His voice was bitter. 'But I've had more than I wish of both. India is hardly a pleasant place at the moment.'

'No, I suppose not.'

He gave a short cough that could have been a laugh, but wasn't.

'You suppose? Well, I advise you that to conjecture about things you've never known—'

'It isn't entirely conjecture,' I interrupted with rising temper. 'I'm not quite ignorant. There are papers — even in Cornwall, and I read. I've heard a lot — about the mutiny; and the Black Hole of Calcutta — I know *that* was a long time ago. But—'

I broke off, breathlessly, as he shrugged.

'Journalists' tales,' he retorted contemptuously, 'and by no means all the truth or even half of it.'

'That's not my fault,' I said, 'and anyway this isn't—'

'The time or place to discuss such macabre matters, I quite agree,' he interposed quickly. 'And no doubt you're wanting to be home and safe from such barbaric characters as myself—'

'Oh no. I didn't mean—'

'Then you should,' he said firmly. 'Educated young ladies have no right to be wandering the moors alone at such an hour.'

I had an impulse to say recklessly, 'I'm not an educated young lady in the way you mean, and I do understand—'

But of course I didn't. And the words never came.

A moment later he raised his hand to his forehead and said, 'Goodbye for the moment, Miss Dorric — until the next time.'

I stared at him, speechless, as he turned to mount his horse. And in those few seconds I noticed something I had not seen before — he had a slight but perceptible limp. Perhaps he'd been wounded in battle, I thought, watching him ride away towards Braggas. If so his hardness was understandable. But was he really so implacable as he'd appeared? I waited, hoping he might look round, but he didn't. And when he'd disappeared round a bend of the moor I went on again towards Carnbrooke, with a curious sense of disappointment in me. For a few heady moments I'd really fancied a warmth and personal interest in his eyes. How blue they'd been — how intent and unswerving on my face. But obviously he had no intention of furthering the acquaintance. His main object in wanting any meeting with me at all had been to enforce his dictatorial assertion that Tharne land was forbidden to strangers. And to him that was obviously what I was — a stranger who'd dared to trespass on his private property.

I was still seething with indignation over the Granite King episode, when I reached Carnbrooke. But as I entered the hall I realised immediately that something was wrong and the duel of words was forgotten. Mrs Crabbe was scurrying to the parlour with a blanket over one arm, and something wrapped by a knitted cover under the other. It looked like Aunt Adela's stone foot-warmer.

'Oh, Miss Caroline, my dear luv,' she gasped, 'I'm glad you're back. She'm took real bad — I've sent that theer Adam for th' Apothecary from St Clewes — oh, but it's a bad business. If your dear papa was here 'twudn' be so frightening. But I doan have the knowledge of such things, an' with her not speakin' — 'et's beyond me I tell you — made her comfortable as I can o' course. But all twisted she is — an' lyin' on the floor like that — what more can I do, Miss Caroline? There edn' nuthen, if you ask me—'

The words rushed out in a torrent of little gasps; I put both hands on her shoulders and shook her slightly, trying to calm her down. 'Who?' I asked quickly, although I already guessed. 'Is it Aunt Adela? Yes it is, isn't it? Here — give me that—' I grabbed the foot-warmer from her, and pushed past into the sitting room.

Just inside the door I stood momentarily staring, shocked and unable to move. Then I ran forward and dropped to my knees beside the stout recumbent form of my aunt. Her neck was twisted to one side, her face contorted, and of an ugly purplish colour, with her eyes glazed and staring. She was breathing heavily, her false curls had fallen off; there was a curious rattling in her throat. I was suddenly very frightened. 'It's all right,' I said with my lips close to one ear, 'we've sent for help.

Mrs Crabbe—' The old servant came forward. 'Get me another cushion for her head, and then find another blanket.'

The old woman did what was asked, and together we managed to raise Aunt Adela into a less cramped position. I'd heard my father say that stimulants should not be given in such cases unless under medical direction, advice that I was grateful for just then. Obviously my poor aunt was suffering from some sort of stroke, apoplexy − or a heart attack. There was nothing else really that could be done until help arrived. So I waited, holding her hand and trying to locate a pulse in her wrist, with Mrs Crabbe peering over us fearfully. By the time I'd found a flicker of a frail heart beat, the apothecary from St Clewes had arrived. He was a portly ageing man dressed all in black except for his white neck-scarf.

He hummed and ha-ad a good deal, suggested bleeding, and produced a bottle of liquid and two small boxes of pills from his bag. But he was evidently uncertain of his diagnosis, and eventually suggested calling a specialist doctor from Penzance.

'Safer,' he said. 'The poor lady is in a sorry state indeed. You leave things to me, my dear, and I will contact Doctor Stevens.'

He drew a deep breath, returned his instruments to his bag, went out, and after heaving himself to his horse − an old nag looking far too small and frail for his great weight − was presently riding along the moorland road in the direction of St Clewes and Penzance. Aunt Adela was left on the floor for a further two hours, and when at last the doctor arrived, he confirmed that she was suffering from a massive stroke, and that recovery − if at all, would only be partial. One side of her body would most certainly be paralysed for life, which would mean constant nursing and attendance.

With the help of Adam she was carried by the two men to her bed. She lay there for two months not speaking or able to do a thing for herself, relying entirely on me and Mrs Crabbe with occasional help from a visiting nurse, to feed her and see that she was kept clean and as tidy as possible.

It was a dreary difficult time.

I seldom went out except for a brief quick walk each day, and then I hardly ever saw anyone. By then the trees were naked of leaves, standing bleak and dark against the landscape. The woods round Tharne emerged mysteriously through the chilly morning and evening mists, although at mid-day sometimes, when pale sunlight spinkled the moors, its towers and windows showed more clearly against paper-pale skies. Once when I was passing I caught the glimpse of a woman's dark face watching me from the drive. She was not near, but close enough for me to note her beauty — the proud lift of head and luxuriant black hair falling in thick braids to her waist. When I paused she lifted a scarf quickly to half cover her face. Then she turned and moved gracefully in her long draperies to the door and went in.

I went down the lane dejectedly, with a crowd of suspicious thoughts niggling at me.

If this was the foreign servant I'd heard about, she certainly did not look like one. Probably what rumours said was true — she had been Garth de Verries' mistress in India, and he'd brought her back with him to continue the relationship.

A wave of irrational jealousy swept through me. He had everything I thought — Tharne, wealth, looks and power, and the company of the exotic creature I'd just seen to fulfil all his emotional needs.

From that moment, though I did not admit it, even to myself, I took an instant dislike to the young unknown Indian woman, and my resolution, to defy Garth de Verries' claim to the Granite King became a firm resolve in my mind.

One afternoon shortly before Christmas there was the clanging of a bell followed by the sound of Mrs Crabbe's footsteps padding down the hall, and a man's voice speaking. Curiosity drove me from my aunt's bedside to the landing. Glancing down, but careful to keep myself unseen in the shadows, I saw Garth de Verries' dark form silhouetted in the doorway. He was handing something to the old servant — something that looked like a bouquet wrapped in tissue paper.

I drew back against the wall instinctively, and waited until the door had closed again and his footsteps had died away down the path. Then I went downstairs.

Mrs Crabbe was in the kitchen already taking a glass vase from a cupboard. On the table was an immense bunch of pink carnations arranged tastefully with maidenhair fern. I went forward, picked them up, and smelled them. Their fragrance filled the air.

'It was him — that theer gentleman from the hall,' I heard

Mrs Crabbe saying disapprovingly. 'I wouldn't have took them, but—'

'Whyever not? They're lovely,' I exclaimed. 'They're for my aunt I suppose. I didn't know—'

'No.' Her voice was truculent. 'For Miss Caroline. That's what he did say.' She paused before adding irritably, 'They never last long – this kind. And why does he want to bother? A fast one he is – that's what they say in Braggas. Queer goings on theer at all times o' the day an' night – lights burnin' when all respectable folk should be in bed. Surely you do know that, Miss?'

Yes I knew. I couldn't recall the number of times I'd got up from my bed when rest seemed impossible and looked through the window towards Tharne – seen sometimes the silhouette of a man's form moving against the glow from an upper window and recognised the profile. Twice there had been, as well, the outline of a woman's shape. Unable to tear my eyes away I'd watched resentfully as their two figures had swayed towards each other, then melted as one – lost in the shadows from trees blowing in the garden and the intermittent darkness of clouds dimming the moon.

Such brief incidents had always left me feeling at first despondent, then coldly, stubbornly aloof and condemning. I tried to dispel the thought of their lovemaking behind the closed curtains – tried not to think of his hard blue eyes and sensuous lips seeking hers in passion. Yet my own limbs quivered; in imagination I became for an unwanted moment that dark foreign woman at Tharne, felt a pulsing of breasts and thighs in spite of all determination not to, and almost instantly was ashamed.

What was he to me? Nothing. Nor ever could be. I had no place in his life, and had no real wish for one. My duty was at Carnbrooke with poor sick Aunt Adela who had done so much for me and for my father when he was alive.

Duty might be a sterile and joyless word, but it was a role I couldn't escape. Though all my instincts might be to race with Flash wildly on some cold frosty night to the Granite King, where I could fling myself into the heather waiting for passion to be appeased – for a strong figure to appear miraculously, wild and dark under the fiery stars, I was bound to four walls and the house where my aunt lay helpless in my care.

In a jumbled kind of way these thoughts raced through my mind again as I contemplated the flowers lying on the kitchen table. I pulled myself together abruptly when Mrs Crabbe droned on again persistently, 'Did you hear what I said, Miss? A fast mysterious one he is—'

'Yes, I heard.'

'Hm!' She paused, then asked bluntly, 'Courtin' you, is he? You just be careful—' My cheeks flamed.

'Mrs Crabbe, you forget yourself. How dare you? As if — I don't even know him. We should be grateful that anyone gives a thought for poor Aunt Adela at such a time.'

The old woman sighed and turned away. 'What I say's only for your own good. A headstrong one you always was, an ef I'd had my way you'd have learned right'n wrong long before this, even ef it was from my hand on your backside. Now don't you go on at me, Miss Caroline. I've been in this house long enough to be able to speak my mind now and then. Knowledge you may have, about med'cine an' such, 'cause of your dear papa — but men's a different matter altogether. An' I care for you, havin' no childer of my own.'

I knew she did, so I held my tongue at that point, and left her to arrange the flowers in her own way.

Christmas was a gloomy one that year. Instead of making any visible recovery Aunt Adela seemed to grow weaker and more helpless as the days passed. I tried to divert my thoughts from sickness and suffering by reading, in what few leisure moments I had. Occasionally I put myself in the place of Jane Eyre, imagining my secret longings to be similar to hers for the passionate dark Mr Rochester. But of course there was little resemblance. Jane had been gentle and meek and entirely self-sacrificing, whereas I was at heart rebellious and selfish, desperately wanting Garth de Verries for my own. No. If I was like any of the Bronte characters, it was Catherine in *Wuthering Heights* — except that she had been free to wander the moors with Heathcliff, while I had no freedom at all.

Selfishly sometimes I wondered how long I would be able to endure such frustration. Once when I was walking home from Braggas I glanced seawards, and in the far distance saw the shape of a man astride a horse riding upwards towards the rugged summit of the Granite King.

I did not have to wonder who he was. I knew. It was Garth de Verries. My heart contracted then bounded on again quickly. I stood still for a few moments, watching him mount the summit, and there wait with his horse facing the glimmer of sea beyond the cliffs. Tearing my eyes away I walked on.

As I passed the gates of Tharne I had a shock.

Why I glanced up the drive I don't know; instinct may be, or mere curiosity. But to my surprise I saw Garth was already back. Although the winter light was not good, his strong features were quite discernible behind the glass of a long Gothic window overlooking the front garden and the lane. Shadows filtered fleetingly from the trees across the drive. One moment he was clear, the next he had disappeared.

I was confused, and in some strange way apprehensive.

Why had he returned so quickly from his ride? And why should he have been so statically watching when I went by? Had he known I was in the village? Was he afraid I was about to trespass on his domain? I dispelled the suggestion immediately. Probably I was making much of nothing. The walk from Braggas had taken me half an hour, more than sufficient time for him to gallop quickly back from the moors. The weather was not really pleasant, – chilly and grey with a thin clammy mist already glistening on the ground. He had probably been anxious to return.

As soon as I reached the house I went into the parlour, and gave a poke at the logs where a fire was glowing.

Then I took off my cape, lit the lamp, and glanced at the weekly paper I'd been to collect. The news was not good. There were depressing extracts concerning the outrages still committed by the Bengal Army in India, and the critical massacre of Europeans.

I wondered how much was true, recalling Garth de Verries' cold comments concerning press reports. In any case, I decided, it was strange that he could be involved so deeply with a woman of enemy origin. Or was it? And were the Indians really to blame? My father had not thought so. Although I was only a child at the time I remembered him referring bitterly to the East India Company, and saying that when it took over the Great Mogul, warfare had been inevitable. Such references then had had no real meaning for me. Even now, at seventeen, events so far away held little significance. If it hadn't been for the Indian girl at Tharne I wouldn't have allowed myself to be troubled at all. So I put the paper down, went to the kitchen and asked Mrs Crabbe to make tea, and was shortly back again in my aunt's bedroom.

She had been sleeping. The sound of the door opening roused her. She glanced at me and smiled lopsidedly. A flood of sympathy swept through me. She looked, suddenly, so old and frail — so completely unlike the fussy fluttering plump woman I'd grown used to since childhood. She could no longer speak or gossip. Any communication between us had to be made by signs and feeble scribbling from her left hand. I could seldom read her ill-formed words, and when, from a glance of her one good eye she indicated what she wanted this time, my heart sank. But I fetched her note-book from the dressing table, placed its metal pencil between her fingers, managed to raise her head a little against the pillow, and waited for her to start on the laborious task.

She only managed to convey three words before falling back again exhausted. I studied, the paper carefully. All I could make out was — 'What will you—' the rest was a jumble, but I guessed she was worrying over me and wondering what I would do when she had gone.

I tried to soothe her, and presently she slipped into unconsciousness again.

I left the room quietly, closing the door behind me softly. Mrs Crabbe was in the hall carrying the tea tray to the kitchen.

'How is she?' she asked. 'Still sufferin', the poor dear?'

I shrugged. 'I don't know. I don't think so. I wish—'

'Yes, Miss?' Her face had a grim expression. Her old voice held a challenge. 'Wish it was over, do you?'

I could feel the hot blood flush my spine and cheeks, because what she suggested was true. I did want things to be over one way or another. Sickness oppressed and filled me with revulsion, although I wouldn't admit it. There were times when I wanted to run away for good from the stifling conditions thrust upon me.

Yet when Aunt Adela died at the end of January I was overcome by genuine grief, remembering all her small kindnesses, her amusing gossiping ways, small vanities, the ridiculous little bunches of false curls lying by her mirror, with smelling salts, pot-pouri and innumerable bottles of cosmetics. Such small things, somehow, were more achingly poignant than the dreary trappings of the funeral later. There was a simple service at St Clewes Church, attended by only two or three villagers as a show of respect, Adam, Mrs Crabbe and myself. The snowdrops in the graveyard glimmered white under the winter sun. As Mrs Crabbe and I walked to Adam's waiting cab following the burial, a bird sang from nearby. Sadness, filled with relief overcame me. Tears lay damp on my cheeks, but my heart felt lighter than it had done for months.

When we reached Carnbrooke I found a note lying on the mat inside the front door. I opened it and read:

> Please accept my sincerest sympathies in your loss. If there is anyway in which I can be of help let me know, and I will do what I can.
>
> Sincerely yours,
> Garth de Verries.

I was aware of Mrs Crabbe watching me as I put the note in my reticule. I was moving away when her curiosity got the better of her.

'Well?' she enquired, 'anything important, is et?'

I could have told her to mind her own business but I didn't.

'Sir Garth,' I said. 'Sending his condolences.'

'Hm! I'm sure you don' need his,' she remarked with withering scorn.

'We never know whose help we shall need, any of us,' I replied ambiguously.

As events proved later, I was right, although I would never have dreamed of it at that moment.

The same week I was informed by my aunt's solicitors that although during my father's lifetime Aunt Adela had paid off a considerable mortgage on our house, she had taken out a further one a year before her death, and that there was little left in her personal estate to cover it.

At first I could not realise the implications of his statement, and when I did I was shocked.

'But why?' I asked. 'She was quite well off. Why did she have to do that? She left money, didn't she? She had shares—?'

I broke off, silenced by the look of gloom on his dry, friendly face.

'My dear young lady, your poor aunt at one time was very ill-advised over investing in shaky companies. She lost over the years a great deal of capital, with the consequence that – it distresses me having to tell you this, but I'm afraid I have to – except for a few valuables, furniture, and a meagre sum in her current bank account, there is nothing to come to you save debts. Of course—' he cleared his throat, forcing a false note of cheer into his voice '—one or two pieces here have value – the William and Mary chest, the silver – oh you will not be left entirely penniless. And if you sell the house—'

'Sell it? But why should I? Where would I live—?'

He didn't answer for a moment, then he said, 'I shall do all I can to assist you and advise, but without the security I'm very afraid the Bank may feel it has to foreclose—'

He looked away apologetically, fumbling with his papers. I knew then what he had been trying to say all the time.

I had nothing.

I was a pauper.

2

I could not accept my position. I would not. The thought of losing my home Carnbrooke which had belonged to the Dorric family for generations was not only depressing but bleakly frightening. What would I do? Where would I go? I was trained for nothing but working samplers and stitching sheets. I had not even the qualifications for taking a post as governess. And I would not want to teach anyway. I hadn't the patience.

During the next few days following my talk with the solicitor several wild plans swarmed through my head – of going to London and somehow pressing a theatrical producer to employ me, if only with a walking-on part in a play at first. I could work, I could learn. I had practised countless roles from Shakespeare before my mirror when I was younger. Once when I was about ten my father had caught me unsuspectingly trying to emulate Lady Macbeth with hands clasped tragically at her bosom.

He had been amused and said, 'You're not really quite the type, my love. Why not Puck? Or Miranda from the *Tempest*?'

I'd flushed and answered, 'Oh, it's only a game, Papa. I'm not any good anyway. And I'm not pretty enough to be an actress.'

He'd thrown me a strange glance then, a very serious look, and said, 'Acting can be painful and wearying unless you get to the top of the profession, and I wouldn't wish such a life for you. Have your games, child, but remember happiness comes first. One day I hope you'll marry and have a kind husband and children of your own.'

'Yes, Papa,' I'd replied meekly. But I'd known he was looking back over the years to the period when his own sister, my Aunt Henrietta — had so spoiled her life by running away with the penniless strolling player who'd afterwards so cruelly abandoned her. I'd not been sure, either, that I wanted only a *kind* husband. Kind people, however worthy, could sometimes be dull, and secretly I'd longed always for excitement and colour — not for any dull routine that continued every day the same — but for the adventure of not knowing quite what was going to happen next.

Well — the last bit had come true anyway, I told myself firmly and a little bitterly, less than a week after the solicitor's unpleasant disclosure. I certainly couldn't foresee any clear picture of the future unless it was as the companion of some rich elderly woman who would probably bully me and have me forever at her heels. I shuddered at the thought, and on impulse got Adam to drive me to Penzance the next day. The accountant there was youngish, and had been to see Aunt Adela several times during the last two years of her life. She had appeared slightly fatuous at knowing him — 'Very well connected,' she'd told me. 'When Mr Daniel, the senior partner, retires, the firm will be Horace Coutts'. Any girl who marries him will be lucky indeed.'

I'd glanced away uncomfortably and changed the subject knowing she was thinking of me. The idea of such a union had seemed absurd and ridiculous. But the last time he'd been to

Carnbrooke I'd certainly seen a glance in his eyes that told me he was impressed, and if he really liked me I thought, and was as well connected as Aunt Adela had suggested, he might be willing to advise me what to do. An idea had been simmering in my mind of making shell-pictures. Obviously painting was not a gift of mine, but from being quite young I'd collected shells and pretty coloured small stones from the beach which I'd arranged and stuck with glue on boards making attractive designs. Adam had framed several of them for me, and there were still two of them hanging in Aunt Adela's bedroom, and one in my father's old surgery.

Hopes rose in me wildly that if I knew the right people I could work up a connection and somehow make a living that would save me from having to sell Carnbrooke. Horace Coutts might be willing to supply the introductions. If I was nice to him he could possibly even arrange a loan with the bank. Oh my head seethed with a number of extravagant impossible notions as I set off that afternoon in my one best gown, a lilac silk, under the black braided cape I'd bought extravagantly for my aunt's funeral. My hat also was of black, made mostly of feathers and veiling, a small affair perched high on my swept-up hair and tied under the chin with black ribbons. I was wearing a pair of black gloves on my hands, which had belonged to Aunt Adela. Very vainly I'd applied a touch of pink to my cheeks from one of her small pots of cream.

Mrs Crabbe had eyed me suspiciously before we set off. 'You look flushed, Miss Caroline,' she'd said disapprovingly. 'Are you sure you haven' a fever on you? Or 'es et——?' the question had died doubtfully on her lips.

I flashed her a bright artificial smile. 'I'm quite well, Mrs Crabbe, and I certainly haven't a fever.'

'Well——' she paused, hoping I'd tell her about my business trip; I knew she was longing to be taken into my confidence, but I was determined not to create an argument, 'Very well then,' she said, tossing her old head in annoyance, 'you jus' tek care of yourself Miss Caroline. 'Tedn' right for young ladies to go ridin' to towns without no comp'ny, that's what I do say — specially now, when you have to be more pertickler than ever 'bout your reputation.'

I lifted a hand in farewell, and a minute later was seated in

Adam's cab, with Adam attired in his best brown coat and stove hat ready for the cross-country journey.

The afternoon was bright, with pale patches of thin sunlight filtering in a networked pattern from the trees. As we passed the gates of Tharne a little further down the lane on our left, I thought I glimpsed a static female form near the drive. I did not turn my head to see who it was, but sat firmly erect, my chin lifted rigidly upwards, my eyes staring straight ahead. I felt grown-up, quite sophisticated, and gratified in making a show of independence. Whatever my future was to be, those few moments marked the start of a new era. Miss Ruana — if it *was* Miss Ruana — would be curious, no doubt, and let her cousin Garth know of 'Doctor Dorric's penniless daughter's outing'. Garth probably would not be interested, but I was sure that the Indian woman would be, and I hoped she had been there. It had become very important to me to make an impression on the new family at Tharne.

The mile to Braggas was an easy journey winding between rhododendrom bushes, high hedges of thorn, willow, and over-hanging sycamores. From there the lane cut upwards taking a high moorland route towards the opposite coast. Derelict mine-stacks and standing stones were silhouetted against the far Western ridge; in dips of the moor small hamlets crouched against slopes of heather and gorse. Ahead, a little to the left, Mounts Bay was a glitter of silver, with the Mount itself rising like a fairy-tale castle from the water. A shiver of breeze had sprung up, and I pulled my bonnet strings a little tighter in case the frivolous contraption was wafted from my head like a balloon.

My heart was already quickening with excitement, and when the cab took the turn down towards Penzance's main road, I searched rapidly through my reticule for cologne to calm and cool me. I must appear very dignified and controlled, I told myself — prove to Mr Coutts from our first moment together that I was quite capable of tackling a successful business venture. The samples of shell-work propped up safely in tissue paper beside me, were those from Aunt Adela's room. One depicted a multi-coloured bird with wings outspread, the other a bunch of flowers minutely made of pearly shells with centres of tiny yellow stones.

After climbing the hill, past the Market Place in the middle of the road, we cut down a narrow cobbled street on the left, and halfway to the harbour arrived at Mr Coutts' office.

Adam stopped the cab with a jerk of the reins and word of command to his tired elderly horse. Then, with one arm round my pictures, one lifting my long skirt carefully above the ankles, I dismounted, leaving Adam to wait for me.

'I'm sure I shall not be long,' I said. 'If you'd rather go to the Inn Yard—'

'I'll wait for 'ee here,' he interrupted stubbornly. 'I'm all right, Miss.'

So I crossed the pavement and went up the few steps leading to the front entrance. The porch, like the rest of the building, was early Georgian and reminiscent of earlier social days. The brass plate at one side was impressive. An ancient official dignity seemed to herald the interior. I tugged at the brass bell-pull. There was the sound of movement followed by the opening of the door.

A thin bespectacled man in sombre clothes eyed me a trifle furtively. But when I'd given my name and told him I was an acquaintance of Mr Horace Coutts he waved me in, directed me to a dreary room lined with yellowish books and told me to be seated while he ascertained whether the time was convenient for Mr Coutts to see me.

It was.

A moment or two later Horace entered — I have to call him Horace, in view of what was to follow. He, too, was thin, scholarly-looking, with gentle manners, a small mouth, and pale blueish eyes that lit up when he saw me. He was dressed impeccably in dull dark clothes that I supposed were correct for his profession. I guessed he could not have been much above thirty, but he seemed much more to me, and my heart sank when he spoke.

'My dear Miss Dorric. I am so honoured to meet you again. I had such great esteem for your much lamented late father. Please do let me know what I can do for you. I presume it is advice you require—'

I explained as coherently as I could the position I was in — my trouble with the mortgage and plans brewing for the future. I spoke quickly, afraid of giving him the opportunity of dashing my hopes in the first few minutes. My voice, I knew, must have sounded breathless, my cheeks were burning, and my hand shook a little as I pulled the shell designs from their paper wrapping; all the time I was aware uncomfortably of his static expression, the pale eyes watching me, the thin lips unmoving as though sculpted into a faint perpetual half-smile. The atmosphere of the room was not encouraging. The yellowish walls seemed to be closing in on me. The tidy desk with its tabulated drawers, files and carefully assorted papers, mocked me in its officialdom. I had a rash sudden desire to jump up, make some random excuse, run out, and flung myself into Adam's cab; but I didn't. Instead I went on and on until the whole disjointed narrative was over. Then I stiffened, faced him very squarely with my back quite rigid, and waited.

He did not speak for some seconds.

'I suppose you think me quite improvident and ridiculous, Mr Coutts?' I said impetuously, 'Perhaps I am. I'm — I'm sorry I troubled you. I just thought—'

'Yes, Miss Dorric?'

I thought you might be able to advise me,' I told him. 'Professionally of course. How to get a loan I mean — to tide me over until I could get properly started with — with these shell things of mine. I know they may not appear very clever or attractive to you — but they are becoming popular. I was reading in a ladies' magazine that a friend of the Queen has quite a collection—' I broke off thinking, 'Oh how snobbish that sounds. How ridiculous and vain.'

Why didn't Mr Horace Coutts speak? Say something? *Anything* — I wondered, with my first anxiety turning to irritation. Unable to bear it any longer I jumped up, pushing the works back into the paper. Two shells that could not have been stuck sufficiently securely on to the background tumbled off, and fell with a thin rattle on to the floor. I stopped down to prevent them rolling under the table but Mr Coutts was too quick for me. His hand was suddenly on my wrist. I glanced up. He was kneeling down, and his face was a shade pinker than it had been, under his carefully smoothed fairish hair.

'My dear Miss Dorric,' he said, 'Please allow me—' He insisted on helping me up, but I couldn't help feeling that his eyes were more on my ankles and disordered skirts than on the runaway shells.

We were both breathing heavily when at last order was restored and I was seated again in the chair facing him. Through
a wave of embarrassment I heard him saying, 'You did quite
right to come to me. Your work I am sure, is artistic, most
artistic, and with perseverance and a little practical help I feel
quite confident you may have an assured future ahead.

Relief surged through me.

'And you mean you think it wouldn't be too long — that I
could get the Bank to give me a loan or something? Is that it?
Would you talk to them, Mr Coutts?' I looked away, confused by
my own temerity.

'My dear, Miss Dorric — Caroline—' His voice was warmer,
almost intimate. 'I will do what I can — immediately. And I can
assure you, you have no need to worry. None at all.'

That was the beginning.

Of course I should have known.

I should have sensed, despite my youth and inexperience,
that men of Horace Coutts' type were not likely to indulge in
philanthropy with no likelihood of payment in some way. I
should have recognised also that my artistic ambitions were
really rather amateurish and childish. I had a sense of colour
and design — a certain originality, that was all.

Fear and elation had dispelled all sense of perspective in me,
and business consideration had never been my strong point.

The consequence of this fateful meeting with Horace Coutts
was that although I got my loan, I also found myself in a most
compromising and difficult situation. At the beginning of May,
through a chance conversation with my Bank Manager, I
learned that Horace himself had guaranteed the finance necessary to lift me out of debt, and when I later confronted him with
the fact, he told me it was of no account, because he wished to
marry me.

I remember the occasion so well.

It was late morning and he had called at Carnbrooke to
inform me that a certain Lady Marston-Green who had recently
come to reside at Falmouth had heard — through him — of my
artistic work, and wished to contact me, as she was most interested in the current Victorian trend for flower creations and
original ornamental decoration for the house. I had been on the
point of thanking him, with reservations on my part, for his

philanthropic gesture concerning the bank loan, when he hastily forestalled me.

He lifted a slender pale hand to silence me. 'Please wait, Caroline——' he said. 'I can guess what you're about to say — and it is quite unnecessary. I have faith in you, great faith — as I informed the bank. Taking a risk on your work is really taking no risk at all——' and he smiled at me benignly, I flushed as he continued, 'I have so many contacts. Lady Marston-Green is just the beginning. What I propose to do——' What this quiet looking, conventional rather prim looking youngish man proposed to do, took quite five minutes to explain, and left me bewildered and flushed, and hardly able to believe my ears.

At last I managed to say cautiously, 'It's very kind of you, Mr Coutts——'

'Horace, surely.'

'Well — Horace then. But——' I swallowed to gain composure. 'I am grateful, truly I am; for the contacts I mean, and for your arranging this — this supper party you propose. But I don't think I should accept finance from you——'

'Isn't finance what you need?' He smiled, reached over, and patted my hand. I flinched. 'Of course it is, my dear. Besides, I'm not giving you money, if that's what you're thinking. Just my word — on your behalf, as your collateral.' He paused then added, 'Do you understand — Caroline — dear?'

In a confused, half-frightened, half-angry way, I did. Horace Coutts meant to imply that for my friendship, — and perhaps a little more than that, though I hoped not — he was willing to guarantee my integrity concerning the bank loan. 'A sort of blackmail' flashed through my mind. But I did my best to smother the suggestion. I had, after all, asked for his advice, and he was giving it freely, plus practical assistance that an hour ago would not have entered my mind. The introduction? Yes. I had hoped for his help there, but to put me under such a personal obligation seemed suddenly slightly distasteful.

I looked away, got up and went to the window. The lane and trees opposite were spattered with young feathery green from mellow sunlight. Gorse shone golden bright against the moorland slopes above, although the slight dip leading towards Tharne on the right was still enshrouded by deep purple shadow. There was no wind. Even from Mrs Crabbe in the kitchen, no sounds echoed of tinkling crockery or rattle of cutlery. I was aware only of the steady ticking of the clock on the parlour mantelshelf, and of Horace Coutts' static figure behind me, watching. I knew, could *feel* him watching, although my back was rigidly turned towards him. My heart was bumping unpleasantly. I did not want his help, and yet commonsense asserted firmly that I certainly did, and that without it I would most probably be evicted from my home more quickly than I could bear to contemplate.

'Oh, let something happen to decide things,' I prayed inwardly, 'please — please let there be a sign—'

I waited, tense and indecisive, crumpling a shred of lacy handkerchief in a tight ball under my fist.

Almost immediately there was the soft tread of a footstep behind, a touch on my arm, and a man's voice saying a little thickly, 'Caroline—'

I turned, with a swish of my skirts, feeling my cheeks redden and a hot stream of perspiration at the back of my neck. Horace Coutts, looking very unlike himself, light eyes burning, slightly prominent, underlip trembling, and the breath coming in little gasps from his thin chest, was bending forward in a gesture of affection. I drew back.

'Oh, Mr Coutts—'

'Horace,' he whispered. 'Horace to you — my dear, my darling—'

I was quite shocked.

'Please don't. You're mistaken. You're — oh you're very kind. I'm honoured, but—' I made a push past him and reached the other side of the table quickly.

'You mustn't say such things,' I protested. 'I hardly know you. Please, Mr Coutts—'

My words must have penetrated. He sat down suddenly, mopping his brow.

'I do apologise for my sudden intrusion,' he said, looking so miserable I could not help but forgive him. 'You're so very beautiful, Caroline. I quite lost my head.' He smiled wistfully, I got up again. 'The last thing I wish to do is upset you. Will you please forget it — or at least try to understand? Then perhaps later when you have had time to think things over you may realise I have only the highest regard for you. You see — I wish to marry you.'

I was so taken aback I could not speak for quite a minute. He hardly moved, just stood facing me, fiddling once with the pin at his neck-scarf. I noticed quite small things — the beads of moisture on his upper lip — a small nerve twitching near his eye. The pause between us was almost intolerable. Then I gasped, 'Marry you, Mr Coutts? Oh but I couldn't—'

He appeared suddenly decisive making a move round the table towards me, with a rush of colour flooding his scholarly features. 'Why not? Because I'm so much older? Because you think me dull and plain? But—'

'No no,' I interrupted, terrified that he was going to try and take me in his arms, 'you're not old at all, and not plain. You're very kind, and I admire you—' I edged round the table and reached the door where I stood with my hand on the knob.

He mopped his brow and returned to his former place by the window. Not looking at me he said very quietly, 'Please sit down. I realise I've shocked you. That's the last thing I wish to do.'

I went back and perched myself rather clumsily on the arm of a chair. He turned, and I saw with relief that he'd gained his usual composure.

'You say you admire me,' he said, smiling wrily, 'Well, that is something, Miss Dorric — Caroline. Something I'm sure I don't deserve. But I shall treasure the words, and hope sincerely that in the end — when you know me better perhaps — admiration may turn to something warmer.' He lifted a hand, 'No, say nothing now. For the moment we will continue as we are. I will do anything in my power to help you, not only because of yourself, but because of the high esteem in which I held your father. So relax I beg of you; have no fear. I'll leave now, and don't worry. There'll be no question of the Bank foreclosing.'

I did not know what to say. As his lean figure passed down the path to the gate a conflict of emotions stirred in me. Apprehension, gratitude, relief, mingled with a curious uncertain fear. Horace Coutts was not a strong looking man physically. But there was something doggedly persistent about him that I sensed would not easily be overcome.

And I was right.

By the end of the month I was already feeling myself trapped. Horace had contrived several introductions for me to individual people who professed an interest in my designs. I sold a certain number of what I now realise were no more than amateurish if original artistic efforts. But it became increasingly clear as the days passed that however hard I worked the enterprise was hardly likely to make me a living. And while I remained at Carnbrooke, I should be indebted and dependent on Mr Coutts' generosity. He made no attempt to enforce his plan, or threaten me into a commitment of marriage, but whenever we met I was increasingly aware of the ardour, the expectancy in his pale eyes.

I did not know what to do.

Worrying and pondering so much over the future kept me from dwelling on other things; this was the only rewarding point about those uncertain days. But at odd moments when my eyes strayed to Tharne, catching a fleeting glance of Garth de Verries in the lane, or riding − a dark erect figure over the distant moors − despair and an aching terrible longing would seize me. I would close my eyes and imagine the rapturous impact of his arms about me, his ruthless demanding mouth against mine − so lose myself in fantasy that I already felt pledged, knowing that however false and wildly ridiculous the image was, no one in the world, ever, but himself would be able to rouse me, emotionally to the full potentials of womanhood.

'Oh Garth − Garth,' I would think then, 'why isn't it you? Why can't you come wooing with flowers and kind words instead of Horace Coutts?'

If Garth had made one simple pleading overture towards me the working out of my life would have been very different at that point.

But he never did. His whole interest seemed concentrated in Tharne, and when I viewed things objectively I had to admit this was quite natural. He had his inheritance, his home and his mistress − more than enough to occupy his full time. There was also the sick relative in the house and his formidable cousin, Miss Ruana. What chance then, or what right had I to expect any part in his life?

None.

And so I tried to shut him resolutely from my mind, and replaced his image wilfully by another − that of existence as the wife of Horace Coutts.

Mrs Horace Coutts! if the idea had been less formidable it

could even have appeared slightly comical. I saw myself seated in a respectable parlour pouring tea for his elderly-youngish friends, imagined the conventional little bows and remarks, and gossipy snippets of conversation, heard myself saying politely — 'How nice you were able to come, Mrs so-and-so. The afternoon has been quite delightful—' charades of similar scenes followed one upon another through my brain. I would be secure of course, and in time possibly grow acclimatised to the new routine. There would be compensation.

I dwelt on the latter, refusing to accept that my true heart and mind were always elsewhere, wild and unfettered, racing across the Cornish moors through sunlight and rain, feeling the sting of rime on my lips, and always another following nearby, a dark shape with the fire of desire in his eyes and whole being — a destiny that in the end would subdue all the rest and claim me, something stronger than gratitude, honour, life or death — oh yes, it was always there, and would be while I lived; yet unreachable, and therefore to be denied.

So deny it I did. Fiercely, with all the defiance and resolution I possessed.

The consequence was that at the end of July I told Horace Coutts that I would be his wife.

Mrs Crabbe at first appeared gratified at the news, then doubtful. She had assumed more power since Aunt Adela's death, and started to probe and question me with the fussiness of an old hen over her one chick.

'Are you sure?' she said at last. 'Tisn' just a mood es et? Men of his age, c'n be set in their habits, and you were always one for goin' yur own way now, weren't you? Another thing — where'll you live Miss Caroline? Sell the old place after all will 'ee? An' go an' live with him in Penzance?' Her small eyes were screwed up, her head set forward doggedly. 'Well, what *are* your plans, Miss Caroline? Seems to me I have a right to know, considerin' Carnbrooke's bin my home for so many years. Am I goin' to be turned out or what?'

'Mrs Crabbe!' I burst out indignantly. 'As if I'd consider such a thing. You'd no reason at all to suggest it. You know very well all I think about — all I'm doing is for Carnbrooke, for both of us—' I broke off realising with a shock, and from the sudden stern look on her face, that I'd betrayed myself, hardly realising the implication of my own words.

'Ah! I thought so,' I heard the old voice saying triumphantly. 'You're selling yourself, bean't 'ee? Marryin' that stiffnecked critter just for what you'll get out of et.' She paused for breath, then continued, 'Don't do it, Miss Caroline. 'Tedn' right. He's older'n you by a big bit. Dotin' on you he may appear at the moment, willing to give 'ee this'n that, and promisin' the earth. But if you marry — then 'et'll be a different story, I'm telling you. You'll be expected to go where he says, do as he wishes, an' live in the house he wants. An' it won't be here, you mark my words. There'll be no place for me neither.'

'There'll always be a place for you, Mrs Crabbe,' I told her impetuously. 'And you're wrong about — Horace — Mr Coutts. He's a kind man, and very respectable. He'll take care of me—'

She laughed jarringly. 'Respec'able? An' tek care—? Of you? You was never one for either of those, I'm thinkin. A wild streak in you — always was. Even from a babe — an' a real little cherub you looked — there was an imp of wickedness in your eyes an' on your shoulder. I saw it, though no one else did. An' I'd think, one day there's goin' to be trouble ahead for 'ee unless you be curbed, chile. Well — curbed you wasn't, and here you are provin' I was right.'

I laughed, and took her hand. 'Dear Mrs Crabbe. Please don't worry. I know about my own devil, and that I'm stubborn and do silly things sometimes. But, believe me, I'm not being stubborn over this. Horace will make me a good husband, and another thing — I know very well my father would be pleased.'

The last remark silenced her, and for the moment I was relieved. Later though, her remark concerning the very important question of where I would live with Horace shocked me to reality. Why had I not thought of the situation from such an angle before? I had just assumed that he would agree to move to Carnbrooke, retaining his own offices in Penzance for business during the week.

When I tackled him on the matter at our next meeting he was encouraging but evasive. 'My dear love,' he said, 'naturally you will wish to keep Carnbrooke as a country residence. Our time can be divided between my own present apartments, which as you know are very adequate for a married couple, and your father's old home.'

'And Mrs Crabbe?' I persisted quickly.

'I certainly would have no intention of getting rid of so old a family retainer,' he said with rather chilly precision. 'I can assure you, Caroline, you have no fears on that score.'

'And the mortgage?' I queried unwisely.

He stared at me, before answering. 'Have you been troubled officially, or by the Bank lately? No of course not. You can take my word that has already been taken care of. Carnbrooke is already safely yours.'

I did take his word. But I was discomforted. Something in the way he spoke unnerved me and made me realise that even if I wished at the last moment to change my mind about marrying him, I could not.

I was pledged in honour to become his wife.

That is what I told myself and made myself believe then, and that is why on a certain day in mid September I was married quietly at St Mary's Church in Penzance to Horace William Coutts, of Coutts and Large, Chartered accountants, and after the brief ceremony, set off with him for Torquay where we were to spend a conventional week's honeymoon before returning to Cornwall.

3

My first night with Horace was not only a shock but a bitter revelation of my own mistake. I should not have married, of course. I'd known I didn't love him, but I'd expected, stupidly, that gratitude for his help might develop from respect into something warmer which in time would blot out the secret cravings of my own wild nature.

How naive and young I was. How blind I'd been.

As I undressed and changed into my night clothes following his retreat into the dressing room of our conventionally sumptuous hotel bedroom, I braced myself to meet the inevitable forth-coming intimacies with outward bravado, although I was inwardly apprehensive and shivering. I loosened my hair from its pins, braided it, and buttoned my cotton nightdress tightly under the chin. It was embroidered at the neck, and had long sleeves fitting at the wrists below hand-stitched frills. Staring at myself through the oval mirror my own reflection looked strange to me. My eyes were dark-rimmed from exhaustion in the candlelight. I appeared jaded yet childish, longing desper-ately to be back alone in my own room at Carnbrooke. For the first time I faced the one stark fact that this could never be. Even when I returned to my old home, I would not be alone. Horace would be with me — the scholarly looking sedate man I had only that day given my pledge to 'love, honour, and obey' for life.

And he was a stranger.

I hardly knew him.

I swallowed nervously, took a tiny pot of pink cream from my reticule — one I had secreted from poor Aunt Adela's collec-tion, and rubbed a little on my cheeks. I must look composed and cheerful I thought. Whatever happened, Mr Coutts — Horace — must not guess my inner fear — my absurd longing to rush to the door and escape from that stuffy exotic interior.

My reflection was not encouraging. The white figure with strained face, wide burning eyes, pink cheeks and set chin was one I hardly recognised — childish, yet prepared to face what lay ahead with adult stoicism.

I decided, as I had before, that Aunt Adela's pink cream did not suit me, and hastily rubbed it off, leaving my cheeks with a natural glow from the friction, and my nose shiny.

I had just laid the lace towel aside when the dressing room door opened and Horace came in. He was wearing a sedate white shirt that reached to mid-calf length, and had a night cap on his head. I had a hysterical desire to giggle. He looked so odd, like one of illustrations from Dickens. Any wild ideas of possible sentiment between us collapsed in that first second to pity, fear, combined with embarrassing ridicule. I smiled auto-matically and made a pretence of tidying my discarded dress, shaking it, then returned to the dressing table to put my brush straight on the glass surface.

Horace coughed.

'You look — very charming,' he murmured rather thickly, coming towards me.

'What? In this thing?' I laughed shrilly, thankful to find anything commonplace to say. 'It's not at all becoming. All night clothes are so — ugly—' Even then I didn't realise what my words could imply. My one longing was to be away — rush out anywhere — clothes or not — and somehow be back on the Cornish moors, racing like a fox to its hole or any wild thing to its hiding place.

Horace Coutts did not understand of course.

Taking my random statement as an invitation, he moved up behind me, and placed his hands on my shoulders. He was breathing heavily. I stiffened.

'What a pretty wife I have,' he whispered, with his face against my cheek.

I made an involuntary movement away. 'Oh, Horace, you mustn't — we mustn't — give me a little time—'

He smiled. I closed my eyes, and could feel myself shivering. Then one hand was moving insidiously from my shoulders to buttocks. 'Oh God,' I prayed inwardly 'help me, please help me—'

But no deity came to my aid. Horace lifted me up deliberately. His fingers had no gentleness in them. They were hard tipped, without artistry or any sense of sensual expertise. As I lay on my back on the bed, he pulled the nightdress up, and bent over me, staring at my nude body. There was a slight rim of foam on his lips. I was suddenly terrified, and would have sprung up if he hadn't flung himself on top of me.

Although a slight man, he was hard and forceful. But my thighs were closed tightly against him. For minutes he fumbled, pushed and panted, while I struggled in an effort to free myself.

It was no use.

In the end he managed to penetrate and possess, leaving me torn, bleeding, and in considerable pain. I jumped up, and made a dive for the dressing room. When I returned he was lying with his arms under his head, smiling again.

It was not a nice smile.

'Come here, Caroline,' he said.

Like an automaton I took a few steps from the bed. He

reached out and grabbed my wrist. Then he remarked, 'You must learn a little self control, my dear. You are my wife, and in future I hope will be more adaptable and forthcoming. Still—' he paused briefly, '—I must be patient I suppose. You are, after all, little more than a child. But remember—' his voice rose shrilly—' children who do not behave get whipped. If you do your duty all will be well. If not — but we won't speak of alternatives—' he broke off, shocked, obviously, to see the hatred in my eyes. He tried appeasement. 'Whatever is the matter? I wouldn't really hurt you. You know that. Caroline—'

I stared at him before saying irrelevantly, 'Your night-cap's fallen off. Won't your head get cold?'

'My head?' he gasped.

'Yes. Your head.' I started to laugh, thinking in my wild disillusionment what a ridiculously unattractive head it was, topped by nondescript thinning hair, and with wide ears sticking out on each side. His Adam's apple protruded from his thin neck. The hatred in me turned to contempt.

Suddenly he began to laugh too. This eased the strain. He yawned, kissed me dutifully on the cheek, pulled the ridiculous cap on again, and turned over.

Minutes later he was asleep, breathing and snoring rhythmically with his mouth open. He was still snoring when at last, towards dawn, I slipped into troubled unconsciousness.

I was woken by the sound of a maid's knock on the door. She entered, carrying a breakfast tray for one. I noticed, thankfully, that Horace had dressed and already gone out presumably for his early 'constitutional', which he had informed me previously several times, was his habit, and one which kept him fit for the day's routine.

I dreaded to think of the endless days — and nights probably — of routine ahead. Anxiety in case Horace should return before I was up and about, made me hurry through a quick cup of tea, and take a few bites of toast. Then I washed frenziedly, and pulled on my chemise, stays, thick lace-edged drawers, petticoat, and three underskirts. I had just stepped into my high-necked blue day dress, when Mr Coutts — or rather, my husband — entered.

He was smiling, and rubbing his hands together with a certain gleeful fatuousness that told me he had satisfactorily dispelled the less harmonious side of the night's events. I noticed his longish nose was slightly pink-tipped, and had the suggestion of a dew-drop gathering.

'Well, my dear,' he said cheerfully. 'Obviously you slept well; good, good! I have already done my daily dozen. So we can look forward to a relaxed day together ahead. A tour round the Marine Drive perhaps? Or a morning in the concert hall listening to good music? Music can be so peaceful for the soul—'

'Whatever you choose, Horace,' I heard myself saying, but my thoughts were elsewhere. Peace for the soul? Horace Coutts' soul? What did I want of that, when all my being and heart were far away with the wind and clouds racing over the Cornish moors? With the gulls screaming, and great waves flinging their fury against the granite cliffs?

Oh God! what had I done?

Many times I was to ask that question during the days that followed. And many many times, secretly, the image of a strong, arrogant, condemning face flooded by imagination, swamping all other thoughts into negation.

Time dragged by – a period in which I constantly made an effort to concentrate on Horace's good points, his dependable qualities, practical shrewd mind, and astute assessment of human beings, his knowledge of classical music and literature, and unfailing patience in trying to educate me to his standards. He could be generous when he considered the cause warranted it, and during those first days seldom refused to allow me any feminine indulgences if I asked nicely, such as perfume or a new dress, provided it was in good taste. But he knew where every penny went. In most frivolous moments I could sense – almost perceive – his mathematical brain precisely calculating the cost to his pocket.

I tried to feel tenderness; in the Gardens one day, watching his profile turned to a pond where ducks swam, I impulsively slipped my hand into his. For a moment he had looked almost young, with the autumn sunlight touching his fine features with gold. He drew his hand away firmly, and looking down on me said primly, 'Caroline my love, not here. It's most unseemly in public.'

The cold reproving look in his pale eyes chilled me. I glanced ahead with anger and disappointment seething in me. My cheeks burned. I wanted to hurl cruel words at him, and throw decorum to the winds — I wanted to race away and join a group of children on the other side of the pool — to throw bread to the birds, pull off my stupid stockings and shoes and dangle my toes in the water. But I walked on very erectly with Horace, chin up and lips firm, controlling my wild impulse, as my heart steadied, and the rush of rebellion faded to inevitable acceptance.

At last the charade of a honeymoon was over, and we left again for Cornwall and our apartment on the outskirts of Penzance.

Though conventionally furnished Horace had done what he could to brighten the rather sombre dining room and parlour with new rugs and muslin curtains which were caught back by looped gold cord to give an impression of light and air. But Horace, I found, did not really like fresh air, having suffered from childhood with a weak chest. So more often than not the heavy brown velvet side-curtains were drawn over the muslin, leaving only four feet or so of restricted daylight into the rooms. I bought flowers which I arranged in china jugs and vases to beautify the sombre mahogany chests and heavy dining table. But Horace said they made him sneeze, so Mrs Pym — his elderly daily servant — took them away with a sniff of her nose and an 'I told you so' look in her eyes. Mrs Pym, although extremely competent, made me more than ever frustrated.

To have looked after the apartment myself would have given me something to do. As it was I had almost the whole day to fret over the dullness of my life.

Months passed. Christmas came and went. In a fit of despair I told Horace one day in February that I felt useless under present conditions. 'Mrs Pym does so much,' I complained, 'I might as well not be here. Why can't we get rid of her?'

Horace stared at me, astonished.

'Get rid of Mrs Pym? Whatever are you thinking about? The idea is quite ridiculous, and most unkind. She's a worthy soul, extremely competent, and knows my tastes so well. Good cooks of her calibre don't come three-a-penny—'

'What a pity!' I said with a sudden spurt of courage. 'If they did we could have one for breakfast, one for lunch, and one for dinner couldn't we? But of course — that might be rather costly. For your pocket, I mean.'

I realised a moment later how outrageous my short speech must have sounded. And — taken in one light, which I certainly had not meant — extremely funny. When Horace did not speak, the humour quite overcame trepidation, and I started to laugh.

Horace did not.

'You seem to have developed an odd and somewhat vulgar attitude recently that I find most distasteful,' he said pompously. 'Try and behave according to your status, Caroline. Remember you are a married woman with wifely obligations.'

My temper flared. 'You've never allowed me to forget that, Horace.'

Neither did he that night.

I went to bed early, but Horace quickly followed.

He did not wait for me to undress myself, but flung me on to the bed pulled my clothes up roughly and clumsily fell upon me. When I struggled and caught my teeth on his palm he put a hand across my mouth, slapped me hard, then turned me over again and took me as though I was some cheap whore.

I felt degraded. Humiliated in a way I had never thought possible. Not only by Horace Coutts, but by myself for selling my body for the sake of Carnbrooke.

Carnbrooke!

After lying numb and frozen with disgust for a few minutes, that one name — the thought of my old home — sent a wave of life through me. I jumped up, went to the wardrobe and took my valise from a top shelf.

Horace had already tidied himself, and was brushing his thin hair in front of the mirror. He turned, regarding me coolly, with a hint of smugness on his face.

'What are you doing?' he queried.

'I'm putting my case ready for the morning,' I told him recklessly.

'You're what?'

'I'm leaving you, Horace. I'm going back to Carnbrooke.'

He did not at first believe me. He simply stared, mouth open, while I watched contemptuously his Adam's apple jerk in his thin throat.

'I shouldn't have married you,' I heard myself saying quickly with a rush of words like those of some automation. 'I thought it would work — that respect for you would be enough — and I did respect you — in a way — until tonight. But not any more—' I was so breathless I had to break off for a moment. The pause was sufficient for him to exclaim, 'What nonsense. You're my wife. If I've been too hasty I'm sorry. But to talk of leaving is ridiculous, just hysteria. Now stop it, Caroline—' His voice had hardened, but there was sudden fear in his eyes. I knew he had believed me. He came towards me purposefully. I backed, and snatched a paper knife from the bedside cabinet.

'If you touch me I'll — I'll use it — I'll kill you — I swear I will. I mean it—' The threat was not true of course. Hatred, terror and intense disgust drove me to the wild speech. My legs were trembling; the room swam round me; I knew that if he approached by one more step I would probably collapse on the floor.

But as we stood there, facing each other like characters in a stage melodrama, something in Horace seemed to crumple. He gasped, grasped a chair suddenly, then sat down, head in hands, breathing heavily. The knife fell from my hand. I still watched him, feeling terror slowly turn to a dull pitying contempt. When he looked up he was very pale.

'What have I done?' he asked. 'Tell me, Caroline, what have I done?'

I swallowed, trying to think of how to explain. But I knew I couldn't. It was too late. Besides, Horace hadn't the quality or knowledge to realise the first thing about the sorry situation we were in.

It was my fault of course. Most of it was — I'd been too selfish and ignorant, and perhaps too young to realise the hurtful crime I was committing in marrying one man when I was already in love with another.

Although I was in no state to assess things coherently, knowledge flowed over me in a dark tide.

I think Horace, in a dim way, also sensed the truth.

After a further brief and chilling conversation he said, 'Very well. If you want a change so soon — a holiday from domesticity, go to Carnbrooke by all means for a time. A breath of country air may do you good and enable you to view matters in proper proportion.' How like a legal document he sounded. 'I shall stay on here, of course, or tongues may start wagging. And

as we are known to have two residences there can be no raised
eyebrows over the fact that my wife's health demands a spell of
peace and quiet. In fact—' he paused, flinging me a speculative complacent glance, 'what could be more natural?'

I was shocked by the implication of his words, realising in the
same moment that his distasteful suggestion was not impossible.
But no, I told myself forcefully, it couldn't be — it musn't be —
to have Horace's child! The mere idea seemed an affront, so
offensive following the recent unpleasant sexual interlude, that
I felt momentarily sick.

I pulled myself together, with a pretence of misunderstanding.

'I'm glad you understand how I miss Carnbrooke, Horace,' I
managed to say coolly.

'I'm not entirely without imagination, my dear,' Horace
answered fatuously. 'And in return of course, I shall expect a
little from you. For instance—'

'Yes, Horace?'

'During the time you choose to absent youself at your country
retreat I shall consider myself quite entitled to call on your
services occasionally—' a grim suggestion of a smile twitched
his lips as I flinched. I waited rigidly until after the short pause
he continued, 'for entertaining or presiding at my table when
we have guests—'

I bowed my head slightly. He rubbed his hands. 'Good.
Knowing you are at least available when necessary will have to
compensate, I suppose, for the time being.'

I didn't answer. But once more revulsion filled me. I had
thought for a brief interim he was going to be generous, make
the parting easy. But I was wrong. The parting would never be
complete until I was legally free for good of my wretched
marriage.

Except by divorce this could not be; and however hard I
pleaded I knew it was extremely unlikely Horace Coutts would
agree to such an unacceptable procedure.

I turned away desolately, feeling suddenly exhausted almost
beyond endurance.

Thinking he had won, he said:

'Now that is understood I suggest you get some rest. In the
morning you may feel different. I shall sleep in the dressing

room, to allow you to regard things from a more objective angle.'

But I did not sleep that night, and in the morning my mind was unchanged.

I left that day for Carnbrooke. It was raining I remember — thin rain that blew shroud-like over the grey hills, encompassing the moors and distant sea into quiet uniformity. But when I stepped from the cab, a thrill of delight flooded me. The moist air though so still, held the fragrance of heather, bracken, and a multitude of wild growing things. The gorse was already a blur of gold on the hillside, and the glittering damp turf was starred with celandines and early primroses.

'Well, my dear soul!' Mrs Crabbe exclaimed as I entered through the front door. 'What a surprise, to be sure. What's this then — a visit? Or for—'

'Yes.' I told her before she could finish. 'A visit — a very long one. I'm home, Mrs Crabbe—'

'For how long then?' she asked, surprise touched with apprehension on her face.

'For ever, I hope,' I replied shortly.

She didn't answer.

I pushed by her and went upstairs to my old bedroom. As though discarding a nightmare, I pulled the curtains wide and opened the window.

To my right down the lane, I watched a shaft of sunlight penetrate the grey rain, and for a second the roof and towers of Tharne emerged briefly tipped by silver.

Then all was misted by cloud again.

I went to my bed and sat down. It was only then in the reaction of relief that a slow welling of tears came to my eyes, and I cried soundlessly, knowing that whatever happened in the future I would never return to Horace Coutts.

Never.

4

Following my return to Carnbrooke I spent most of the first week wandering about the house and garden, revelling in the new contact with beloved and precious things. There were times, often, when I paused in some small household task to touch walls and furniture with a kind of gentle reverence, unable fully to comprehend that I was there again, back home, and that everything was the same − solid, comforting, real.

Rufus, too, shared my delight. Since my absence in Penzance he had been mostly under Adam's supervision in the stables, or confined for very short periods with Mrs Crabbe in the kitchen. Now he was free again to race upstairs when he felt like it, to fling himself on the quilt or sit by the fire in the parlour. After breakfast each day I took him for a walk over the moors at the back of the house, where he'd snuffle inquisitively, nose down, through the bracken, then pause a little ahead of me, tail wagging, teeth gleaming in his shaggy face. He was no longer young, but affection and familiarity with old habits seemed to imbue him with renewed youth.

In my first reaction of freedom from Horace I was content for a time to live entirely in the present, shutting the painful past and any fears of the future away. But a sudden unexpected meeting with Miss Ruana one afternoon when I was walking to Braggas, jerked me to reality. Rufus ran at her round a corner of the lane, causing a sudden jerk of her basket. She had obviously been shopping. A loaf and some buns spilled from their bags to the ground and rolled towards the hedge.

'I'm so sorry,' I said, red with confusion. 'Oh Rufus, you bad boy—' I broke off, staring at her apologetically. Her severe face was unsmiling. Her mouth was tight in her red face. 'You must let me go back for more—' I continued. 'If you got them in Braggas—'

'I did not,' she said coldly. 'They were made specially for me at the farm. Still——' She drew herself up very erectly. 'Accidents will happen. It's not a major disaster.'

'No, but——' I bent down to pick up the bags. She stopped me immediately.

'Don't trouble unless you want them for your dog. None of them now will be fit for human consumption.'

'No, I suppose not.'

As I paused uncertainly she said, 'I heard, quite by accident that you were back at Carnbrooke. Nothing wrong, I hope, Mrs — Coutts. It *is* Coutts, isn't it?'

'Yes,' I told her, both flustered and angry.

'Hm.' She eyed me shrewdly before turning away. Her cold hawklike glance was so insidiously condemning, that my annoyance turned to acute discomfort. I knew what she suspected, and had an irrational desire to deny it, to cry defiantly, 'I'm not having a baby, if that's what you think, and I'm not living with Mr Coutts any more. I've left him — *left* him, do you hear? We're nothing to each other. Nothing.'

Mercifully I managed to keep control of my tongue, and the hysterical statement never fell. I sensed her disappointment with brief satisfaction. But when, after a moment, she passed on, giving a slight formal nod, my faint triumph quickly crumpled to gloom.

Everyone in the district would soon know of my marital plight, I thought dejectedly, and what they did not know they would make up. Some would pity me, some condemn.

And Garth?

I could hardly bear to think of him. I couldn't expect him to understand. Although no word of love had passed between us, no commitment, or declaration of passion, the mutual awareness had been there; the spark, however sudden and unexpected, had been a flame between us. I had recognised it, and so had he.

'You fool,' I said to myself — 'oh you fool and traitor, Caroline Dorric. How could you? How could you demean yourself by allowing that stick of a man to defile one inch of your body?'

The question may have been absurd, melodramatic, and unfair to Horace. But the truth remained. I had sold myself. And in doing so had sacrificed any possibility of Garth and I ever coming together. As I walked on the memory of his face — the stern set chin and bright blue eyes shocked the beauty of that early spring day into aching longing. He would despise me now; how he would despise me. It was no use thinking, 'But why should he? He has his own life, his foreign mistress—' In any case I didn't actually know that. I had no proof. Besides, laws for men differed from those for women. Women were supposed to be pure and dutiful and beyond reproach where marriage and love were concerned.

I was already exhausted when I reached Braggas and went into the village shop.

I bought a few unnecessary trivial things, aware of Mrs Biggs, the owner's curiosity, but displayed sufficient composure to keep her guessing. When I left, I felt a little better. Tomorrow was another day, I thought, tomorrow anything could happen.

And it did.

In the morning I had a letter from Horace:

Dear Caroline,

I trust by now the country air has restored your nervous health enabling you to view matters in proper proportion. Your absence has been regretted by my friends — if you remember I had arranged a small supper party at The Queens for last Friday which was to have been honoured by the presence of Lady Marston-Green. However I was able to explain your absence with the minimum of discomfort. She sends you her sincere sympathy, and wishes you a quick recovery from your 'disability' — which I put down to a mild infection of the grippe. So please do pull yourself together now, and return at your earliest convenience. I should very much regret having to come to Carnbrooke myself to enforce my rights.

His rights, I thought, with a wild quickening of my heart, his *rights?* — I stood for a moment gripping the table, trying in vain to supress my sense of revulsion and fear, then I continued reading:

Believe me my dear, my deep affection for you remains unchanged. I beg you to be reasonable and not strain our relationship unduly.

Your devoted husband,
Horace Coutts.

My pulses gradually steadied, waves of chill replaced the burning heat of my body. I smoothed the damp fringe of hair from my forehead, and patted my chin with a shred of lawn handkerchief where perspiration had gathered. My spine was suddenly cold. The bodice of my dress clung to my flesh. I couldn't see him, I thought, I wouldn't. I hated him. But — why should I? As quickly as the wild emotion had flared, it died again into a deadly logical assessment of the situation.

Horace was only being himself — Horace Coutts, an average Victorian husband complying with accepted moral standards which demanded a wife's obedience and response to his demands: her presence at his table, and her body at night.

I was the one out of line with society — the rebel who dared to defy. The unprincipled cheat refusing to pay for her privileged marital status.

Privilege! I winced. If only Aunt Henrietta, the family outcast and sinner, was alive, to give me comfort and encouragement! or my father! — a stab of pain seered me. What would he have said?

There was no answer to that. I knew he wouldn't have wished me pain, but if he'd not died I would never have married Horace. It was as simple as that.

Suddenly my head grew blank and weary of argument, and on impulse I changed into my riding habit, went downstairs to the back of the house, and got Adam to saddle Flash for me.

I thought at first of cutting up the moors to the back of the house, and taking a route leading over the far ridge. Then half way down the lane I changed my mind. On the left I noticed the wall already being built bordering Tharne property. It cut from perhaps fifty yards beyond the narrow strip of roadway, and from there was obviously going to run down in a straight line eventually encircling the base of the hill topped by the Granite King. Indignation flooded me. So Garth de Verries had really meant it. With everyone else was I to be entirely denied access to my favourite retreat? Would the wall — when it was completed — be topped by that horried jagged glass that was used sometimes to ward off trespassers from a private estate? Or would there be savage watchdogs prowling about?

The very suggestion revolted me.

With my anger intensified I kicked Flash to a sharp canter

down the lane, and when we reached Braggas took the track up the slope on my left and rode sharply towards the towering Carn.

The gorse and heather smelled sweet; the early sun cast a silver net over the landscape. Gulls dipped and wheeled overhead. The windless silence gave a peculiar sense of being alone in a newly-born world. I paused half way up the moor, reined, and looked back. The clustered roof tops of Braggas above the winding street dropping towards the small harbour, had the misted quality of a mirage. Nothing appeared quite real or tangible. I thought of ancient legends, and Celtic warriors about to take shape from the glittering damp air. Gone was the dark reality of Horace Coutts — vanquished like magic from my life. I was back again in my own territory — myself, a part and being of that mystic Western land, Rhianuon, Gwenhwyvar, or the fateful Morgan-Le-Fay, free spirit of cliffs and sea and ancient dolmen, of flying clouds and rustling streams; of rain and tears, and blossoming earth.

'Oh Garth,' my heart cried, as Flash reared slightly, whimpering in response to the elements, 'where are you?'

That I had met him so briefly was of no account.

Recognition had been between us in our first few seconds together. Not only physical, but through something beyond time — beyond the boundaries of commonsense. Fight him I might for what was mine. But the fight would unify, because we were already as inextricably bound as the flying spume to the sea and the granite rocks to the throbbing earth.

So I was not really surprised — unconsciously I must have expected it — when I saw him approaching from the other side — the Tharne side of the hill. He was astride his stallion. They climbed easily through the haze, blurred at first, then clearly recognisable as the pale light broke the damp air to a million sparks of shattered dew. Dew seemed everywhere — bright on hair and face, and horse's mane. Like legends from the past they rode towards me. Yet real, so real my heart pounded, and a rich glow of warmth rose in me. I quietened Flash and waited. The steam of life and animal breath exuded fire from the morning chill; and fire raced wildly through my veins.

At last he was there, and we faced each other. The darkness of man and beast loomed, large — formidable. But his face was hard and vividly bright above the glimmer of a white cravat.

And even in those first few seconds the eyes registered — their blue brilliance lit by sparks of gold.

I kept my gaze steadily upon him, conscious of my neck and muscles stiffening.

'Good morning, Caroline — Miss Dorric,' he said. I was momentarily taken aback. Surely he'd heard of my marriage? Or perhaps he'd been away.

'Good morning,' I answered politely. 'It's going to be nice, I think.'

'So you decided to visit your favourite haunt — from the other direction?'

There was a hint of irony in his voice. I did not reply.

'Well, I don't entirely blame you. But I rather thought after what I'd said you'd have been accustoming yourself to some other wild retreat — Castle Cromme perhaps?' He paused questioningly. 'Well — Miss Dorric?'

'I often go to Castle Cromme,' I told him. 'It's — I like it there too—' which was true. The ancient ruined remains beyond the high ridge at the back of Carnbrooke had been a chosen haunt of mine since childhood — 'But it's not the same as this. I—' Oh what could I say, how explain my feelings and hidden motives, when I was not even completely sure of them myself?

'I understand perfectly,' he remarked in colder tones. 'This patch of moor interests you because it's forbidden, and therefore you have to ride it. Rather childish, isn't it?'

'No,' I answered. 'No. You're completely wrong. I told you — it's always been common land—'

'It's Tharne land; and I don't want any trespassing.'

'But—'

'In six months,' he continued, very deliberately, 'the wall I'm having built, will completely encircle this property round the Braggas side of the hill. It will be a high wall, heavily enforced against the gales and weather, and will safely cut off the very dangerous precipice on the northern sea-side. This is not only for the well being of my family and any visitors I have at Tharne — but for the sake of people like you who consider they have the right to ride and wander willy-nilly over my lands whenever they choose. In a mist you yourself could easily kill yourself by riding over the cliff there, or even be taken by a bog pool. Do you understand?'

Feeling suddenly reckless, I said, with a short defiant laugh, 'I know every inch of this land. Every inch. I've been here since I was a little girl. Always — whenever I felt like it—' I broke off recklessly.

'Without your elders knowing no doubt,' he said grimly. 'You should have been caught and soundly spanked. And if I ever find you here again that's what you'll get.'

'You wouldn't dare—' I gasped.

'Oh, yes, I would. Make no mistake about it. I'm a man of my word, as all who've known me have discovered—'

'Including your — your Indian servants I suppose—' I broke in heedlessly, 'and that woman of yours you bought back—' suddenly, realising what I'd said, and with a hand to my mouth I gasped, 'Oh, I didn't mean—'

He dismounted from his horse, sprang forward and grasped Flash's bridle.

'Get down,' he said. 'Or shall I assist you?'

Hardly realising it, I obeyed him.

The next moment his hands were on my shoulders.

'Now. Tell me what the devil you're talking about.'

'Just what I've heard,' I said.

'Or thought?'

'Both.'

'I see.'

My whole body was trembling, although I tried not to show it.

'Whether you've heard it, think it, or have merely concocted a sordid little jealous story is of no account,' he said. 'It might have been, if you were other than what you are — *Mrs Horace Coutts.*' The words cut me with the sharpness of a sword. 'But under the circumstances — since you took it into your head to marry that dry-as-dust stick, I hardly think it's your business to comment on my private life.'

His grip tightened. I strained away from him, but he held me close. My head whirled. All my senses seemed to merge and quicken into overwhelming desire. Yet still I struggled.

'Why did you do it?' I heard him saying close against one ear. 'Why, darling — why? *Why?* You didn't want him. He was nothing to you. Was he — was he?'

Suddenly, as I gasped, I was free, and nearly fell to the ground. When I'd recovered my balance, I shook my head and turned away dumbly. In a second he'd caught me and turned me round again. Our two bodies were hot and vibrant and hard against each other. His lips, like fire came down, burning my own. I reached out to him then, and the kiss was sweeter, lovelier, more cruel, and bitter than anything I'd ever dreamed of. I'd imagined it so often, through sleeping and waking moments. But the reality was a shock — encompassing me in a brief throbbing oblivion more wonderful than heaven and more terrible than hell.

With abrupt release it was over.

He tore himself away, and before I'd recovered had mounted his horse, and with a hand hard on the reins, said, 'Go home, Caroline — wherever that may be — and never come this way again.'

A second later he had gone.

Paralysed of movement I watched him plunging down the track to Tharne, kicking the stallion to a dangerous speed. When at last the thud of hooves had died and horse and rider were no more to be seen, I turned and found Flash grazing placidly by a nearby rock. I took her bridle and led her a few yards towards the cold throne of the Granite King.

Hard and relentless the giant dolmen stood bleak and arrogant against the sky. Resolute, merciless. Unfeeling of love or human emotion. Something of its icy indifference penetrated my own spirit. I was young yet, but one day I would be old, with my deep secret self unfulfilled. Garth's kiss still burned on my lips. But my heart was chill; and as though in response to my desolate mood, a drift of clouds suddenly dimmed the sun.

I shivered, and a few seconds later was riding back to Carnbrooke.

The next day I got Adam to drive me into Penzance for a meeting with my bank manager. Before I saw Horace again — which was inevitable sometime — I was determined to know exactly how much I was indebted to him, and the amount he'd gone to in guaranteeing Carnbrooke, whether the mortgage was completely covered, or if he was making regular payments to retain the property.

I was not looking forward to the encounter knowing that I had no funds at all to face my own commitments.

To my surprise I was greeted with considerable deference, and most flattering smiles.

'My dear young lady — Mrs Coutts,' the manager Mr Thorpe-Waston told me, beaming over his spectacles, 'but Mr Coutts has no control over Carnbrooke at all. It is yours alone to live in. Did you not know this?'

'Well I—' I hesitated, swallowed nervously, then continued, 'I realised of course that before we were married my husband had pledged security, but I—'

'Your husband?' The heavy eyes arched above the gold rims. 'Mr Coutts certainly came along to offer any reasonable help within his power, but by that time everything was being cleared. The property was being transferred to its new owner, with you named as having sole rights to live there.

'But — how?' I asked, completely at a loss. 'I don't see — you must be mistaken surely?'

'No, no. Men in my position do not make mistakes,' the genial voice went on, 'can't afford to. I can assure you the letters of agreement giving you sole rights of occupancy, are safely deposited in your single name — perhaps that should be remedied, of course, now you have a wedding ring on your finger.' He smiled disarmingly.

'But who owns it then? You must tell me,' I insisted.

He stared at me owlishly. 'You have more good friends, obviously, than you imagined,' he remarked, 'including an extremely generous one.'

'Who?' I demanded curtly.

'I don't think he wished you to know—'

'But it's my right,' I persisted.

'Very well.'

He got up suddenly, went to a desk, opened it and returned with a file of papers. Producing one he returned to the table and said, 'The deeds are here, if you insist in persuing them. The name of your benefactor is de Verries, Sir Garth de Verries, and the transaction concerning Carnbrooke was finally completed a fortnight before your marriage.'

I didn't need to peruse the paper. If I had I hardly think I would have been able to decipher it. My head was swimming, and I had to grip the table as I got up, to steady myself.

Through a dream, I heard myself saying, 'I can't go on living

there of course. It's impossible. I shall have to—' I didn't know
how to finish. The word 'leave' was on my lips, but I held it
back. How could one walk out of a house that had been a gift?
And if Garth de Verries wanted to help, why should I refuse —
unless he expected something in return. What? Through my
confusion only one explanation registered, and the thought
made me both angry and suddenly wildly excited. My skin was
burning with elation, yet at the same time I felt subtly
humiliated. Garth must have had a motive at the time of his
philanthropic gesture. As with Horace, there must have been a
cunning plot in his mind. But then he probably had not heard
of my forthcoming marriage. Perhaps if I'd not taken such a
rash step in my life everything would have worked out properly
between us. The suggestion was too wild and improbable to
contemplate properly. Myself — as Garth's wife. Was that it?
Could it ever really have happened?

In a quick tide of rising hostility against Horace Coutts I
wished in one reckless moment for revenge, and knew myself
capable of emotion that I'd not realised existed. Then, as I
pulled myself together I heard Mr Watson remarking reason-
ingly. 'Oh no, Mrs Coutts, you can't possibly abandon the
property. It was a gift. Sir Garth, I know, would never take it
back for himself. Besides — my dear young lady — why should
you wish to appear so ungrateful?'

Why indeed!

Presently, having gained composure, I asked, 'Did my — did
Mr Coutts know of the arrangement at the time?'

'Oh almost immediately, naturally. I had to inform him at
our next meeting concerning your — liabilities. And I naturally
assumed he would put you in the picture.' He paused, eyed me
shrewdly, and continued quickly, 'If I'd envisaged your unwel-
coming reaction to Sir Garth's generous gesture, I'd have
contacted you. But Sir Garth was clearly against you knowing.'
He sighed. 'Sometimes, in my position, it's very difficult knowing what to do for the best.'

'Yes, yes of course.' By then my nerves were under control,
and before I left I was at least outwardly composed and polite.

Two days later Horace appeared at Carnbrooke. It was about
eleven thirty that Mrs Crabbe ushered him into the sitting
room. He was conventionally dressed in sombre professional

attire, and carried his tall hat in one gloved hand. His hair was sleek above the fairish side-burns, his pale eyes expectant, his mouth slightly pursed.

'Well, Caroline,' he said, 'you look much improved in health I must say.'

'Thank you,' I answered formally. I tried to smile, but the effort was not very successful. I could feel his gaze travelling my body, and resented it. No doubt he was critical of the blue cotton dress I was wearing, which though flowing and falling from the waist, was tight about the breasts and cut rather low at the shoulders for day wear. Yet his gaze also held something else — something that filled me with distaste — a covetous anticipation of asserting his 'male-rights' — of ravishing me with his greedy hard hands.

I shuddered.

'What's the matter, Caroline?' he asked. 'Aren't you a little pleased to see me? Or are you cold? Shall we shut the window?'

He made a gesture to close it.

'No. Please,' I said. 'I like the fresh air.'

'Of course.'

He took a chair near the table, and waved a trifle irritably to one opposite. 'Oh, do be a little helpful and relax,' he said. 'There's no need to be nervous, you know. I am your husband.'

I sighed.

'Don't let us fence, Horace. Tell me why you've come please, and then——?'

'*Why?*' he interrupted shrilly. 'To take you home, of course. Obviously you're quite well, and have had more than sufficient time to recover from your strange nervous malaise. At first I decided to leave you to make up your own mind concerning your return. But on reflection I have found I was wrong. Women are moody creatures at the best of times — wayward sometimes——' he smiled coldly, 'and in need of male guidance. So here I am. And I would be grateful if you would pack immediately, as soon as possible. I have an appointment with an important client at three o'clock. This will allow us just sufficient time to have a meal in Penzance before I return to the office——'

'No, Horace,' I interrupted firmly. 'I'm not coming with you.'

He jumped up. 'What do you mean?'

'I thought I'd made myself clear before,' I told him firmly, as my heart started pounding. 'Our marriage is over.'

His temper flared. He took a step towards me. I sprang from the chair and faced him, with both hands clenched at my sides. 'Don't touch me. I'm sorry you've had the journey for nothing. I'm sorry too—' and this was quite true — 'that I took advantage of you in the first place when I accepted your help. I thought it was very generous of you, and I was grateful. But—' I tried to soften the blow '—it was only through gratitude, I married you Horace. I didn't realise it at the time. I thought we could make a success of things if we tried hard, even learn to — to care for each other, in a kind of way. But love isn't like that—' my voice trailed off uncertainly. 'It's—'

'Yes?' His iron hand grasped my wrist. 'What is it? Perhaps as you know so much about it, you'll clarify your highly irrational and melodramatic concept of the word and explain. Or is it so irrational? Have you, in my absence, been indulging yourself with some rustic paramour? A roll-in-the-hay, don't they call it? — a—'

I wrenched my arm free.

'You insulting creature,' I exclaimed. 'Leave me alone. Go away. Go — or I'll call Mrs Crabbe. I'll scream—' The glaring prominent eyes narrowed. His pale face seemed to narrow and grow whiter. Suddenly he straightened up and said in deadly threatening tones, 'You'll be sorry for this, Caroline. If there's another man I'll find him and make him pay—'

Without thinking, I cried — 'But he's paid already, hasn't he? And you never told me. Garth, Sir Garth de Verries — you deceived me, Horace. It was *Garth* who bought this house — Carnbrooke — my home—' I was breathing so heavily the room felt to be closing in on me.

Horace gaped, and for a moment, in a threatening fit of hysteria I thought he looked almost funny. I started to laugh. Then he said, 'Stop it,' and slapped my face hard.

'So he's the one,' he remarked. 'I see. You are aiming for a higher catch. Well well! I might have known.'

He took his hat from the chest and walked to the door. 'You'll hear more of this — both of you,' he threatened, with his hand on the knob. 'I may have no handle to my name. But I have power.' Not realising, in the heat of the moment, the implication

of his words, I said recklessly, 'Do whatever you please, Horace.
There are some things that can't be bought. Oh – please—'
Emotion, a feeling of mingled guilt, frustration, desire for one
man and dislike for another, dimmed all sense of proportion in
me. I stared at him blankly, longing for some sign – however
faint – of understanding.

But there was none. Only bleak condemnation.

A second later he had turned abruptly, and gone, closing the
door behind him with a sharp snap.

I listened to his footsteps receding down the hall, heard a
click of a latch followed presently by the sound of horses' hooves
and carriage wheels echoing from the lane. Then all was quiet;
everything except the monotonous sound of the clock ticking,
and a bee buzzing from the open window to the flowers on the
table.

5

The following few days became for me a blurred time of
bewilderment and realisation of what I'd done. One moment I
was shocked by Horace's implication concerning Garth, and the
fact that I'd not denied his accusation – the next I was unable
to believe the sordid interim had really happened. When at last
I was able to face matters honestly, I told myself Mr Coutts had
been merely bragging when he'd threatened to involve Garth de
Verries. But the memory of Horace's cold voice – the mean
malicious glint of his eyes suggested I could very well be wrong.
Then I thought, with a renewal of commonsense – nothing
could be proved. There had been nothing wrong in my association with Garth.

Nothing except – a kiss.

And a kiss? What was a kiss?

Not everything of course. But so much; oh so much. And I
shivered; my whole body trembled when I recalled those few
passionate moments by the Granite King.

For a week I hardly went out, but busied myself about the house, finding things to do which prevented me from dwelling too much on my own predicament.

Mrs Crabbe was puzzled.

Once she said, 'Changed you are, Miss Caroline — or should I say, Mrs Coutts — since you got wed. Why you do stay on here s'long, though, when your husband's in Penzance I can't for the life of me mek out.' She paused, then added, poking her old face forward, 'Expecting are you? You do look a bit peaked like.'

'No,' I replied sharply, almost shouting. 'No.'

And thankfully, I knew by that time it was true.

'Hm!' She looked disbelieving for a moment.

'If you hear any rumours of that kind please contradict them immediately,' I went on in my most arrogant tones. 'I am not expecting a baby, and — well, you may as well know it — I am not returning to Mr Coutts, ever. Our marriage was a mistake. It's over.'

She took me by the arm then. Her jaw was set, her old eyes glittering with condemnation in her wrinkled face. 'Now look here, Miss Caroline, ef things are that wrong you jus' tell me 'bout et, see? As far as I c'n make out I'm the only one now you do have to confide in, an' I'd be lacking in my duty — duty to your dear papa, — ef I didn't speak. Come now, luvvie—'

I pushed her away relentlessly, deliberately turning my face away so she would not see the tell-tale tears in my eyes.

'Please leave me alone, Mrs Crabbe,' I said. 'Later perhaps we'll talk — when I can see things more clearly. There's no need to be distressed. I'm quite all right.' Even to my own ears the last words sounded formal — cold.

She muttered something, and went to the door, paused there and said, 'You can't bottle things up for ever, and what you're doin' now edn' right. So you jus' think about et, and when you be done thinkin' come an' tell me.'

The latch clicked.

She was gone.

I did not tell her anything at that time of course. I was becoming increasingly aware of the wrong I'd done in allowing Horace's accusation concerning Garth de Verries to go undenied. I felt like a trapped wild creature trying to hide from justice, and because of it kept well out of sight of Tharne.

My occasional strolls took me only a short way along the lower path at the back of Carnbrooke, never down the lane to Braggas. Just once when I was closing the parlour curtains for the evening, I was attracted by a shaft of gold light striking the towers of the de Verries mansion above the trees. I paused involuntarily. Something moved — a shape behind the glass of a top window. A second later a face appeared, briefly illuminated by the fading sun's last ray. It was a dark face surrounded by massed brilliant blackness — a child's. Almost immediately a small form was spread-eagled grotesquely, arms wide, nose pressed against the shining surface. I nearly screamed, thinking she must fall. But of course the window was closed. Supposing the glass shattered?

I held my breath, and then, suddenly the form and face disappeared, leaving only an impression of shadows moving fleetingly. A hand appeared and a blind fell down. All was dark. Simultaneously the lingering light died behind the rim of the distant horizon, and all was hushed and still, and curiously without life.

A vague cloud of unease filled me. Mystery seemed to thicken round the walls of Tharne, enveloping the household into forbidden territory — a world of its own with all doors closed to strangers of which I was one.

I drew the curtains tight, and at that moment Mrs Crabbe entered with the lamp. I was tempted to confide in her about the child, but did not. Whatever I said would only have evoked some kind of criticism, and I was suddenly overwhelmingly anxious for peace between us. If Horace carried out his threats I should have more than sufficient haranguing to face later. So the least said about the de Verries family for the moment, the better. I thanked Mrs Crabbe for bringing the lamp in, and she remarked a little sourly that she'd had to trim the wick herself. 'That girl get lazier every day,' she told me pointedly. 'If you're thinking of stayin' much longer mebbe 't would be best to look for someone else. I don't get younger, an' Adam's only here when he thinks like et—'

'Leave things as they are for the present,' I said. 'I've enough to think of just now without — without domestic upheavals.'

'Hm!' Her voice was gruff. 'I can well b'lieve that. An' the sooner you get your mind straight the easier it'll be for all of us. That's for sure.'

She left the room still muttering. I tried to ignore her comments, but it wasn't easy. So much that I had done during the last year seemed to have gone wrong. The sense of guilt not only depressed — but irritated me. My body felt rebellious too; not only through longing for Garth, but because of the enforced isolation and lack of exercise.

Tomorrow I thought, I'd go for a ramble — take the narrow sheep track behind Carnbrooke that led eventually to Castle Cromme. The castle — which was merely a relic left from far ancient times, lay just over the moorland ridge — a desolate wild place consisting of a half-circle of tall stones, some fallen, surrounding the faint indications of what could have been a prehistoric village or one massive fortress. There were beehive huts in the vicinity, and the atmosphere was of forgotten life and a world long dead, although broom and heather thrived there, and it was a favourite haunt for badger and fox. There was no suggestion any more of defiance against the passing of time. Unlike the rough savagery of the Granite King on the opposite slope bordering Braggas, the atmosphere was forbidding, cold and remote.

I had never particularly cared for it, feeling too many dead lay buried beneath the tumpy mounds. Yet sometimes, in lonely moments I had felt a morbid kinship with the area. Ghosts? No. I did not believe in ghosts. But the sense of 'place' had an identity of its own, as though mocking the wild irrational stirring of blood in my veins. There, if anywhere, I thought, I might be able to get matters into proper proportion. All things passed. Eventually all longing for Garth would die.

It must.

So the next morning, quite early, I set off with Rufus, on the four mile walk to Cromme.

It was a clear day, although a faint glitter of mist still persisted as I climbed the first slope. The tang of autumn hovered in the air, and the foliage of bushes and undergrowth was already tinged by russet and brown. Soon it would be the fall; soon tumbled blackberries would lie crushed and rotting among the damp dead leaves and wet earth. Dank pools of black bog would appear, and the inky holes of deserted mine shafts would loom treacherously below the bare tangled network of bramble branches and weeds. High winds would later sweep in from the Atlantic, driving heavy rain from sullen clouds. All would be grey and desolate. Yet underneath life would be stirring again. The roots of fern and fresh spring turf would be pulsing and pushing through the last year's decay. And in February the buds of aconite, celandines and primroses would glimmer gold by stream and stone. If only the next few months could be jumped I thought, or slept through so that I would wake up then, and find all my problems solved, and know what the future was to be.

Rufus suddenly started barking and tugging at my skirt. I picked up a twig and threw it for him. This happened several times. But when we turned the brow of the hill his attention was diverted by movement on the ancient site. I followed, and saw a horse — a dark brown chestnut — tethered by one of the standing stones. When its head lifted my heart contracted. He was a magnificent beast, with a white star on his forehead: from the de Verries stables, I guessed.

I looked round and at first saw no sign of any rider. Then Rufus cut to the left, yelping with excitement. I stood quite still, watching. Garth's figure presently appeared climbing the slope between the rocks. He was wearing a black jacket and fawn breeches, but against the sunlight all was dark except for a spatter of gold striking sideways across the clear hard lines of cheekbones, prominent nose and jaw.

I had an impulse to turn and walk away, but before I could do so he had taken a few long strides towards me, and stood as motionless as myself, looking down on me.

'Well, well,' he said at last. 'The errant young wife! What a pleasure.'

My cheeks burned beneath the brilliant blue eyes. There was something in his voice that warned me he already knew; Horace's threat had been no idle one. He had somehow contrived to make trouble between Garth and myself. My first reaction was of shame, my second of anger and irritation that Garth should speak in such tones to me.

'Good morning Sir — Garth,' I said, lifting my chin an inch higher. 'I — I didn't know you came this way.'

He laughed. 'It's permissible, I believe. I'm thinking of buying the land. Matt Cadmin has no use for it except for sheep, and I'm interested in the site.'

'I see.' I meant to keep my tongue under control, but before I was aware of it I said, 'You seem anxious to purchase a good deal of property round here — including Carnbrooke.' Once started I could not stop. 'I didn't know until recently that it was you who paid off the mortgage. I should be grateful to you, and I am. But — you ought to have told me—'

'And you,' he interrupted, 'might have warned me of your devious little plot to entrap me.'

My heart thumped painfully. I felt the colour drain from my face. My whole body trembled with indignation and shock.

'I don't know what you mean,' I managed to say coldly.

He gripped me suddenly by the shoulders. 'Oh, but I think you do. Your pleasant little concoction of a love affair — the persuasive whispers and admissions of — intimacy, don't they call it, and — good God!' His grasp tightened. He was shaking me. 'What was it you actually told that dry-as-dust spouse of yours? And what did you hope to gain by it?'

'Nothing,' I gasped. 'I said nothing to him, or to anyone else. There was nothing to say. What do you take me for?'

A hand went from my shoulder to his pocket. He took out a piece of paper and waved it before me. 'You recognise the writing, I suppose? The address?'

One glance told me it was my husband's.

'It looks like Horace's, but I don't know anything about it. He did threaten me, and I said—'

'What did you say?'

'I don't know. I don't know,' I answered helplessly. 'It was all so ridiculous I couldn't think properly—'

'So you let him assume his chaste young wife was also my private mistress and most charming whore. How delightful!' The blue eyes were fiercely condemning. I was suddenly frightened, and made a wild attempt to free myself. But both arms were about me, and though I kicked and struggled he held me close for a moment before flinging me down where the bracken was soft and springy under my body, tangy with the mingled scent of heather and wild thyme. He knelt by me, his face a bitter mask of disillusion and desire. 'As you've already taken so much that was freely given, and laid claim to far more, I take it you won't mind paying the price now?'

His intention was clear. I had wanted him — longed for

him — so much, so much. But not like this — oh not like this. There was no tenderness on his face, no compassion or understanding — only a thwarted terrible determination to possess me at any cost; to take in revenge what I would so willingly have given in warmth and sweetness if he'd asked.

My whole body stiffened. My fists pummelled his chest. Then suddenly the hardness of him was in and of me, a raging fire that burned relentlessly until all energy and passion was spent. I lay faint and weak at last, too exhausted and bewildered for some moments to pull the rumpled skirts and underwear over my thighs. My eyes were closed. For some reason I didn't want to open them. When I did Garth was standing a yard or so away staring down at me. His expression was remote and cold, though one side of his lips twitched wrily. He pulled me up by one hand. Then he handed me my cape.

'Quits,' he remarked.

I said nothing, just stared at him. There was a long pause, in which for a second something warm flooded his eyes then as abruptly died again.

'Would you care to ride with me?' he asked after the short interim. 'If you're tired—'

I drew myself up coldly.

'No, thank you. I would hate it. I'm well used to walking.'

He laughed, but the laugh held no humour.

'Spare me the dramatics, Caroline. And for God's sake—' He turned away, mopping his brow as he did so. 'Don't look like that. You got what you—'

'Wanted?' The sneer in my own voice shocked me.

'Deserved, I was going to say. Things might have been different, but we must be rational, mustn't we?'

'What do you mean?'

'The three of us are properly in your neat little triangle now, aren't we? You, myself, and your so-canny Horace. Oh don't underestimate him. I can assure you this isn't the end of the story; merely the beginning. A bitter, very eye-opening beginning, I'm afraid.'

He walked quickly to his horse, untethered and mounted him, and the next minute was cantering sharply down the slope towards the valley.

Hurt, humiliated, still smarting from physical and emotional pain, I started walking back to Carnbrooke.

My skirts were soiled and draggled when I got there, my hair a tumbled mass, tangled with spikes of undergrowth.

Mercifully Mrs Crabbe was nowhere to be seen.

I went upstairs and flung myself on the bed. Only then, did the sobbing start, and it seemed for a time that it would never cease. When it did, I dragged myself from the bed and went to the window. Down the lane I saw the Indian woman turn in at the gates of Tharne. I was surprised; had she been looking for Garth I wondered; A quick spasm of jealousy shot through me. I quickly dispelled it. What did it matter? Garth de Verries obviously thought he had a right to take any woman he wanted.

I shivered, feeling suddenly sick.

It was only very much later that I began to wonder about his reference to the 'neat little triangle', and his blunt assertion of the bitter beginning of our association.

A fortnight later I had my answer.

Garth had admitted intercourse with me.

Horace was going to sue for divorce.

6

At first I was too numbed by shock fully to realise the implications of the terse communication. So cold and practical! So legal, and — deadly somehow. The document was headed Frayne and Bannisters, Solicitors and Commissioners for Oaths; the address Beach Street, Penjust. I read the stiffly worded document several times before accepting that Horace and Garth between them could have done this to me both acting out of revenge.

For a little time I was actually frightened. Divorced women were considered outcasts in conventional society. Cornwall was not exactly that of course — beneath the facade of what gentility existed, the free wild spirit of its Celtic people was still there. But Methodism was strong with village folk. Fallen women and whores could still be stoned and driven from their homes. Being Doctor Dorric's daughter I would not be treated in such a way, but the condemnation would be there, the dark looks and sneering whispered conversation. Small calculated disasters could happen — a smashed window on a dark night, a tumbled rock blocking the front gate, anonymous notes pushed through the door. Oh, so many unpleasant frustrating things. Neither would Garth escape entirely. But he wouldn't worry. He was suspect already — he and his foreign mistress, Kara. Yes, that's what her name was. I'd heard it from Adam who had a nephew, a bit of a simpleton, working in the stables. No one generally took any notice of what the lad said, which was why, probably, he was employed at Tharne. The rest of the servants, except for Miss Ruana's personal maid, had been hired elsewhere or brought with the family from India. Either they couldn't speak English properly, or wouldn't. I guessed they were paid well for their silence, though what the mystery was I couldn't imagine. I no longer troubled myself about it. That summer the hard facts of reality had to be faced, and they were not pleasant.

As the days passed, however, my nerves became more adjusted and I concentrated on one aspect only. Freedom! freedom from Horace.

This was what I had longed for since my flight from Penzance. There would be a sordid bleak period to go through first, but when it was over — yes, when! What would I do then?

I tried desperately not to think of Garth. For a month following the letter from Horace's solicitors, there was no sign of him. Obviously he did not care about me at all. Well, I told myself defiantly, the feeling was mutual. That was not true of course. I did care about him. Cared so much that longing for him was submerged as the days passed, my bitter fierce resentment holding more hatred than love.

So when Mrs Crabbe announced sarcastically one afternoon that 'my friend from over theer at the big house' had called wanting to see me, my first instinct was to refuse.

'Tell him I'm not well and wish to speak to no one,' I told her haughtily. She mumbled something and turned away. Then I called her back.

'No. It might be something important. You'd better—' I looked round the room fleetingly, and caught a glimpse of my reflection in the mirror. I was looking pale, in a high-necked olive green dress bought in Penzance shortly after my marriage. My hair was drawn back to a pile on top of my head, but loose tendrils had escaped forming a thin wayward fringe over my eyes. I made a quick effort to tidy it away, and continued, 'Give me a moment or two, Mrs Crabbe, then show Sir Garth in.'

She shuffled slowly out. I straightened an embroidered antimacassar over the back of an arm chair, pushed a few odds-and-ends from the table under a cushion, dabbed a little cologne from my reticule at each temple and moistened my dry lips with my tongue. Whatever happened, whatever the interview entailed, I had to appear cool and composed, and mistress of the situation.

When Garth entered I was rigid as a beanpole, and determined to show no flicker of nerves or fear.

He was dressed in fawn except for a black jacket and a white cravat at his neck. He appeared stern and forbidding, and I was instantly on the defensive.

'Do sit down,' I said coldly.

He gave a slight inclination of his head. 'After you.'

When we were both seated, he remarked, with formal precision, 'No doubt I should make an apology for not having called before, but I was waiting until the legal position was quite clear.'

'I don't see why you should be so concerned,' I answered. 'If you're referring to my marriage, which I suppose you are, the problem's mine and you needn't be involved in any way.'

He jumped up. 'Don't be ridiculous. And please don't use those haughty tones to me—'

I stood up and faced him, feeling the warm colour flood my face. 'I'm merely stating facts,' I said, hoping desperately the violent trembling of my legs would not be obvious under the layers of petticoats and stiff material of the dress. 'Horace is divorcing me. I don't need pity, or understanding – or – or anything. And I suppose it's the same with you. If it wasn't you wouldn't have been so eager to let Horace know just what happened—' I broke off, breathless suddenly and outraged by his attitude. 'It was very mean of you,' I continued quickly. 'But then I should have known—'

'Known what?'

'That you were not really a gentleman.' Before I realised it the flat statement fell damningly from my lips. I put up a hand to my mouth as a wave of cold chilled my spine.

For a second nothing happened. Then he took two strides towards me. His hard hands gripped by fore-arms, his breath was warm against my cheek, his blue eyes blazing.

'That's good then, isn't it?' he said in lazy yet threatening tones, 'because a gentleman, my darling, would certainly not know how to deal with you. Thank your lucky stars I'm the kind of man I am, with a firm hand and hard head on me. You need both, Caroline, and I shall make it my business to see, in future that you get them—'

'*You!*' I exclaimed hotly. 'You're presuming a great deal I think. How dare you come here to my own home, and – and—' I broke off, infuriated yet secretly thrilled by his audacity.

He laughed. 'Oh spare the dramatics. Don't pretend, Caroline.'

'I don't understand you. I—'

'You don't need to. Time for that when we're married—'

'But – marry? I wouldn't marry you if you were the – the—'

'Last man in the world?' He laughed again. 'You wouldn't have to, would you? With no wagging tongues, no sly gossip or religious frills – what use marriage lines?'

I stared. 'You insufferable—'

His lips came over my mouth. My head fell back, as his kiss burned me, drawing all resistance into a tide of welling sensuous desire.

The contact, though overpowering, was brief. A minute afterwards he walked to the window, and stood staring out, with his back to me, while I recovered my breath. Then he turned and said, 'If marriage to me appears so hateful to you, perhaps you'd say so now, and save us a deal of embarrassment at the last moment. But I think you'd find life easier under my legal protection. For myself it's neither here nor there. I don't care a damn for my own reputation. I'm quite aware, anyway, of its shortcomings. Do what you like, Caroline, only I'm certainly not going to plead with you. And romantic pledges of eternal devotion definitely aren't my line.'

I could feel the nails of my fingers cutting fiercely into my clenched palms. I didn't know what to say. Such a short time ago, months merely, I would have given anything in the world to have heard Garth asking to marry me. But this nonchalant insolent proposal! There was no affection in it, no regard even. Only a harsh contemptuous challenge that stung me to reply, 'How right you are. I quite see your point.'

His eyebrows lifted perceptibly. My cold statement, I knew had mildly shocked him.

There was a short pause before he said, 'Good.'

He came towards me; but careful to avoid his eyes, I turned from him, and walked to the mirror, patting my hair with an air of assumed calm. 'So it's understood?' I heard him saying behind my shoulder. Through the mirror a sudden shaft of light caught the brilliance of his eyes watching me. His face, partly shadowed, was knife-edged and hard, the reflection loomed tall and motionless, like a dark emblem already foretelling my future.

'What?' I enquired provokingly.

'You will be my wife.' The words came as a flat announcement, holding no question, giving no opportunity for fencing or reprieve. 'When the formalities of the divorce are completed and eventually finalised, you will come to me — gracefully and dutifully, and share the marriage-bed with the minimum of protests and tears—'

'Stop! stop. You sound like Horace—'

A hand touched my buttock.

'No. I shall not be like Horace at all, which you well know.' I shivered.

When I faced him again there was the hint of a smile about his mouth which momentarily made him suddenly softer, more vulnerable.

I must have shown a certain weakening. He took one hand briefly in his, and said lightly but with a catch in his voice, 'Cheer up, Caroline, all is not lost. You may not find life with me so bad after all.'

Little else passed between us that afternoon. I was too dazed by his unromantic proposal to fence or argue. Without formal acceptance from me Garth had skilfully manoeuvred the suggestion into a fait-accompli.

It was only a week later that I learned when the day came I should not be living at Tharne as I'd expected, but would remain at Carnbrooke, which would be our mutual home.

'The house is still yours for the moment,' Garth told me unemotionally, 'but when we marry it will be ours.'

'But—'

'I don't intend Ruana, my cousin, or other — dependents to have any change in the household routine,' he continued firmly. 'Tharne is my own responsibility and will remain so. There I shall continue with what business I have in hand—'

'You mean your fencing off the Granite King?' I interrupted impetuously.

His glance was hostile. 'That and other things.'

'Kara, I suppose?' I continued hotly, ignoring all danger signs.

The piercing eyes seemed to darken.

'Kara also,' he said. 'And I don't like your tone, Caroline — or the way your devious little mind runs, for that matter. Watch it, my darling, or there'll be trouble. And by the way—'

'Yes?'

'It will be a good idea, I think, for you to move from Carnbrooke for the time being.'

'What do you mean?'

'Pleasanter for all concerned — especially you. Divorce can be a slanderous dirty business. My cousin Ruana will be able to recommend some suitable place for you to stay in London — Kensington, perhaps. We can be married in town when everything is settled. In the meantime I shall be free to continue with my business here undiverted by — your presence.'

I bit my lip.

'Do you mean Miss Ruana — your cousin — knows about us already?'

'I shall tell her tonight,' he said.

I laughed shortly.

'She won't like it.'

'Whether she does or not is of no account.'

His voice was cold.

I realised for the first time that Garth de Verries would be quite ruthless in getting what he wanted, provided he wanted it enough.

'I see.'

'Do you?' Without watching his expression I knew it had changed, softened. 'No, I don't think you do.' His manner had become remote — far away. I sensed his mind had temporarily diverged from me to other things — to a life in which I had no share, nor ever would have. 'How could you? Understanding only comes from experience; and apart from your stupid marital adventure — you've had none. There are bound to be difficulties between us — great gaps I shan't expect — or want you to explore. But with luck I think we'll be able to make the best of what we do have.'

'I hope so,' I managed to say stiffly.

'And I'm not a tyrant, Caroline. If I've sounded domineering, abrupt and stern, it's because I've had to be. There are more than ten years between us. And for me those years have been hard and bitter. While you've played and woven your childish dreams round the Granite King, I've dealt with men; defeated, dying tortured men. I've seen woman and children massacred, homes burned, leaving only mutilated and charred bodies behind. I shan't speak of this again. I've no wish to remember, God knows. But the legacy will be with me always, and it's one I can't share. Neither can I shirk the responsibilities laid on me.'

I wished to ask, 'What responsibilities?' But I did not, knowing just then, there was no point. He wouldn't tell me. One thing though was starkly clear to me; sometime the mystery of his past and of Tharne would have to be explained. Not only because of my stubborn determination to know the best and the worst of the man who seemed destined to be my husband, but because without trust our future would be a sterile thing. However passionate our longing, however rich and wild physical fulfilment, there was, or should be, something else; something that Garth was always too quick to sweep aside; the heritage and spiritual kinship with the land we trod — the land, I'd been born to. I wanted not only to have Garth's arms round me, to feel his body pulsing strongly against mine, but to stand with him on the highest point by the Granite King, feeling contact with flesh and earth, knowing that nothing — ever — could come between. The carn, in a way, was a symbol of my deepest most primitive self; the self that I was completely willing to surrender provided he did the same.

And he must, he must, I thought constantly. Then the rest would not matter. Even Kara I would somehow subdue and dispel from his life.

I had not realised at first how fiercely I resented her. The knowledge was a shock. But I managed not to betray it, and presently Garth left, after returning once more to the mundane more practical matter of my proposed sojourn in London.

I departed a fortnight later under the severe disapproving chaperonage of Miss Ruana, who made it quite clear to me that although she considered Garth's intention of marrying me was the greatest mistake of his life, she would see that the proprieties were observed where she was concerned. Acid remarks from her implied that despite his becoming involved with such a 'fallen' creature as myself, my immediate future would be under strictest surveillance and discipline.

I dreaded the thought of even a week in her company, and was thankful that when she'd seen me properly settled in at the Guest Home for Single Ladies — her own choice — she would have to return to Tharne and her household duties there.

I saw very little of Garth during the period before leaving Cornwall. It seemed to me frequently that he was purposefully keeping out of my way. Those last days were strange and lonely. Mrs Crabbe, having learned the truth, was off-hand and disagreeable. November mists increased a sense of desolation that hovered round the grey walls of Tharne like a pall. I did not go to Braggas very often. News of my disgraceful 'situation' had somehow got about, whispered from one to another with highly-coloured additions. Sly glances suggested that I had become involved with dark things at the big house. I was already regarded as an outcast who had brought shame to my father's name.

There were moments when I myself was half afraid of the future. However hard I tried to convince myself that there was nothing really abnormal about Tharne, and that life behind those narrow oblique-looking windows was no different from that of any other rich colonial family returned from abroad, I could not dispel my suspicions.

Several times following my first glimpse of the child briefly silhouetted against glass, I had seen her shadowed shape again moving past a top floor window. There were evenings when the wild, yet sad strains of a violin drifted on the winds soughing among the trees.

I had asked Garth if his invalid friend was a musician. He had glanced at me strangely.

'Why?'

'I've heard music sometimes. Like violin strings.'

'Possibly.' His voice had become non-committal. 'We're a musical family.'

'Oh. I didn't know.'

'There's a lot you don't know about the de Verries clan,' he'd retorted coldly.

'Yes. I'm sorry.'

'Oh Caroline,' he said more gently, 'don't pry and probe too much. Don't try and make mysteries when there are none.' His hand had involuntarily closed about my waist, moving gently upwards to a breast. Doubt had instantly died in me consumed by a mounting thrilling passion, stronger than reason or fears. It was always the same. By a single touch Garth could inflame emotions that transformed for an instant the whole world.

Just as quickly it would be over, leaving me uncertain of my own identity, and angry it should be so. I was, after all, myself — me. And some day, however deep our longing for each other, he must surely come to realise it.

7

The guest house was grey, flat fronted, of early Georgian design, extremely respectable with rules for 'residents' including 9.30 p.m. as the latest hour for retirement, when outer doors of the premises were locked. This meant no theatres or other social enjoyment in the evenings, and that the dozen or so 'ladies' there were elderly, wishing nothing more entertaining than a hand of whist at night, when they sat amid the palms in the stuffy drawing room gossiping over cards and their cups of hot milk.

When I was not strolling about the vicinity of neat squares and gardens, occasionally finding a certain glamour in misty explorations of the locality, I retired to my own room and read a book, or wrote letters to Garth and to Mrs Crabbe. They were stilted notes dealing with and describing the local scene. I was very bored indeed. If my bedroom had not been comfortable and pretty, with a view of Hyde Park some distance away I should probably have walked out of the place and informed Garth I had no intention of staying there any longer. But I restrained such wild action, buoying myself up with anticipatory excitements of the future.

Once a month Garth generally managed to make a brief visit. Although my whole being was on fire when we met, our conversation seemed stilted and forced. He gave me any necessary news of Carnbrooke and occasionally referred to matters involving the divorce which was proceeding to plan. The latter did not really interest me. All I was concerned in was to be free of Horace and to be able to return to Cornwall. What Garth paid for my upkeep at the 'boarding establishment' I never knew, and I did not ask. The place had been his choice for me, or rather Miss Ruana's; and privately I was chagrined that I hadn't been settled in more colourful surroundings. Of course whenever he was in London we had outings — Kew, Hampton Court, The Tower — even Vauxhall, and the Cremorne Gardens. But I had explored most of these on my own, although I did not tell him so.

The months dragged by. I had hoped to return to Carnbrooke for Christmas, but Garth had insisted on my remaining in London. I made no real friends, and at that time my chief diversion was touring the shopping centres of the West End. Garth insisted on providing a limited personal allowance which I frequently squandered on a single item of extravagance. The fogs that winter were thick and oppressive, hanging with yellow squalor over the city. Of course there were intermittent bright days when the networked branches of the plane trees were patterned delicately against the sky, dangling their small dark fruits over the embankment. The river, then, subtly excited me. I would watch the squat tugs and great ships, dreaming of freedom and escape. Not from Garth, but the frustrating cloying atmosphere of city life. At nights I would lie for a time unsleeping, with eyes closed, seeing in imagination not the well-furnished comfortable bedroom but the wind-swept moors above the sea where the Granite King stared bleak and grey across the Atlantic.

Once as I stood motionless watching the light fade over the water, I heard a man's voice saying behind my shoulder, 'Are you in need of company, ma'am. Can I direct you anywhere?' The tones were cultured, the implications suave. I turned my head quickly and looked at him. He was youngish, — middle-aged perhaps, with handsome features, a florid complexion, and quite elegantly dressed in a frock coat, with a tall silk hat and white neck-scarf. His lips were sensuous and lascivious, his eyes small.

'No thank you,' I said very clearly and firmly. Something in my expression must have startled him. He muttered a confused apology, gave a brief annoyed jerk of the head and walked smartly away.

My feelings were mixed. Obviously he had thought me some available 'lady of leisure', or professional prostitute, which angered me. On the other hand something about me must have evoked his interest.

What?

I made my way back to the boarding house and took a good look at my image through my bedroom mirror. The curtains had already been drawn and the candles were lighted on either side of the dressing-table. I was wearing a small tilted forward boat-shaped black hat with bunched velvet ribbons at the front, and a shred of veiling falling behind — one of my major extravagances — and a tightly waisted maroon coatee with a full crinoline skirt to match. Both were embroidered with ribbon. My wine and black patterned tartan cape fell almost to the hem, and from back view could not have appeared particularly seductive. But in profile, outlined against the river and fading light I realised I could quite easily have given a wrong impression.

A hint of humour rose in me, combined with a touch of titillating vanity. Supposing I had accepted my admirer's invitation? Allowed him to take my arm and escort me to some coffee house or glamorous retreat of ill-fame? It would have been amusing leading him on and then at the last moment leaving him chagrined and outraged at his own mistake and my playful deception. But then matters might not have ended in quite such a way.

The thought sobered me. I decided no more to risk solitary strolls after twilight. In future I would resign myself to boredom in the company of the respectable whist-playing ladies, and to act decorously — as decorously as possible — under the eagle eye of Miss Mitty, the proprietress of the boarding establishment.

From the beginning she had made no secret of the fact that she had implied to Miss Ruana that I would be kept under what careful supervision she could provide. I knew I had been a trial to her, and I think Garth knew too. But he hadn't attempted to exact promises from me.

'You're not a child any more,' he'd said once. 'You must know the pitfalls of London night-life. You can't be watched every moment. Just be as wise as you can, and try and retain any decent reputation you have left.'

'I'll try,' I'd said, with a hint of defiance.

'Good. I have to accept the Horace interlude, but in future—'

'You needn't say it,' I'd interrupted. 'What do you take me for?'

And he'd smiled.

'God knows.'

All the time, I'd known though, during that frustrating period that he trusted me; simply because the feeling between us held such mutual all consuming passion.

And at last it came to an end.

Garth de Verries and I were married on a late October morning in London, 1860, and that same day we started the long journey to Cornwall.

Miss Ruana was waiting to receive us in the large parlour at Carnbrooke. Although late — it was almost ten o'clock — there was the conventional wedding spread prepared on the table, including an iced cake. I thought this rather odd, especially as she was so obviously averse to the marriage. Her strong features were set and cold, her fine eyes hard and condemning as she said, 'You must both be tired. I hope you have a good meal and feel—' her voice rose slightly, '—restored in the morning. Mrs Crabbe and I have been busy most of the day. There's a fire in the large front bedroom.'

My father's bedroom, I thought, with a jerk of the heart. Mrs Crabbe, who had been standing motionless in the shadows, came forward then.

'I've seen the big bed from the spare room's bin' put there,' she told me. 'Didn't seem right, somehow, to have the doctor's left. An' his chest's bin taken to the back too. Seein' things is goin' to be so different here from now on I thought none of us'd be wantin' too many reminders—'

Her glance at me was belligerent; it was as though she was saying, 'How could you have shamed your father's memory by bringing such disgrace on us?'

My lips tightened.

'Thank you for trying to arrange matters. I shall have to see what I think of the change.'

Garth made an effort to brighten the conversation by re-marking, 'Well, now, let us leave domestic details and enjoy some of this excellent food. Steam trains have their uses, but they can be damn tiring. I'm sure my wife needs a wash, and so do I. But before that, what about a toast, Ruana? Aren't you going to wish us luck?'

His cousin smiled bleakly, although it was more of a grimace holding no trace of warmth or good-will.

'Naturally I wish you luck, Garth. I'm sure you'll need it.'

His face darkened. 'Why?'

'We have had difficulties at Tharne this week, in your absence. Kara—'

'What about Kara?'

'We shall have to get more help.' Her lips closed like a clam, then opened again automatically to continue, 'When you have time to listen I'll explain.'

'Tomorrow then,' His tones were final.

'Of course. I hardly expect you to become involved with business affairs so promptly.'

Although her short speech held no rebuke, her manner did. I could feel her dislike – almost hatred of me – chilling the atmos-phere, and I wondered why. Her disapproval of the situation should by then have abated, or at least settled into resignation.

But perhaps it was not only myself but the fact of Garth's inheriting her old home that she found impossible to accept.

Yes. Surely that must be it.

The thought calmed me a little, and I did my best to be nice to her. Presently she left, leaving Garth and I both tired and a little on edge to face the emotions of our first night together at Carnbrooke. I was grateful to him for not insisting on going across to Tharne that evening. Although I'd faced the possibility — after all there would have been nothing natural in it, rather the reverse — I'd determined to do everything I could to keep him away. He was my husband now. Carnbrooke was to be our home. I knew if any confrontation between us rose over the matter I would fight in any way I knew, play all my charm and inner reserves, of strength to have him unreservedly by my side during those first hours.

I accepted in that first realisation of my own jealousy, that I was not at all the innocent nice young woman I'd believed myself to be before my marriage to Horace. Somewhere beneath my fawn-like exterior was the potential irrational wildness of a young tigress. This was not a comfortable sensation. But it gave me courage. So I consciously tried every device to intrigue him. When his eyes and mind momentarily wandered towards Tharne, I diverted him quickly by some haphazard question that instantly broke his trend of thought. When he relaxed for a moment into brief speculation, I made a sudden movement that brought his blue eyes once more upon me. I had never so deliberately played the siren before. But that night I did; I was careful to show my profile to advantage, to move with my neck arched and chin up, and when his glance strayed from me, to waft my lacy handkerchief very subtly on the air. It was sprayed with perfume from my reticule. How had I learned such feminine tricks in so short a time? — I do not know. Perhaps they are inherent in most women who love passionately.

It was only later when we entered the bedroom and I noticed my father's photograph staring from its silver frame on the dressing table, that resolve faltered, making me suddenly vulnerable and perhaps even a little ashamed. Just inside the door I paused, as childlike memories flooded me, filling me with an aching longing. Why had Mrs Crabbe put it there, I wondered. Surely she could have left it in my old room where it had always been?

I didn't move until Garth said, 'What's the matter, Caroline?' adding after a second with wry amusement in his voice, 'Frightened?'

I tore my eyes away. 'Of course not.'

I went forward, hearing him close the door quietly and turn the key. My pulse quickened. How very funny, I thought. There was no one to disturb us. Mrs Crabbe certainly would not. My valise lay open on the bed. I touched the frilled lingerie automatically. There was movement behind me, and suddenly I was in Garth's arms. His eyes, hot and blue as burning steel, blotted out the room. I longed for him utterly, yet somehow, gentleness was missing. One hand slowly but firmly unbuttoned my dress.

My head fell back.

He lifted me up and laid me on the bed.

'No need for games any more, darling,' he said. 'No lies, no acting, no pretence, and no — Horace.'

'Horace?' I echoed in bewilderment.

'What do you think I am?' he muttered, 'you married him—'

'But—'

'—For what you could get,' he told me ruthlessly. 'So I must give more, mustn't I — much much more — until I blot him out—' There was no smile on his face, no compassion; only a deep dark hunger intermingled with a kind of bitter anguish. I did not struggle against him, but closed my eyes. My throat felt choked. There was no longer time for words. Our union was fierce and sweet, yet lonely because of apartness and misunderstanding. It was as though a wild sea had claimed us and thrown us as so much jetsam on an angry shore.

Long after it was over I lay rigid and wakeful staring into the shadows. Once I shivered, remembering the shock of another marriage night. Little more than a year ago. Yet Horace's influence had persisted and had somehow managed to mar what should have been a fresh and vital beginning. I half expected his form to emerge accusingly from the shadows at the end of the bed.

Mercifully it did not.

Next day, though, something insidiously unpleasant happened. I was in the hall when a letter was pushed through the door. I picked it up, and thinking it was addressed to me, was about to open it when I paused. Something about the name, and post mark had halted me. The stamp was a foreign one, and the initials were not correct. I could feel the colour ebbing from my face as I read.

Mrs Kara de Verries,
Carnbrooke,
Nr Braggas,
Cornwall.

I stared at it stupidly for quite a minute, then put it on the hall table.

Garth appeared a moment later.

'There's a letter,' I told him, indicating the envelope. 'I thought it was for me, but I was wrong.'

He gave me an intent swift glance and picked the note up. I waited for an explanation. There was none.

After a second he slipped it into his pocket nonchalantly. 'I'll take it over when I go.'

'But—'

He put both hands on my shoulders and kissed me.

'Don't worry your head about my affairs, Caroline. I'm quite capable of dealing with them.'

He gave no explanation, and I did not ask. But my suspicions and jealousy grew, and a gnawing unhappiness that I'm sure Mrs Crabbe sensed.

When Garth had left for Tharne half an hour later, she said, 'You seem restless. Anything wrong?'

She did not call me 'maam' or Milady, or Miss Caroline, which she would have done in Garth's presence. But I pretended not to notice. I was taking a few withered chrysanthemums from a vase on the hall table.

'Certainly nothing's wrong,' I answered, 'except these faded things. I hate dead flowers.'

'Hm!' She tossed her old head. 'You can't expec' me to have my eye on everythin' – there's a lot to do, an' havin' that Miss Ruana fussing round these last days has'n helped either.'

'Oh well, you needn't worry about her any more,' I remarked. 'Now I'm back I'm sure she'll keep her distance.'

'An' so will most folk, I shudn' wonder,' Mrs Crabbe told me darkly.

I spun round.

'Just what do you mean by that?'

'You surely doan' expec' friendly neighbours to come callin' after whats bin' goin' on? Nor to tek to that wild furriner livin' in the old doctor's house?'

I smiled grimly.

'Sir Garth is hardly a foreigner, Mrs Crabbe, and we've had very few visitors since my aunt died. In my case you're probably wrong. I may have caused a scandal as Mrs Horace Coutts. But "Lady de Verries" is quite a different matter—'

There was a gasp.

'*Lady* de Verries?'

I laughed. 'Of course, as the wife of Sir Garth that's what I am now. And I think you'll find it makes quite a difference.'

She stared at me for some moments, then told me bluntly. 'Not to me 'et won't. Not ever. An' I edn' goin' to call you milady either, not in private anyways.'

Somehow I suddenly wanted to cry. I put my hand on her shoulder and murmured, 'I don't want you to. I just need your companionship and help – as I've always done. And I think my father would want that too.'

She softened immediately.

'Oh lovee dear! I jus' don' know what's come over us all, an' that's the truth. But you c'n count on me, as you do know. Never doubt et, midear.'

And I never did.

That same morning, trying to dispel a depressing feeling of self-pity and resentment at Garth's determination to leave me alone while he concerned himself with Tharne affairs – especially Kara – I saddled Flash and cantered down the lane to the turn, taking the route through Braggas leading seawards round the base of the Granite King.

Although I had been prepared for changes, the sight of the wall enclosing the tract of moorland shocked me. It was almost completed. Less than a hundred yards of open land remained, giving access to my favourite haunt. I took it, cutting directly up to the Carn. At the top I reined Flash to a halt, and stood in the shadow of the great stones, facing Tharne.

The roofs and towers of the house were faintly filmed with mist in the distance, half shrouded by trees in their valley. But when my eyes became accustomed to the fitful light I saw with surprise that the copse and a strip of land beyond the building had also been completely enclosed by a higher wall. Massive gates were closed against the moor. Inside what had obviously been made into a kind of paddock, a horse grazed. So not content with asserting his rights over the Granite King Garth had made doubly sure of complete privacy by having this inside circular erection built.

Why? *Why?*

As I paused, a small dot of a figure darted from the trees, followed by a taller one, — a man — who rushed after it and swept her up into his arms. Then a haze of cloud dimmed the gleam of sun, and when all was clear again they had gone. I guessed the child had been the one I had seen behind the top windows of Tharne. And despite the distance between us, I was uncomfortably certain that the man had been Garth.

Confusion and resentment deepened in me.

What was their relationship? Was she Kara's? And the father — could it be my husband?

Suddenly jealousy intensified into anger.

I turned, kicked Flash to a sharp canter, and made a quick detor round the Granite King downwards. When I reached the lane I paused again and looked up. As usual, the landscape seemed dominated by nature's stern effigy of its stone monarch. The stark silhouette loomed dark and clear against the sky — wild locks tattered beneath the jagged crown. A wind had risen during the last quarter of an hour, and from the rocky throne a defiant moan whined through the heather, asserting, 'I am here for ever — created from rain and sun; from storm and thunder; lord of the moor and all I survey. Nothing can change or vanquish me. No foreign power or plundering feet. From the deep dark heart of the earth I was born, and remain supreme — supreme—' The wild cry went on and on, caught up by the shrill high screaming of passing gulls. On the far side of the hill the precipitous rocks thrust as black jagged glass into the mountainous sea.

Somehow the wild scene restored my confidence. Whatever Garth might achieve, this tract of territory would in the end defeat him, and when that day came both the good in us and the worst, would be one; and our commitment to each other complete.

8

By the end of November a certain pattern to my married life had become established. After breakfast Garth went over to Tharne where he remained until the evening. There were exceptions of course, occasions when we drove to Penzance or Penjust for shopping. Once Garth took me to Falmouth for a meeting with elderly Sir George Trecarron and his Lady who had been friends of his uncle. The house was large and rambling, set in woods above the river; the grounds were vast, echoing with the screaming of peacocks from the lawns.

Although I was treated outwardly with old fashioned courtesy, the atmosphere was chilly and disapproving. Sir George was something in politics, − a subject in which he tried to involve Garth, but meeting with no response was obviously relieved to let the matter drift, and turned instead to military affairs and the glory of the British Empire. A good deal of wine was drunk. I toyed with mine, keeping my head sufficiently clear to realise that beneath Garth's non-committal comments concerning India, irritation and anger were deepening in him.

I didn't really blame him. Sir George was pompous, boring, and a snob, revelling in the British Crown having acquired complete control over that vast country. Our portly pink-faced host spoke as though Queen Victoria had emerged peacefully and naturally as some gracious magnificent flower symbolising Britain's rightful superiority over the rest of the world. War though, was still seething in India. There was still poverty, distress, sickness, and great resentment. The Queen herself could in no way be blamed of course. She was revered by her own people and abroad. But the fact remained that power and glory had sprung from roots of bitterness − including the seven years war from 1756 to 1763 when Robert Clive had defeated the Nawab of Bengal. Later, there had been the East India Company's avarice in assuming sovereignty over the Empire of the Great Mogul. Then in 1857, there was the mutiny — the bloody outbreak of Sepoys in the Bengal Army.

All this was history. I had heard snippets from my father, but only since my marriage to Garth had this stark picture registered, and although I wished desperately he would confide more of his personal involvement to me, explain the aftermath, and mystery enshrouding Tharne, I knew in some way he had been badly hurt, not so much physically as mentally. His facade of strength — and on occasion ruthless irony — hid wounds too deep to talk about. So I was not surprised that he allowed Sir George to go smugly rambling on while Garth forced himself to silence. If he had not, there would have been an explosive incident.

Whether Lady Trecarron sensed the true situation I could not tell. But I was relieved when she escorted me to the drawing room following the meal, leaving the two men to their own devices.

In spite of the room's rich elegance — perhaps because of it — I felt smothered and imprisoned. The air was close, smelling too heavily of pot-pourri and perfume. There was a great deal of silver and crystal about.

The furniture was mostly of rosewood and gilt; the upholstery and curtains of heavy silk in a cream and rose Regency design, lined with velvet. The thickly piled carpet was also cream, and valuable china glittered behind enclosed glass. Miniatures painted on ivory stared imperiously in gold and ebony frames from the satin-papered walls. In the centre of the immense marble mantelshelf a French clock with a gold pendulum ticked melodiously between china figurines of a seventeenth century shepherd and shepherdess. Opposite the fire-place a large portrait — doubtless of some bygone female ancestor — gazed imposingly from its intricately carved surround. On the top of a cabinet two very large China Dogs sat sneeringly remote from human contact.

The dogs appeared out of place somehow, and I wanted to giggle. Whether Lady Trecarron sensed it I didn't know. We were discussing trivialities, but her eyes narrowed, her gaze jerked suddenly upon me when she commented in cold level tones:

'I was quite — surprised — when I heard of your marriage to

Garth. I knew Sir Bruce very well, of course. In his younger days my family and his were quite closely acquainted. Garth went into the Army early and being only a nephew we naturally did not see so much of him. But I always considered him a responsible young man. Perhaps traditional would be a better word—'

'To what — Lady Trecarron?' I asked boldly, 'socially?' I forced a smile. 'You mean you didn't expect him to marry an ordinary country doctor's daughter?'

'I did not say that.' Her lips closed primly. 'It was the — circumstances.'

I looked away trying to hide the angry rush of colour flooding my face.

'I know. Divorce is considered very wicked. And I don't expect anyone in your position to understand. The point is—'

'Yes?' The short icy word was like a challenge.

'How we came to marry is our own affair I think.' I forced myself to face her boldly, continuing quickly, 'If you'd ever known unhappiness like mine, Lady Trecarron, you wouldn't bring things up again or try to revive the past. It's over; and I want to forget.'

My hands were damp, my spine was prickling uncomfortably, and I could feel the lace at my neck rising rapidly up and down with my quickened breathing.

'My dear girl,' the well-bred pompous voice continued, almost as though she was addressing some erring serving maid, 'I've no wish at all to upset you. To the contrary. But a little advice is surely to your advantage.' She took a delicate sniff from a small glass bottle, obviously smelling salts.

'Advice? About what?'

'Not to become flustered when you are not received as cordially as you may have anticipated in some circles of de Verries acquaintances. Women in — our station — and I say '*our*' since you now bear a noble name — must expect to be ostracised on occasion when they defy convention.'

'And men?'

'Men are different, as you well know.'

'Yes, and that's quite wrong.' Without meaning to I flung the rash statement in her face.

She flushed.

'I hope you're not emulating the frightful opinions of women like that disgusting so-called liberated creature George Sand?'

'You mean Choplin's mistress?' I queried with an imp of wickedness rising in me.

'Until she destroyed him.'

'I suppose it was his own choice.'

There was a perceptible pause. Then, in a booming voice Lady Trecarron flung her bomb-shell.

'She smoked *cigars*!'

The humour of the situation quite overcame me. Perhaps it wasn't really funny, but I laughed, and for a few seconds couldn't stop.

'Oh dear. Please forgive me,' I said. 'It was, just — just my own stupid imagination. I'm sorry.'

Lady Trecarron, looking rather like one of her disapproving china dogs, appeared at that point to ignore me altogether. Then she said coldly, 'I can see you're quite a character, Miss Dorric — I mean — Caroline.' The slip of name I knew was intentional. 'Well, I hope you won't find life at Tharne too difficult, and I mean that.'

'I don't think so,' I told her. 'Garth and I aren't living there.'

The information clearly startled her.

'Not? I understood — then where?'

'At Carnbrooke. My old home.'

'Indeed. How very odd.'

'Not really,' I said, grateful to have the conversation diverted to more normal channels. 'Garth has a great deal to do at Tharne — alterations, renovating — that sort of thing, and we thought we should have more privacy at home.'

'Your home.'

'Ours,' I corrected her.

She gave the pretence of a smile.

'Yes, I can see that. And of course it would not be really fair to uproot Ruana from the rightful position she's held for so long. A strong character, with a genuine sense of duty. I have always admired her.'

In spite of my determination not to be intimidated by such half-veiled jibes, irritation in me deepened to dislike. I wondered how long I'd have to tolerate Lady Trecarron's barbed comments, and took the first opportunity of turning our conversation to more general topics, praising the Trecarron home, its situation, the grounds, the drawing room itself, especially the paintings and miniatures. The latter I discovered were her weakness, and I was forced into hearing a historical account of the characters so skilfully and delicately depicted. I trailed behind her as she indicated with a wave of her silk fan different ancestors of the Trecarron family, including some of her own.

By the time Sir George and Garth appeared I was smothering a fit of yawning.

I think Garth guessed.

There was a glint of humour in his yes when he said to me later, on our return journey, 'A bit much for you, was it?'

'Not very stimulating,' I told him. 'Lady Trecarron did all she could to humiliate me — in a very well-bred way of course; and when she found she couldn't — well, she did, but I tried not to show it — she gave a lecture on the family tree. It went on and on—' I sighed.

He laughed; for once easily; and I relaxed, wondering if at last things were going to be frank and friendly between us.

'I'm afraid you'll have to put up with a bit of that sort of thing,' he said. 'But you'll get used to it.'

He slipped an arm round me.

It was a wonderful feeling having him so close and protective beside me. But as we neared Tharne his mood changed. He withdrew his arm and his body stiffened. I'd hoped we would go straight into Carnbrooke together.

But when he'd helped me from the chaise and seen me through the door of the house, he touched my hand and said, 'I'll have to look in at Tharne for a time. Not too long I hope.'

The next moment he was gone.

Resentment gnawed me again.

Tharne!

Kara!

Would they always come first?

9

During the next few weeks Miss Ruana — I could never think of her as just Ruana — invited me to have tea with her at Tharne. Garth did not join us, having told me beforehand that it should be 'a woman's affair'. Obviously he was hoping we would both become resigned to the situation and grow to like each other better.

This didn't happen. Her manner, though polite, retained its icy disapproval. The heavy atmosphere of the parlour was even more smothering than Lady Trecarron's drawing room. The furnishing was of dark mahogany, the velvet curtains and upholstery deep brown. A stern-looking oil painting of some bygone de Verries, one hand on a Bible, hung over a carved chest. Relics of India, including black carved elephants and a sword, threw distorted shadows against the yellowing heavily embossed wall-paper. Antimacassers draped the backs of the high-backed chairs. An aspidistra in a large cream pot by the window shadowed the stream of thin light filtering through the lace curtains which were already half hidden by the sombre thick side drapes.

The meal itself was served from a silver tea set, delicate bone china, and consisted of wafer-thin cucumber sandwiches, iced biscuits and home-made 'fairy cakes.' Yet I could not enjoy anything. Our conversation, concerning current Royal affairs in London, the political scene, and Garth's ideas for re-planning the gardens and having plants in the conservatory replaced by new varieties, not only bored but worried me.

'I noticed,' I said at one point, 'that part of the moor's already been taken in?'

'You mean the fence?'

'No. Inside that.'

She glanced at me sharply.

'How did you know?'

'From Braggas,' I replied unthinkingly. 'When I was there I went up the hill — well, part of the way — near the Granite King, and it was obvious.'

'You're not supposed to go there,' she said flatly. 'I'm surprised Garth did not tell you.'

'Oh he did. But—'

'He did?'

I was confused.

'I suppose it's been such a habit with me I forgot.'

'Then I advise you to try and remember his instructions.' Her voice was cold. 'My cousin does not appreciate being thwarted, which I'm sure you will learn for yourself if you disobey.'

I did not reply, and a little later, thankfully, the strained session ended and I left.

The hall was already wrapt in evening shadows as Miss Ruana ushered me to the front door. At the top of the first flight of stairs I thought I saw movement, briefly, from the darkness. Then there was a throaty sound, like that of a child's smothered laughter, followed by a scamper of light footsteps that could have been those of a mouse scuttling, or human.

It was impossible to tell.

Miss Ruana almost pushed me through the doorway.

'You must come again,' she said, with no welcome in her voice. 'For Garth's sake we must try and forget the past.'

But I knew she never would. And I knew, also, that this would not be easy for me.

As matters turned out it was more difficult than I'd anticipated, because the following day after breakfast, when Mrs Crabbe was in the kitchen and Garth had already left for Tharne, I saw a white envelope on the doormat.

I picked it up. It was addressed simply in block capitals to 'CAROLINE DE VERRIES' CARNBROOKE.'

It was stamped, and the postmark was Penzance.

Puzzled, I tore it open.

It read, in the same characterless inscribed capitals, 'VENGEANCE IS MINE, I WILL REPAY, SAITH THE LORD.'

And underneath:

'DOOM TO SINNERS.'

I went suddenly cold and rigid. It was as though my spine had turned to ice. In those first few moments I was certain no one could have sent the offensive communication but Horace. Then, when I thought again, it seemed doubtful. Horace was crafty, as I had learned to my cost, an accountant with a sharp and calculating mind. Surely he wouldn't resort to such primitive and dangerous tactics when he was so well used to plots of this kind. No doubt it would give him pleasure still to discomfort me, but his methods would be subtle, and of no threat to himself. Besides, I'd heard that he was already directing his amorous attentions elsewhere. The plain daughter of a barrister acquaintance of Lady Marston-Green had been seen dining with him in Penzance more than once, and his manner apparently had been quite devoted.

The news had been told me by Mrs Crabbe, whose niece ran a boarding house overlooking the bay. 'A man of his kind with plenty of money and a profession won't find et difficult to wed respectable,' she'd pronounced, eyeing me disapprovingly. 'He'll get on, Miss Caroline. The young woman may not be a beauty, but she's got other things to tempt a man.'

'Oh I'm sure,' I'd answered, with withering scorn. 'A handle to her name probably and wealth to add to Horace's — although I'm not certain he's so flush as you seem to think.'

'Flush? What a word!'

'Well — you know what I mean.'

She had tut-tutted, and left the room. I'd realised then that despite my new status as Lady de Verries, poor old Mrs Crabbe was too set in her ways to accept the divorce. In her mind still, I had not only disgraced the Dorric name but made a vast muddle of my life which might mean ultimately I would end up like my sinful Aunt Henrietta.

Because of her attitude I said nothing to her of the anonymous note. I also decided not to worry Garth over it. When my first revulsion and shock had worn off I was almost convinced it was nothing more than a tasteless practical joke played by some ill-wishing villager wanting to frighten me. Being posted in Penzance was nothing. On Market days the town was crowded with country people from all parts of the locality. There would probably be no more of the warped threats. And to have even remotely imagined Horace might be concerned was quite ridiculous. Mr Coutts, if rumour was true, had far more important matters on his mind.

The sensible thing I suppose, would have been to tear the offensive words up and then burn them. But something held me back — instinct, or perhaps a vague idea they might be needed some time as evidence. So I put the paper in a private drawer where some of my most precious mementos of days with my father were kept, locked it safely away, and determined to dwell on it no longer.

But the memory persisted. I couldn't shake off the niggling sense of depression shadowing my spirits.

So on impulse I found Adam and asked him to drive me into Penzance on the pretext of having shopping to do. He agreed grudgingly, and presently we set off. It was a cold day; I wore a maroon velvet cape over a grey jacket and dress trimmed with velvet ribbon and founded on a style created by Worth for the Empress Eugénie, one of the most fashionable figures in European society. My hat was small, tilted forward with a shred of veiling falling behind. I knew the outfit was unsuitable for day wear in remote Cornwall — it was one Garth had insisted on buying for me during my period in London — but I felt defiant; and flouted it, I suppose, as a sort of armour; in challenge to the past, and the malicious perpetrator of those ill-wished notes.

When we reached Penzance Adam deposited me at the yard of an inn where there was accommodation for the vehicle. I told him an hour would be sufficient time for me to make my purchases, and left him ostensibly attending to his horse, knowing that as soon as I was out of the way he would be making for the tap room.

There was no market that day. A fish cart rattled by as I walked up the main street, and a number of sea-men lingered about. They looked like Bretons in their coloured jerseys, and I guessed a ship had recently berthed in the harbour. Local women wearing the traditional black shawls over their dark skirts passed with baskets over their arms. I felt conspicuous in my fashionable attire, and after purchasing ribbon and thread at a haberdashers, I took the first chance of calling at a coffee house which I knew was popular with the more élite of the district.

The interior was lit discreetly with oil lamps behind diamond-paned windows. Several customers were seated at small tables taking refreshment. There was a tempting odour of freshly baked cakes, and coffee. My appetite was suddenly titillated. I found a chair in an alcove and sat down on my own, spreading my full skirts carefully so they would not crease. A girl in a mob cap and white frilly apron over a blue dress took my order, and when I had loosened my cape and taken off my gloves, I looked round.

At first, through the frail light of restricted beams from the window intermingling with light and shade cast by the lamps, faces appeared hazy and unreal. Then, as features and forms gradually registered, I had a shock. I think I remained still as a statue for a moment, hand half-lifted to my cheek.

It could not be, I thought. That disc of a countenance lit briefly to clarity — not Horace's. Oh surely not. Yet I knew all the time it was. From a seat near the window Horace's pale eyes were turned upon me coldly, with such chilling dislike I almost winced. There was a woman with him — a rather large fresh-complexioned plain woman who must have been only slightly younger than Horace. She was swathed in furs, and held a coffee cup elegantly aloft, displaying the flash of diamonds on a hand and wrist. Obviously Horace's latest amour, the financially and socially elegible relative of Lady Marston-Green.

Yet such observations registered only automatically. Horace, though so pale and insignificant in appearance, emanated a force so concentrated with hatred for me I was momentarily consumed with revulsion and a longing to rush away into the street — anywhere in escape from proximity of the man who had once possessed my body.

I half rose to leave, then controlled myself, sat back again, and wilfully, with difficulty, tore my eyes from his.

I was shivering, and knew I must have gone pale. So I stared down at my saucer, hoping he would not have noticed. My heart was hammering. If he came over, I thought, I must appear composed and in complete control of my manners and emotions.

I need not have worried.

A few minutes later I saw him chivalrously ushering his companion to the door, and as my pulse steadied was aware of her, flattered, gazing up at him devotedly when they passed.

He gave one further violent glance in my direction before they left.

The next moment their silhouetted figures moved as shadows against the glass outside, then they were gone. It took me a little time to relax. When I could think calmly again I had to accept that Horace Coutts was my enemy for all time. In his eyes I was a creature beyond forgiveness or mercy. Yet I still could not believe that he would endanger his own reputation by writing nasty notes. He was sufficiently acquainted with the law to realise that such offences were generally traced eventually to those who'd sent them. Only an insane man, in his position, would resort to such means of revenge.

Insane?

My heart jerked. Perhaps Horace was mad — perhaps that was the answer.

The overwhelming longing to be out of Penzance, as far away as possible from that hateful period of my past, intensified.

I paid my bill, left the coffee house, and found Adam still at the inn. We were soon jogging along the lanes leading up hill and down towards Carnbrooke. We reached home by twelve-thirty. Garth still was not back, and I wondered what was keeping him at Tharne. From unpleasant worries of the morning's events, my thoughts turned to Kara and the envelope addressed to 'Mrs Kara de Verries' which had been mistakenly delivered at Carnbrooke following my marriage to Garth. The recollection had niggled and tormented me from time to time, but I had pushed it to the back of my mind telling myself it had probably been meant for Miss Ruana de Verries, that it was possible she had been helping Kara over some personal or business matter, and the two names 'Ruana' and 'Kara' had got mixed up. Yes. Miss de Verries — that could be the answer. But there could be another — the one I dreaded — that Kara indeed was his mistress, and had been using his name before their arrival at Tharne. He could even have gone through some primitive ceremony with her in India enabling her to call herself his wife. Such things had been known. This explanation could be the reason for my being debarred from the house which I should rightly have shared with him.

It was as though a dark cloud overshadowed me. I felt bleak, cold, and depressed. I didn't really believe Garth would enter into any unlawful bigamous commitment, but emotional ties could sometimes be more binding than lawful relationships;

and the bitter fact remained that he spent more time at Tharne than at Carnbrooke.

I was unresponsive when he attempted to make love to me that night. Fretting had exhausted me, and for the first time I had no desire for physical contact. I turned my face away when an arm slipped over my body, wishing to fondle a breast. All I wanted was comfort, and words from him to sweep my fears away. There were tears under my closed eyelids, but I managed to hide any sign of emotion. After a moment or two he withdrew his hand. I heard him sigh.

'What's the matter, Caroline?'

'Nothing,' I answered flatly, 'I'm just tired. I wish—'

'What?'

'I wish things were simpler,' I told him.

'In what way?'

'It would be easier if I was more welcome at Tharne,' I said bluntly. 'People must think it funny I'm with you so little.'

'People? Who?'

'Mrs Crabbe, Adam, the servants, and villagers.'

'But they know nothing about our private arrangements.'

I looked at him then. He was staring at the ceiling. His profile set, expressionless.

'Of course they do. And gossip gets about. If I had a reason — from you, Garth — it would help when they exchange glances and nudge—'

He gave a short contemptuous laugh.

'They? Glance? Nudge? Oh Caroline, what do you expect from country people under the circumstances? A brand new Lady de Verries — ex-Mrs Horace Coutts — suddenly appearing as a ravishingly dramatic figure in their midst?'

'I wish you wouldn't bring Horace's name into it.'

'I don't see how we can ignore him completely since he's the primary cause of the scandal—'

'And Kara,' I said rashly. 'What about Kara, and that strange child? The visitor you never allow me to meet? Don't you see? It's all so — so abnormal—?'

There was a long pause in which I could sense him struggling for control. Then he said very quietly but firmly, 'When we married you knew exactly where you stood. We made a bargain, which I expect you to keep. One day, inevitably, you will know

more of my private affairs, but until I choose to enlighten you
please don't persist in probing. For once in your life try and
think of others.'

His harsh tones hurt me.

'I do. Of course I do. That's why I want to share. Oh Garth!' I
longed desperately to touch him, to feel him soften and relax in
love. But there was no relenting. He was as remote from me as
the cold Granite King on the wild moors above Tharne.

Presently he said, 'Go to sleep, Caroline. This isn't the time
for argument.'

He sounded tired. Knowing further pleading was useless I
tried to induce unconsciousness. But for hours the effort was
futile. Long after Garth's steady breathing told me he was
asleep I lay wakeful with my eyes on the window curtains which
were lit to fitful swaying shadows from the moonlight. Sometimes the contorted semblance of a pointed profile seemed to
take shape, mocking me malignantly — the thin nose elongated, the chin sharp under twisted lips. The long neck swayed
snake-like, darting towards me with each movement of the
curtains, blown by the penetrating wind.

I closed my eyes and looked away.

'Imagination,' Mrs Crabbe would have said, 'you've got too
much of it. Who'd want to harm you?' Horace? Maybe. His
expression had implied it that morning. But perhaps I was
being unfair. When I'd needed help he'd offered it, and I'd
grabbed it, unheeding of consequences. I could hardly expect
him to like me now; and probably seeing me in the coffee house
had unnerved him in case I'd insisted on an introduction to his
new lady friend. Well, 'friend' was hardly the right word, and
he should have realised I was the last person in the world
wanting to meet either of them.

Arguing in this way helped to subdue fear and the memory
of the wretched communication, and at length, as dawn
approached I slipped into uneasy sleep.

Of course times were not always stressful between Garth and
myself. There were occasions when worries seemed to slip away
magically, and he would suggest an outing or that we ride
together to Castle Cromme where he'd sweep me into his arms
and hold me warm against his chest, with his mouth firm and

demanding on mine. The moorland wind would be fresh and
stinging on our cheeks, the air keen with the sharp scent of dried
heather under the first frost, and high above our heads the gulls
wheeling and crying over the standing stones. I would feel
young again then, and break from him, running like a child
down the opposite slope. And when he caught me he'd fling me
down, laughing, in the rough undergrowth, his blue eyes
suddenly serious and hot with love. My arms would be raised to
his neck; for a moment we'd be close — so close, our hearts so
thunderously beating, he'd jump up saying, 'Come along, up
with you—' or something like that. 'Time we got back, darling,
I feel like bed.'

Our union at Carnbrooke, later, would be fierce and sweet
then, and for a brief interim afterwards I'd be able to forget the
shadows haunting my life.

But always they returned.

One afternoon only a fortnight before Christmas, Garth
came back unexpectedly from Tharne and suggested we rode to
the Granite King, taking the Braggas route.

'I stared at him. 'But I thought you said — I thought—'

'The wall will soon be completed,' he said, 'and thank God for
that. Then there'll be no entrance at all from that end. So as
you've got such a passion for that rocky tump—'

He paused.

I didn't speak at first. Rebellion rose in me again. 'Rocky
tump'. What a way to think of the Granite King! and I wasn't at
all sure I wanted to go there like that — just calmly, on Garth's
invitation. It was my place. It always had been. I loved Garth.
But he had stolen my sanctuary and my retreat; I could see
things in no other way, and I wished just then he had not
reminded me of the wall. Every time I'd gone down the lane I'd
tried not to notice it — it was of Cornish Granite, and in some
lights merged into the landscape. But it was there, all the same.
And at the Braggas end where the labourers were still working
in the day time, the enclosure operation was all too evident.

'Well?' I heard Garth saying. 'What about it?'

'All right,' I answered, almost offhandedly.

I could feel his eyes on me.

'If you're not keen, forget it.'

'Oh but I am,' I remarked quickly. 'It's just — I don't know why you have to put a barrier up just there. No one ever goes, except me, and—'

'They could. And as I've said, it's dangerous. Now, Caroline, if you're going to get awkward again I shall wish I'd not suggested us going.'

'I'll be ready in five minutes,' I told him, ignoring the tones of his last remark. 'Give me time to change into my habit.'

When we set off, a thin stream of late afternoon sunlight silvered the distant line of winter clouds. A few crows with a solitary gull wheeled over the sullen landscape. The men had left the site of the unfinished wall when we reached Braggas; an odd light or two already flickered from cottages in the steep cobbled street leading to the harbour. Boats were preparing to set out for a night's fishing.

We took the track to the left upwards to the carn. The great boulder loomed almost black against the cold horizon, lit fleetingly to a towering semblance of life by the last glow of fading light.

I could feel Flash's instinctive response to familiar ground as we reached the rocky summit. She whinnied joyously, wanting to take the easy canter downwards to the track encircling the copse and Tharne. But I halted her, as Garth reined.

For a moment or two we both stared at the distant roofs and towers of the great house.

'You wouldn't think, from the road, that the place lay in such a dip, would you?' Garth said.

'No.'

'Too damp to be quite healthy,' he continued. 'Somehow better heating will have to be installed. Look how quickly the mist's coming up.'

'Yes,' I did not add, 'And there's something moving down there — among the trees,' although I was quite certain my eyes were not deceiving me. A thin clump of silver-birch where light should have still penetrated, was completely black with shadow, and as I watched there was a wavering furtive parting of cloud and mist, and a furred shape disappearing into the undergrowth. It could have been a dog of course, a fox or a badger even. Or human? Was the gate of the property's circular inner wall open? Had the form retreated inside? Garth must have noticed my concentration.

'What are you staring at?' he asked suddenly.

'I thought I saw someone moving.'

'And if you did, what of it?' He laughed lightly. 'A gardener or one of the men probably.'

'I suppose so.' But I doubted it.

'You can never stop wondering about things, can you?' Garth commented with just a hint of irritation. 'Come along now, we'll get back. The light's going quickly, and I don't fancy riding bog-ridden land in the dark.'

'But bog isn't round here. It's over there,' I told him, pointing to the right. 'I know exactly every danger spot.'

'You may think you do, but land shifts. There are constant geographical changes going on in this part of Cornwall, and to take risks is just stupid.'

I was wise enough at that point to hold my tongue, and a minute later we had turned to cut down the track towards Braggas. It occurred to me that just for once Garth might have allowed me to use the old way bordering the house, especially as we were together. Was his refusal mostly stubbornness. A determination to show me his word was law? Or did the sick visitor at Tharne account for his attitude? I tried to rid my mind of the old haunting question, but uncertainty — a strange feeling of being caught in some inextricable web of intrigue — made me silent and withdrawn.

When we reached Carnbrooke, Garth also was quiet, and presently went over to Tharne.

The following week Christmas cards began to arrive. In spite of niggling worries, the old childish excitement and anticipation of the festive season started to rise in me. I took a walk to Castle Cromme one day, dressed in my thickest cape and warm button boots, carrying a basket for holly which grew on the hillside in thick glistening clumps, bright with red berries. There was a family of gipsies living in two vans by a thicket over the ridge.

As I approached a hollow where the bushes crouched dark, a woman darted out. She was lean featured, brown skinned, wearing a black shawl over a red skirt. Her dark hair was pulled back by a spotted handkerchief. Under one arm was a bundle of mistletoe. From the other hand dangled branches of holly tied by string. Her bright dark eyes flung me a glance of appraisal, then, standing quite still facing me, she said, 'Greetings, dordi. Kushti Rawni, and what's a fine gorgio lady such as thee doing all alone in such a place?' She hesitated, and smiled, showing the gleam of very white teeth. 'Here, dordi – a piece of mistletoe for luck lady – and holly to protect thee from the evil ones.' She handed me sprigs of both. I took them, and feeling she might wish payment searched for coins in my pocket. But when I handed her some small silver, she refused.

'Oh no, dordi. Brooms I sell, and posies when the cowslips come. But a gipsy gift's for luck dordi, needing no 'lovel' from gorgio folk.' Her thin brown palm shot out. 'Your hand, lady.'

Before I had time to think I had removed my glove, and my palm lay upwards in hers. She stared a moment then let it go. Her eyes were clouded when she glanced up again.

'Beware, lady,' she said. 'I see darkness and light in thy dukkerin; a long night threatens thee. But take this, and have it always under thy pillow for sleeping, and o Del shall protect thee. There is a Rai who loves thee well, remember that, and blessings lady. Blessings of the gago folk!'

She wove a sign in the air, and a moment later had cut with the speed of a wild creature towards the left of the hill where a path wound in the direction of Penzance.

I paused irresolutely for a minute, wondering why I should have been chosen to be 'gipsy-blessed'. Then I recalled that she had also warned me. Of what?

Still clutching the sprigs of mistletoe and holly I took the scizzors from my basket, placed the greenery in, and went on to the thicket of twisted trees where the berries were most profuse. I spent a little time cutting and pulling, but as the wind freshened under the grey sky my hands grew cold, and I was soon hurrying back to the house.

After closing the front door behind me I looked down at the mat and saw the postman had been. I picked up two or three envelopes – obviously containing cards, – and opened them.

The last one gave me a shock.

The contents were stark and clear, printed in bold capitals.

'ADULTERESS. HOPE YOU GET WHAT YOU DESERVE.'

Waves of fear chilled me. I dropped the holly on to the floor and ran upstairs. When I reached my room and sat on the bed I was trembling so violently I could hardly breathe.

Mrs Crabbe had lighted a fire in the grate. Mechanically I tore the paper up and dropped the pieces into the flames. In two seconds they were no more than charred relics blown with the smoke up the chimney.

So the gipsy had been right. Danger threatened. It was only later when my nerves had quietened a little that I remembered she had also said that someone loved me. Garth, I told myself determinedly — it must be Garth. Oh God let it be. Let his love be so strong nothing would shake it; otherwise I knew I would want to die.

10

Christmas that year was strange and quiet. Except for the one spent in London before my marriage, the festive season had generally been one of homely excitement, cheerful voices and laughter, with Mrs Crabbe, Adam, and any servants we had joining in.

With Garth it was quite different.

The love between us for those few days seemed to be enriched and more glowing. But behind the warm glances, passionate interludes, and touch of hands and lips there was a certain constraint. Occasionally I caught an anxious look in Garth's eyes, and at those times I knew he was briefly remote from me, and was concerned with Tharne.

I tried not to mind; did my best to smother my jealous streak, knowing there was nothing commendable in it, and that my father would have disapproved. This was what was lacking — the wisdom and affection of his comforting presence — the guidance of the good man I still missed deeply.

Once when Mrs Crabbe came into the parlour and found me staring at his photograph which I had had removed there from the bedroom, she said, 'Yes, 'tedn' the same es et? Never has been since he were took.'

I wished she wouldn't speak that way. In level tones I managed to point out, 'Things are always changing, Mrs Crabbe. Every-thing altered when my aunt died, too. We have to get adjusted.'

'Hm! you're a fine one to talk. Out of one marriage into another—' she sniffed, and added quickly, 'I shouldn' have said that. Forget et.'

'I'll try. But please — please don't forget who I am—'

'Lady de Verries,' she interrupted before I could finish, 'I know, I know.'

'The wife of Sir Garth,' I told her firmly and as quietly as possible. 'I realise it's difficult for you. But — do try and look pleasant. My father wouldn't want us to be miserable all the time now, would he?'

She lifted a corner of her apron to one eye. 'I s'pose not. And don't think I'm against that fine family you've got into. A respecter of the gentry I am — always have been. Miss Ruana I c'n understand, for all her haughty ways. But those black-eyed furriners lurkin' 'bout — they give me the shivers they do.'

'Why?'

'Not like us. That's why.'

'Oh—' I forced a laugh. 'That's just ridiculous. Of course they're like us. They're human beings, people who've been through a great deal of suffering. Life is still terrible for millions of people in India. There's famine in parts, and killing, and great distress. My husband has merely shown kindness in bring-ing one or two suffering servants with him.'

There was silence for a few moments; then she asked bluntly.

'How d'you know 'twas kindness, Miss Caroline? You don't, do 'ee? That dark one — that Kara creature doan' look like a servant as you call 'et, to me. No. Nor a nurse neither, whatever they do say 'bout her lookin' after some invalid or other. An' 'tes my b'lief there edn' so many servants there either. Just one girl, folks say, an a funny lookin' man wearin' a balloon on 'is 'ead — an' a boy and gardener.' I couldn't help laughing.

'A balloon? Oh, Mrs Crabbe — that's a turban. He's probably a Sikh.'

'An' what's that, may I ask?'

'Sikhs are of a certain caste and religion,' I told her vaguely, not adding, 'and warriors.' Anyway,' I continued quickly, 'where did you get this information? From Adam's nephew?'

She shook her head.

'Everyone's talkin'. In Braggas Miss Penny — her at the shop — wus saying the Indian man — the one with the funny hat goes walkin' at night, and that's the only time. Billy Grage's sister met 'en in the lane one evenin' an' she thought he was a ghostie — ran for her life she did; nearly had a fit.'

'Well, it wouldn't take much to give Nellie Grage a fit, would it?' I said bluntly. 'She has them regularly.'

Mrs Crabbe flung me a withering glance. 'You've got a streak o' hardness in you, Miss Caroline. Just watch it, or it'll be enough to raise your dear father from the grave.'

She went to the door and before leaving turned there, and said, 'There's sumthen' else too. At Tharne there. A child. A dark one they do say. Now what d'you think o' that? Or do 'ee know all about it?'

'I've heard,' I said uncomfortably, 'but the people living there aren't my affair. This is my home, Mrs Crabbe, Carnbrooke. Miss Ruana's the mistress of Tharne. You must try and remember that.'

There was the sound of a latch snapping, and she had gone. I tried to shut her grumbling and insinuating suggestions from my thoughts, busying myself during those few days with the decorating and cards, the preparing of presents, and seeing there were extra boxes of sweetmeats in case we had callers or unexpected visitors to the house. I kept well away from the kitchen. It had for so long been Mrs Crabbe's responsibility to reign supreme there at that time, I knew she would be offended at intrusion from me. The parlour and hall looked cheerful and attractive when I'd finished arranging the holly and greenery in every available niche and corner — on the tops of pictures, and furniture, helped by Adam who stood on steps to suspend the mistletoe from the lantern hanging just inside the front door. There was a 'kissing bush', coloured candles glowing from dark places, and silver ribbons stretched from corner to corner of the hall ceiling.

On impulse I went into Penjust on the afternoon before Christmas Eve (purposely avoiding Penzance in case I met Horace) and purchased a large box of sweetmeats for 'all at Tharne'. Although Garth and I were to have Christmas Day on our own at Carnbrooke — I felt a friendly gesture could not be out of place.

'What a child you are sometimes,' Garth said, when I showed him. His lips had softened. His blue eyes were glowing.

'I want things to be as happy as possible,' I told him feeling his hand enclose my waist. 'I've something for your — for Ruana too.' It was a round glass ball enclosing a winter scene with snow that fell when it was moved. 'Do you think she'll like it?' I suddenly felt absurd. 'No, of course she won't. It's for someone young. I should have known. Never mind, I'll give it to Lily, farmer James' little girl—'

Garth's lips brushed my hair. 'You'll do nothing of the sort,' he said. 'It was a kind thought. It will go to Tharne. Ruana will know what to do with it.' I knew then that he was thinking of the child I'd glimpsed there, but never met.

'Very well,' I said docilely.

'Caroline—'

'Yes?'

'It must seem strange to you that we were not invited to join the family for Christmas Day.'

'I've grown used to it,' I said truthfully. 'And really I'd much rather be just with you. Mrs Crabbe too. She'd have missed having us here.'

'Of course. Mrs Crabbe makes things much easier.'

I frowned slightly. 'What do you mean?'

'I shall have to pop over there for part of the time,' he said bluntly. 'Afternoon would be best obviously. Knowing you're not alone will ease my mind.'

'Will it?' My voice rose tartly. I was suddenly annoyed. 'I shouldn't have thought your mind could be all that concerned with my feelings. Especially over such a minor matter.'

I knew I was being petty, but I couldn't help myself. It seemed so unfair.

'Darling.' He took me by the shoulders and forced me to look at him. 'Don't spoil things please.'

'Spoil things? Me?'

He kissed me, gently at first, then forcefully — a long lingering kiss draining resentment into negation. Passion rose in me on a wave of longing. A minute later he released me. He was smiling. I told myself then that nothing mattered except being his wife. Those others didn't count; not Tharne, Ruana, or even Kara. But deep down disappointment still lingered, because I knew they did.

And the next morning following a visit to the village I had proof.

A single letter lay on the mat.

With tembling hands I picked it up and slit the envelope.

'WHORE,' the letters read, 'VENGEANCE IS NEAR. GET OUT.'

I was still staring at it when Mrs Crabbe appeared from the kitchen.

'Oh. Another of en',' she muttered. 'Who's et from this time?'

I started at her blankly. 'Who? How do I know?'

Her brows went up over her beady eyes. 'Well, cards generally have a name on 'en, doan' they?' She tossed her head and sniffed. 'Oh 'tedn' my affair, I s'pose. I shouldn've asked — Lady de Verries.'

Realising my own mistake I hurriedly pushed the offensive paper into my pocket. 'There wasn't a name,' I said coolly as my thumping heart steadied. 'That's why I was surprised. And another thing—'

'Ais?'

'You shall see all the cards I have, every one. In the morning I'll start arranging them and you can help me.'

Whether she believed me completely or not I don't know. But her expression relaxed, and her voice was mollified when she said, 'Tek no notice of an old wumman. I do forget meself sometimes.'

'No you don't, and I want you to share everything possible, Mrs Crabbe — just like the old days when my father and Aunt Adela were alive. And for goodness sake—' I touched her shoulder, 'no more of the Lady de Verries.' I waited a moment before adding, 'I don't even like the Lady business myself.'

And it was true.

Mrs Garth de Verries would have been more intimate somehow. How much easier things between Garth and myself could have been if Ruana held the title leaving him free to follow his life as he wished with me beside him.

Then another thought struck me. If that was the case he would probably be still in India, and we would never have met at all.

What a tangled problem life was.

As twilight was fading in a milky greenish glow behind the western ridge, I had a sudden longing for exercise. Garth was not yet back from Tharne, so I went upstairs and put on my bonnet and cloak. The odious note rustled in the pocket of my dress. I took it out and did not tear it up this time, but laid it away with the other one in the drawer.

Then I hurried downstairs and out of the front door.

The lane was already filmed with faintly rising mist. At the end of the short drive leading to Tharne, gables and chimneys at the back of the house rose indiscriminately of architectural design above the trees, — appearing in the fading half light like absurd concoctions of a fairy tale. The original building Garth had told me had been mediaeval, but in Tudor times the frontage had been elevated, and simplified to give an impression of symmetry and harmony. The result had not been entirely happy. Although from the front, the balusters round the large roof mostly hid the hotch-potch of differing period styles, the effect at certain angles was incongruous. Sideways, through the tangle of trees the place gave an impression of something imagined from *Beauty and the Beast*; and it had this effect on me that evening.

I had just passed the drive when the faint insidious whine of a violin playing made me glance back. There was already a light glimmering from an upper window of Tharne. Its glow lit the filtered mist to milky pallor, completely obscuring the shadowed building below. I had the impression of phantom turrets floating above the real world. The wan shapes of naked trees occasionally lurched in the thin wind like some fantastic ballet of nature staged to the moan of eerie elemental music. A blurred shape passed behind glass, — a man's, bearing an uncanny resemblance to Garth. A second later the mournful tune ceased. A pair of thin childish arms waved briefly upwards, like night-moths newly-born and poised for flight. Then there was a sudden high scream. The light wavered and died. All was dark and lifeless again.

I shivered, and realised I was icily cold.

Drawing my cape round me I turned and hurried back to Carnbrooke.

If only Garth would quickly come back, I thought despondently. Probably I was imagining a good deal, but it did seem to me that the secret of Tharne — whatever it was — held unpleasant implications that could easily be connected with the terrible anonymous letters I was receiving.

Kara?

But I had no proof. If I suggested or attempted to ask anything about her from my husband I knew he would be very angry and I should learn nothing. That it should be so was quite wrong and irrational. As his wife I had a right to be in his confidence.

Or had I?

The shadow of Horace still hovered over our mutual life, and I, also, in withholding the fact of the anonymous communications was contributing to the barrier between us. So the fault was partially mine, and I had to accept the situation.

From that moment I steeled myself to face Christmas as best I could, putting fear and uncertainty behind me. It wasn't always easy. But the facade of 'all being well' was interspered with moments of true festivity and passionate interludes that temporarily obscured the worry.

And very soon it was over.

11

The New Year came with fine hard weather that sprinkled the moors and trees with frost. Snowdrops starred the crisp turf in the garden, and as the morning sun lifted to the cold horizon of moors and sky, shafts of silvered light shivered above the valleys where veils of frozen mist hovered.

Sometimes, before Garth went over to Tharne, we had a morning canter together up the slope to Castle Cromme, pausing there briefly before a quick gallop along the ridge. As we returned, my eyes would wander to the opposite hill where the Granite King stared implacably over the Atlantic. The wall was finished now, enclosing the whole area except for the far end where precipitous jagged spikes of rock were their own barrier. The carn from just there was unapproachable. Anyone who attempted to climb round would be mad. But a strange kind of exultancy filled me when I thought of it. For those fifty yards of wild terrain the stone image was monarch still, and would remain so, surely, long after Garth and I had gone. This was important to me. Why I did not quite know, except as a symbol perhaps of independence, and a deeply rooted determination to be more than just a feminine commodity in Garth's life.

'Still resentful, aren't you?' Garth said one morning as we waited, looking northwards over the valley facing the sea. 'Still blaming me for having things safe. You're a funny girl, Caroline. I was mostly thinking of you when I enclosed that place—'

'Not only me,' I corrected him. 'If you'd never met me you'd still have done it,' I paused. 'Wouldn't you? You'd said so.'

'Of course,' he answered lightly. 'Tharne property's my own responsibility.'

'Well then!' I smiled brightly at him. 'Let's not argue. Let's get back now. I'm sure you must be eager to see your — invalid.'

Immediately following the tart remark I wished I'd never said it. Garth's lips tightened. He kicked his mount to a sharp canter, and side by side we cut down the moor towards Carnbrooke.

As usual I felt restless when he'd left for Tharne. I didn't feel like sewing or attending to household matters; Mrs Crabbe was becoming increasing possessive of the kitchen. She took a firm line with the daily girl, and made it clear to me I must not interfere with her duties.

'Oh botheration,' I thought, 'what use am I at all except as Garth's wife in bed? A wife should be more than that.' All the same a warm glow like that of a rose opening to the sunlight suffused me when I thought of those precious interims. But the hours between morning and night were so tedious. It was then that the doubts and conjectures rose to torment me. So on impulse I changed into my oldest thick brown serge dress, pulled on boots and a waist-length tartan cape. Then after tying a scarf over my hair I went to the back of the house, found a fork and trowel in the shed, and carried them to the front. The ground looked solid and hard, and a little raking and digging would certainly help the primroses, aconites, and crocuses to come through.

The cold air stung my face as I plunged the trowel against the frosty surface. Soon, in spite of my efforts I found I was making no progress at all. The earth was far too frozen. I was about to get to my feet when I heard Mrs Crabbe's harsh old voice.

'What d'ye think you'm about? You! s'posed to be a lady, on y'r knees like any tinker's brat. If you was a bit younger I'd teach you to behave proper in th' good ole fashioned way—'

I jumped up, shaking soil from my skirt. Mrs Crabbe's face was bright red with indignation.

'Well,' I said, 'I'm not a lady; merely human that's all. You're Queen of the kitchen, Garth's King of the Castle, and I'm just Mrs Nobody-with-nothing-to-do.'

I glared at her.

Her temper slowly died. She nodded reluctantly.

'Ais. I s'pose 'tedn' much fun for ye with him way over at the big house all the time. An' o' course I've spek out of turn agen. But seein' you in them good cloes muckin' 'bout in all that grime!' She gave a deep expressive sigh. 'I jus' couldn' help thinkin' of those who've nothin' respectable to wear at all—' She touched my arm, peering up into my face, and as we moved towards the front door, said, 'Did ye know Wheal Crane's closed? Leavin' all them miners out o' work, an' hardly one of them with an idea where to go or turn for work. There's rumours goin' about that many are thinkin' o' packin' up an' takin' off to Americky.'

I was shocked.

'No, I didn't know,' I said. Wheal Crane, owned by William Venn, a wealthy land-owner with an estate to the west of Penjust, was one of the oldest copper mines in Cornwall. For some time there had been rumours that its ore was running out. Even during my childhood things had slowed up there. Sometimes after completing his doctor's round my father had returned home depressed because of sick cases resulting from bad conditions in the mine, poverty due to lack of work, silcis, and families with too many mouths to feed on too little money, and poor housing conditions without sufficient heat or proper sewerage.

Once or twice I had driven round with him, and it occurred to me I might get Adam to take me over one day to see a family I knew, the Breames. There had been a baby and several children considerably younger than I had been then. The eldest, Tom, had been about seven, and it had already been planned that in three years time he would join his father at the mine, although only to work 'at grass' for the time being.

I knew my father, if he'd been alive, would appreciate any gesture on their behalf, and I decided to take some eggs with me, a cake perhaps, made by Mrs Crabbe, and even possibly a fowl if I could get one from the farm.

Mrs Crabbe of course was not cooperative, neither was Garth at first, when I told him.

'Why not leave Venn to attend to his own affairs and look after his own responsibilities?' he said a little sharply. 'I don't like the idea of you mixing with sickness — and there *is* sickness in that area, I've heard. If you want to play Lady Bountiful to miners' wives there are plenty at Wheal Daisy who'd be grateful—' Seeing my mutinous look he broke off.

'But Wheal Daisy hasn't any problems, has it?' I said. 'Everything's going well for you there — and for the workers. Adam was saying there's hardly a more prosperous mine in all Cornwall.'

'And you should be grateful for it,' Garth told me. 'It helps enable you to retain Carnbrooke.'

I bit my lips. 'I didn't ask you to buy it for me, and I don't see what that's got to do with whether I go to see the Breames or not. You twist things about so. It's just that I—'

Garth's face softened. 'That you're father's child; daughter of a doctor,' he conceded. 'Very well. Go if you must; but don't go inside — not any of those wretched hovels, even the Breames'. And see you keep away from any stinking cesspit. They say the epidemic is just a form of influenza, but I've an idea it could be something worse.'

'No,' I told him. 'The doctors would know if it was, and people wouldn't be allowed near.' I paused before adding placatingly, 'I won't take any risks, Garth; none at all; and I won't go into a single cottage. If you like I'll give the basket to Adam and let him leave it at the door.'

'Oh, all right,' Garth agreed, pulling me to him and kissing me. 'But that's a promise, remember? Just you stay put in the cab, and let old Adam deliver the goods.'

I gave my word reluctantly. I'd looked forward to having a word myself with Mrs Breame, and seeing the children. However, the project stopped me fretting so much about Tharne and the anonymous notes. It was stimulating having some sort of purpose ahead, and I wished I'd thought about it before.

On the morning we set off it was cold, and although I wore my fur bonnet, thick cape and carried a muff, I was feeling quite chilled when we reached the mining area. The row of drab cottages mostly of clob, though a few granite buildings were scattered on the outskirts, lay on a desolate stretch of moorland half way between Penjust and Penzance. There was no sign of the sea or either coastline; just a brown stretch of scarred land interspersed with massive boulders poking from straggling bushes, and the gaunt shape of a mine-stack and engine-house a quarter of a mile away. The pumping rod was motionless. No smoke or steam billowed towards the grey sky. I felt suddenly downcast and apprehensive. When we reached the track leading to the Breames' home I told Adam to stop. He reined his horse in, and I peered to the left. A man was picking up wood in the distance, and a child's form emerged from a doorway huddled into a kind of shawl.

'I think the cottage is the second down,' I told Adam. 'Yes, I remember. I'm sure it is. If I take the reins would you mind giving the basket to Mrs Breame, tell her it's from—' I hesitated. 'Lady de Verries' sounded ostentatious. Besides there was no knowing what local gossip she'd heard. So I resumed, 'Tell her it's from Doctor Dorric's daughter, Caroline. You can call it a New Year present. There's a chicken inside, and some cakes.'

Adam grunted and rather unwillingly did as I said. I watched his sturdy squat form walk down the track to the cottage. He banged. For quite a minute nothing happened; then a woman's pale face with something dark over the head and shoulders appeared through the half-open door. She glanced towards the cab once, took the contents from the basket, and after a brief conversation with Adam went back into the house.

'What did she say?' I asked the man as I clambered into my seat in the cab.

'Nuthen' much,' he said settling himself behind his horse. 'Thanked 'ee o' course. But it was a grim way she had with her, and grim news too.'

'What?'

'Tom, the eldest boy's, had an accident at the mine an' lost a leg. His father's th' only breadwinner now, an' what with losing 'is job an' havin' the miner's disease — what they call 'et? — Silis—?'

'Silcis,' I told him, feeling my heart sink. 'Oh dear. How terrible. What will they do? And where's Tom now? In hospital?'

'Back home. Havin' to be cared for. The parish is helpin', I do s'pose. Mebee Mr Venn'll do sumthen'. He's rich enough an' master. Trouble is when mines fail owners think mostly of their own pockets.'

'It's quite wrong.'

'It's life, Miss Caroline — I mean m'lady.'

'Oh don't, Adam. I hate being called that.'

He said nothing more, and moments later we were on our way back to Carnbrooke.

On the first opportunity I sounded Garth about the Breames. He expressed sympathy, but was unco-operative with any practical suggestion. 'I'm sure the poor woman will be grateful for the gifts,' he said, 'But if you're thinking of any regular donation, Caroline, please don't. As I said before the responsibility is more Venn's than anyone else's. Certainly not mine. If you keep popping over there you could easily provoke jealousy with other families. And in the end it's up to the authorities.'

'What authorities?'

'The Church; Venn; the Welfare. The law.'

'The law's very unfair then,' I said bitterly. 'And don't say I know nothing about it, Garth. I do. My father thought so. He used to come up against a terrible lot of misery that shouldn't have been allowed.'

I broke off, conscious that Garth's intense glance at me was changing slightly to one holding a hint of amusement.

'Maybe you should have been a politician rather than a wife,' he said drily. 'I can imagine you causing quite an emotional furore. A woman in the House! God save us.'

I tightened my mouth. 'I don't see why not. You never know what will happen in the future.'

'Don't I?' His arm slipped round me. 'Shall I demonstrate, my darling?'

Realising what was in his mind, I blushed.

'Oh, Garth. You're just trying to put me off——'

I saw the flash of his white teeth momentarily, as the fire in his blue eyes deepened and he lifted me up.

'No, no. To the contrary. Quite the reverse.'

He carried me to the door and up the stairs as though I'd been a kitten, his strong heart pumping against mine. As we reached the bedroom there was the clatter of a tray from below telling me that Mrs Crabbe was somewhere about.

Garth slammed the latch hard and laid me on the bed. Then he sprang lightly away and turned the key in the door.

He was not smiling when he returned.

'Mrs Crabbe must have heard,' I whispered.

'A good thrill does no one any harm,' he murmured. He caressed me gently, then with fierce ardour as he unloosed my bodice. 'Why do you wear all these confounded things?' he muttered. I had no chance to reply. His breath was already warm about me, the thrust of passion claiming all that I had to give.

There was nothing anymore but Garth and I swept into the dark wild tide of utter forgetfulness.

It was only during the aftermath of culmination that I felt mildly ashamed. Though physically satisfied, my mind was not. Garth had used the one and only weapon he possessed capable of silencing me into subjugation. I could fight him with words, but not in passion. It was wrong, I told myself, wrong and unfair that things should be so onesided. But then, who was I to judge? I had already broken all standards of accepted social behaviour by becoming his wife. If I had continued living hypocritically as Mrs Horace Coutts, seeing Garth secretly as his lover and mistress, whispers might have got about and tongues wagged, but I had a shrewd idea none would have condemned me openly. I could have worn a cloak of respectability, lulled by inner self-martyrdom. As it was, everything was flagrantly clear. I had sinned conventionally, and the knowledge of it put me forever at a social disadvantage. Yet I knew also that I could not have acted any differently.

If the last eighteen months could come all over again I would behave in just the same way.

'Stubborn and strong-willed as a young colt,' my father had said when I was a child, and it was true. When I wanted anything sufficiently passionately I had not been able to rest until I got it. Marrying Horace in the first place had been my blunder. But when I looked back, I recognised that all the time I'd known he was merely a means to an end. Not consciously — intuitively, as a primitive means of survival until Garth and I had somehow come together.

Generally, after such times of self-analysis, I felt better, and more free to enjoy life.

It was the same that spring. How fragrant and verdant it was that year. As the woods and lush ditches came to blossom with primroses and violets followed by wild cherry and may foaming along the hedges, I left the house as much as possible and took to wandering. The moors then were purple and gold from sun-splashed heather and gorse. Gulls wheeled and dipped against clear skies. The distant sea was an iridescent quiver of silver in the early mornings. By April the memory of the unpleasant letters and niggling fretting over Tharne were becoming just occasional shadows that disappeared as quickly as they'd risen. A curious sense of elation and fulfilment rose in me. Because I so enjoyed walking I began not to miss the hours Garth spent apart from me. There were times even when I felt him in a strange way very close and by my side. Mrs Crabbe eyed me suspiciously at times.

'You go too far,' she told me once. 'There's funny folk around. Castle Cromme edn' the place to tek off to on y'r own. What about them gipsies roamin' the place. Thieves, they do say in Braggas. Nuthen but sly tinker pickpockets out to trap anyone with a mite o' silver in their wallet. You watch out more, an' kip 'way from theer.'

'I'll be careful,' I'd assured her, not divulging I'd seen the woman of my earlier meeting more than once. She was busy at that time of the year picking wild daffodils, cowslips, and gathering a quantity of the large-belled pink heather, which she afterwards bunched and took into Penzance or Penjust to sell.

One afternoon I was caught in a storm that broke quite un-expectedly from the West. I was nearing the high ridge, and with the first clap of thunder followed almost immediately by heavy spots of rain, I turned, pulling my cape close to my chin. I hurried down the slope, carelessly pushing past stones and through en-tangling furze. Then, suddenly, I tripped and fell. It was not an awkward movement, but for a moment my head whirled. I was unhurt, not even a twisted ankle; yet a feeling of sickness filled me. I sat up, and then fell back. Brief darkness claimed me. I waited for a brief pause of time, then hearing a voice, looked up.

The lean brown face of the gipsy woman was staring down on me. The glint of long ear-rings registered, even in the sombre rain-spattered light. Her voice was filled with concern and a kind of penetrating instinctive 'knowingness' when she said,

'What ails thee, dordi? Hurt?'

'No,' I answered. 'Not really. It's just—' I put my hand to my forehead, thinking again I might vomit.

She smiled faintly. 'With chavi, are thee, rackli?' she asked, and it was as though the breeze stirred slightly, rustling the dampening undergrowth with a momentous rising expectancy.

'Chavi?' I echoed. 'What's that? — Chavi. I don't—'

'Child, darling. Child,' the woman said. 'In gorgio tongue, is thy womb heavy with new life of the one to come?'

I felt the blood drain from my face. What was she suggesting — that I was pregnant? The thought had hardly occurred to me. And yet — why not? It would be the most natural thing in the world. And in a flash, thinking back, I recalled recent moments of fleeting giddiness that had passed almost instantly and been as quickly forgotten.

I said nothing. Her hand went out to help me up, and I brushed my skirt free of twigs and soil, looking down to hide my expression. When we faced each other I replied ambiguously, 'I think the fall just shocked me.'

Her smile widened; she gave me a pat on the shoulder, took a sprig of mistletoe from her basket and thrust it at me. 'Take it,' she said. 'With Romany blessings, take it, dordi; hang it over thy door and no thunder, lightning, or any kind of evil shall harm thee in thy days of fertility.'

She inclined her head slightly, made a gesture in the air, and the next moment was speeding lightly through the rain towards the encampment under the fold of the moor.

I returned to the house, awed, and thoughtful, not yet certain whether to accept the gipsy's prediction.

But the next week I knew.

I was to have Garth's child, and for the first time following our marriage, I felt really secure.

The doctor confirmed things on a day in late May, and as I left the consulting room in Penzance, the world — the very air I breathed — seemed rich and heady and full of promise. Summer lay ahead, and if my calculations proved correct the baby was due sometime in the middle of October. I walked with a light step in the direction of Adam's cab which was waiting in its usual place near the inn. There was only a faint ruffle of wind blowing small baby clouds across the clear sky. As I crossed the main street, the moorland hills beyond the town glistened gold in the distance. I had just reached the pavement when I half collided with a dark figure.

I looked up with apology on my lips. 'I'm so sorry—'

My heart jerked.

Horace's pale, set face, stared down on me. He waited rigidly for a moment, while I tried unsuccessfully to think of something polite to say. Whether he sensed my discomforture I didn't know. He said nothing; neither did he even raise his hat, but his expression during the fleeting interlude was so concentrated with dislike my whole body felt suddenly chilled. A second later — two, perhaps three — he had passed on, and with relief I half ran to the cab.

During the journey back composure returned; but the earlier joy and warmth had gone. Doubt niggled me, though of what I couldn't exactly determine. Horace? But Horace no longer counted in my life. He had no power or right any more to interfere. Yet his shadow persisted. And when I entered Carnbrooke it was intensified.

Before I was properly inside the door I saw it; an oblong envelope bearing my name lying clear in a shaft of sunlight.

I picked it up, wishing irrationally Mrs Crabbe or the dog had seen it first and destroyed it.

I picked it up, and was about to tear it open when Mrs Crabbe herself entered the hall from the kitchen.

She came towards me.

'I thought I heard sumthen',' she said. 'Letter, es et? Generally the postman doan call at this time.'

I said something automatically, feeling her eyes boring on my face. 'Not bad news. I do hope—'

Making a pretence of scrutinising the envelope I answered, 'Oh no. Just something I was half expecting.'

'Hm!' She hobbled away.

I took the offensive thing up to my bedroom, and hesitated a moment wondering whether to tear it up unread or perhaps put a match to it.

I did neither. Curiosity and a determination not to be intimidated made me open it.

'GET OUT WANTON,' it said. 'BEFORE WE TAKE YOU.'

The postmark was indecipherable and blurred. I tore the envelope in half, and automatically put the pieces in the drawer with the others. My first thought when I'd recovered was to tell Garth. But for some unknown reason I didn't. Neither did I let him know about the baby. It was as though the two incidents — the shock of running into Horace and the offensive threat, had temporarily frozen me to silence.

So the days passed; early summer days filled with promise and the richness of living growing things, days that could have held such beauty and sense of fulfilment had it not been for the undercurrent of doubt gnawing my heart.

Many times I was on the point of confiding in Garth but when the moment came I delayed, deterred by the longing somehow to have everything straight and clear between us, and the wretched business solved so that no shadow could overhang the baby's birth.

In early June I had to face the fact that I would be unable to hide the truth much longer. So far the developing bulge of my figure had been unnoticeable under the full crinoline of the period. I had been as skilful as possible in keeping Garth unaware of it, although he'd commented once that I was a little more plump than when we'd married. I'd laughed and shrugged the remark off carelessly. But it was more difficult to deceive Mrs Crabbe. Her eyes frequently had a shrewd glance in them which told me she suspected, and she very often flung out sly suggestions which I purposely ignored. Obviously the facade could not go on much longer, and it was imperative that I had an easy mind for the coming months. Dread, however faint, lurked in me, that any day another note would arrive. And perhaps Garth would find it first. That would be unthinkable. Somehow I had to act before it was too late. Yet how? I thought and thought, and eventually came to a decision.

Kara.

She might *not* be the perpetrator of the letters; she could be guilty, or completely innocent. The same applied to Horace. Neither might be involved. But Kara knew things I did not, concerning the reclusive invalid and child at Tharne. She had

knowledge of the mystery there, was part of it; she must be. So
far I'd had no contact with her, we had not even spoken.

Why not?

Why had Garth somehow always contrived to keep us apart?

Mrs Kara de Verries!

Had the name on the first mysterious letter been merely a
malicious dig at me? Or had it been a genuine mistake? Remembering the off-handed way Garth had taken it, I was
suddenly depressed.

I must see Kara, I thought recklessly. I *would* see her, with or
without Garth's permission, preferably when he was not there.

The opportunity came sooner than I'd expected, on an afternoon when Miss Ruana had set off in the Tharne chaise, presumably for Penzance. Garth had gone to Bristol for a few days
on some business or other concerning shipping, which meant I
was free of any dominating presence to debar a polite call at the
house.

I dressed with care in my most unassuming clothes – a
waisted grey cotton bodice fitted at the neck with a simple lace-
edged high collar, and a skirt to match, conveniently full, without embroidery or adornment. I wore nothing on my head but a
shred of lacy ribbon tied circular-wise at the back, to keep my
curls bunched tightly in place. Over one arm swung a gold-link
reticule – a present from Garth, containing smelling salts, one
or two keys, and an embroidered handkerchief; also perfume.

There was a slight drift of wind stirring when I hurried lightly
down the lane to the entrance to Tharne's short drive. I had no
clear plan of what to say when Kara and I were face to face. But
my determination to learn the full truth of her relationship to
Garth was firm in my mind. Once I knew that, other things
must emerge and fall into place. At the same time I meant to be
dignified, and as courteous as possible, keeping my quick
temper in check.

I felt almost buoyant when I reached the front door.

I rapped sharply. There was no response; nothing but the
faint soughing of the breeze in the trees and a bird's chirruping
through the undergrowth. I knocked again, with more force.
Still no reply. At last it occurred to me that with Miss Ruana out
any servants employed might be at the back or in attendance on
the invalid. So I decided to try another door. I made my way

down the drive, and came to a side entrance set in a recess with steps leading up to it. I rapped tentatively; again no answer, although a faint murmur sounded from the interior.

Stubbornly determined somehow to make contact, I went on for quite a distance, until a bend in the path cut suddenly to the left about fifty yards above the stables. I followed it, past a kitchen garden where a narrow track between dark shrubs led to yet another door. This was not encouraging. It had a forbidding look. I ignored it, taking the way round the side of the house which was now bordered on the far side by a wall.

Once I turned briefly and glanced round. Beyond the stables I could see the enclosed paddock and two horses grazing. The wall there, cutting it off from the moor, resembled that of some small fortress. The gates were thick and I guessed padlocked. The moors beyond rose bleak and steep towards the towering image of the Granite King.

Suddenly depressed, with a sense of loneliness deepening in me, I turned and hurried on. My own footsteps, though light, seemed to follow me. Each tap on the gravel echoed uncannily through the quietness.

Then, without any warning, I came upon a conservatory. In contrast to the drab granite walls of the house where ivy trailed in darkening masses, the glass erection caught a glitter of sunlight — of reflected plants and greenery inside. Even the door was painted green. I peered as closely as possible, my face pressed against a pane. The interior was large; and on the far side was another door, half open, leading into a room — a parlour perhaps — since the shadowed suggestion of heavy furniture caught an intermittent flicker of light from either a fire or far window beyond.

I tapped, listening intently. At first I imagined there was a faint sound indicating I'd been heard. Then all was quite still again. Seconds passed. I was about to leave and return to the front of the house when I suddenly glanced down and saw the key in the lock. That was odd, I thought; the door must be unlatched. I tried the knob, but it didn't move, so hesitating no longer I turned the key and went in. It was warm inside, steamy and pungent from ferns and flowering plants. A heavy sweetness wafted the air as a drift of wind stirred it with my entrance. I went back and closed the outer door, still holding the key.

Then I walked sharply towards the inner room thinking a good tap would probably be heard.

I didn't have to wait. Before I reached the parlour door — if it *was* a parlour — a man's figure suddenly stepped from the shadowed interior, and stood looking down on me, his features pale and clear from the greenish-gold light.

My heart bumped against my ribs. I was shocked, and at first too confused to speak. The face was so like Garth's. The same clearly defined features — arrogant bone-structure and sculptured lines of nose and chin. The same unswerving glint of eyes; but no — there I was wrong. These eyes were of a deeper blue; not blue at all really, but dark smouldering jade, as though a film of amber had been superimposed. He was thinner, too, than Garth, and a little taller, a height emphasised by the black embroidered wrap he wore, which was far too exotic to be called a dressing gown. This must be the invalid then, and a relative obviously. Quick as lightning the thoughts flashed through my mind. A murmur of apology broke from my lips, but with a wave of a hand he silenced me.

'No, no. I'm delighted to meet you at last, and quite grateful you've taken the initiative.'

So he recognised me?

His voice was quiet and gentle; his manner cultured, as he continued, quietly, 'Do sit down, please—'

I hardly hesitated before easing myself on to the white painted garden-seat, placed conveniently against the wall, between the two doors.

He smiled, shaking his head reflectively.

'What an old granny my brother is,' he went on, 'so protective, and — and damn boring on occasion—'

'Your brother?' Although startled, I didn't for one moment doubt the statement; everything suddenly seemed so obvious. The likeness — the extreme thinness of the drooping figure under the ornate dressing gown. But why hadn't my husband said? Why had he gone to such pains to hide the relationship?

My confusion must have showed. I was about to make some random remark when the stranger made a little bow, offered his hand, and said, 'Manfred de Verries; and you, I'm quite sure, are Caroline.' For a moment our fingers touched. A formal contact, no more.

Everything so normal, so easily explained.

'Yes. How did you know?'

He turned, picked a crimson flower from a mass of shining leaves and brought it to me. 'Ah! I have eyes,' he said. 'I watch — even from this prison. Besides I've heard things.'

'What things?'

'How beautiful you are.'

I could feel the warm blood staining my cheeks, and was embarrassed because of it.

'Not everyone thinks so. Oh — I didn't mean — please, Mr de Verries, don't think I expect compliments. And the reason I called was to find out — was to — to—' I broke off suddenly, quite at a loss for words, aware that there was no adequate explanation for my intrusion. I'd just trespassed where I wasn't wanted, blundered in 'where angels feared to tread' — that was what Aunt Adela would have called it.

He sat down beside me and put the flower into my hand. Then he said, with a touch of sadness, 'You don't have to explain to me, Caroline. I'm not very good company for a young girl, and my brother no doubt wishes to protect you.'

'From what though? If you're recovering from an illness I don't see why I should have been kept in the dark and forbidden to come here. It's so odd. It's — it's—'

'Unnatural? Yes.' He seated himself beside me, and for a fleeting moment a hand touched my shoulder. 'But then you see, tough characters like Garth and my cousin Ruana regard sickness — any kind of sickness as rather shameful.'

My spine bristled with indignation.

'How ridiculous!'

'Yes. However, we are as we are.'

There was a long pause. When he spoke again it was in softer tones, almost a whisper. 'Put the flower in your hair, Caroline. It's a very rare species. In India it blooms only at night—'

I lifted the blossom to my nostrils. 'How sweet it smells.'

'Yes.'

'You said India — did you bring it with you?'

'Kara did.'

'Kara.'

'My wife.'

'Oh!' relief surged through me. 'I see.'

'What?'

'I haven't met her of course. But we've passed once or twice, in the lane. And I've seen her in the garden.'

He shook his head.

'Poor Kara.'

'Why?'

'Away from her family, imprisoned in this mausoleum of a place. And our child—'

'The little girl?'

'Jessamin. Yes. She's wayward, poor little thing. And rather − difficult. Kara is quite wonderful with her. But Heavens above! what life is it for a child to be shut up and restrained all the time?' He broke off bitterly, got to his feet suddenly, and walked to the far window. I could feel my hands gripping the edge of the seat. When he turned his face was set and hard. The light struck sideways across the fine features emphasising uncannily the resemblance to Garth. I stood up, and as he came towards me the momentary anger seemed to drop away in a flash, leaving him wearied and gentle once more.

'Forgive me, Caroline,' he said, lifting both. arms, palms upwards in a gesture slightly foreign, and more Eastern or French than English. 'I should not have let my temper get the better of me.'

I took an involuntary step forward.

'Oh but, Mr de Verries—'

'Manfred please,' he said, taking my hands.

And that very moment the last thing I'd expected happened; the inner door leading from the parlour opened with a sharp sound followed by a voice saying imperiously, 'What are you doing here?'

I turned, and saw Ruana's cold face staring down on me. She wore a small, brimless black hat, high on her severely dressed hair. Her black bodice and skirt emphasised the rigid erect figure. Condemnation blazed from her eyes. Her thin mouth was drawn down disapprovingly. Before Manfred could speak I jumped up, in a flurry.

'I'm sorry,' I said helplessly. 'I merely looked in to − to—'

'Looked in? You mean you came prying in my absence?'

'No, not prying,' I answered as indignation replaced my momentary embarrassment. 'I paid a call, as they put it. Is that wrong? I'd never met Kara — I mean Mrs de Verries, and—'

'So you thought you'd take the opportunity while Garth was away, and Mrs de Verries resting with a headache — to steal in behind my back, and force yourself on Manfred—'

'Now look here, Ruana' — Manfred's voice seethed with anger, though he did his best to control it — 'You're not being very hospitable. Since this is my house now, as much as yours — I think I've a perfect right to entertain my sister-in-law if I wish.'

'You have every right, Manfred, but in Garth's absence you know very well I'm supposed to watch your health. Supposing you develop a temperature? Supposing you'd overtired yourself — which you could easily have done if I hadn't returned far earlier than I'd intended?'

His lips curled derisively.

'What a bore you are, Ruana. What a goddammed, poker-faced bore—'

Ruana turned dead white.

'How dare you, Manfred!'

His jaw tightened suddenly. The intense dark greenish-blue eyes narrowed. I was afraid at first he might strike her. At his sides the hands were clenched, the skin stretched tightly over the prominent knuckles.

'I must go,' I said, wanting at all costs to avoid a scene. 'Please — oh please don't be angry on my account. Coming here was a mistake. I—'

'Yes, it was.' The flat statement fell like a knife, subduing argument to sudden silence before the harsh tones continued. 'A very deliberate one, though, on your part.'

I swallowed hard and ran to the door of the conservatory. With my hand on the knob I turned once, before rushing up the path towards the lane at the front.

Manfred and Ruana stood perfectly motionless, like two effigies watching.

I did not realise at the time that I had left my reticule behind on the conservatory seat. It was not until I reached Carnbrooke that I discovered it.

Under normal circumstances I would have returned immediately to fetch it; but I decided it would be better to wait until a more opportune and tactful moment arrived. There was nothing of importance in the bag except my back door key. Somewhere I knew I had another which would turn up if I searched thoroughly; but I felt too emotionally exhausted to bother looking that night. Thieves were very rare in the area; frequently, in the past, the door had been purposely left slightly open, either for the cat, or in bad weather for the farmer to place the milk inside.

Little I guessed as I went up to bed on that certain evening, what the next few hours were to bring.

12

I slept fitfully during the first few hours of the night. Then, as a train of thin cloud obscured the eerie pattern cast by brilliant moonlight against the curtains, deeper slumber claimed me.

Suddenly though, I was awake; startled by a sound and the uncanny sensation that someone was in the bedroom. At first I lay perfectly rigid, with my heart pumping uneasily, trying to locate familiar objects such as the looming shape of the wardrobe − the glint of the glass-topped dressing shelf − even the knob of a bedpost. But the uncertain wavering light through the gloom was too confusing. The moon occasionally glittered bright again from outside, and as quickly died into massed blackness.

I stirred; and there was a furtive creak from somewhere near the door. I sat up quickly, clutching the shift at my neck. Cold streams of sweat trickled down my spine.

'Who's there? What do you want?' I managed to whisper.

No reply.

After a few seconds of complete silence I nerved myself to reach for the matches and candle on the bedside table.

There was a muffled sound, and in that same instant the atmosphere seemed to thicken and merge into a form − greater darkness intensifying against the darkness of room and furniture. The shape bore down on me. Like a wild animal cornered I huddled myself into the sheets cowering to the far side of the bed. But the bed was against the wall. Escape could only be from its far end. The warmth and steam of male breath intensified. I made a wild movement and opened my mouth to scream. No sound came. There was a throaty murmur of low laughter, a man's, from nearby — the touch of a hot hand on one thigh. I kicked, and raised my arm wildly, could feel my nails tearing at flesh.

'Wild cat — wild cat—' The words came as a hiss; for a terrified moment I saw the gleam of teeth, very white teeth, in a sudden splash of moonlight. Then everything was obscured again. The low laughter started up once more, dying into a grunt of desire. I shuddered, trying not to let faintness overcome me. But the thing — or whatever it was — was hot on top of me, lusting and tearing, ripping my clothes. I made a feeble cry for help, knowing it was useless. Mrs Crabbe slept at the far end of the house. She certainly would not hear. And if she did, what could she do? Oh God! I thought, oh God — help me.

I struggled and fought, while the sibilant undertones turned to cajoling threats. 'Come, darling — come — Manfred wants you, and you want Manfred—'

Manfred? Manfred? It couldn't be. And then, suddenly, I knew. Knowledge and wild uncontrollable anger gave new energy for a moment, dispelling terror. I lunged out, as my teeth sunk into a thin hand. The next moment I was free, scrambling instinctively from the bed and rushing to the door, knocking the candle over and sweeping a glass to the floor. I plunged through the shadows and wavering light to the stairs, taking the turn blindly to the kitchen and through to the back, only half aware of Mrs Crabbe's distorted face peering from the landing as I passed. Thank heaven, the back door was open I thought, as I reached the scullery. Once out of the house I could find shelter and hide. But could I? Thudding footsteps were already close behind. As I dashed outside into the darkness, I heard Manfred stumble, and a stream of curses follow. I screamed then; scream after scream, disturbing gulls that echoed my cries with their own shrill shrieking.

I ran on, taking the route intuitively towards the moor; and always the footsteps followed. Once I looked back and saw the long thin figure outlined starkly against the hill, face greenish-white in the moon's pale glare, hands outstretched and clawing. I cut to the left, remembering there was a dip over the hill if I had the energy to reach there. Boulders too; and trees. Bent twisted trees interspersed with a wilderness of tangled furze and heather. With the breath tearing at my lungs, I forced myself on, climbing and clutching undergrowth, unaware of cuts and scratches, of the blood trickling from my hands and forehead. And still the relentless nightmare figure was in pursuit. My mind reeled from exhaustion. Every moment that passed I felt must be my last. Yet somehow, I went on again. Several times I had to wait for a second, leaning and gasping against a stone or withered tree trunk.

Once, thinking I was free at last I sank to the ground. Then I saw him again, bent almost double, head thrust forward, grappling with bushes only a few yards away. Mercifully the clouds came up again at that point, and with a great effort I was able to continue – gasping and moaning, as tears of exhaustion streamed from my eyes, half blinding me.

How long the dreadful race continued I never knew. All that registered was a miasma of dark flying shadows and shapes, of seering brightness, a gulping for air, and always – always Manfred on my heels.

Then, suddenly, it was over. I fell, and the earth took me to its heather-bed. Stars seemed to dart up and down in my head for a second, until unconsciousness came in a dark tide of peace.

When I came to myself I didn't at first remember what had happened. As facts half registered I shivered and my teeth started chattering.

I looked round. I was lying on a soft bed. The interior of the room – if it could be called one – was small, and the door was no conventional one, but more of a gap in large curtains. A reddish glow crept in from outside and I realised I was in a tent, and that the woodsmoke scent came from a nearby log fire. As my eyes grew accustomed to the light, I saw the glitter of a single star from the sky where the smoke lifted.

Slowly my head began to clear. I remembered the gipsies and cutting to the dip where their encampment lay; before that, the running, running, and the footsteps on my trail, footsteps of a nightmare — Manfred's.

Manfred.

My whole body lurched. I sat up abruptly, eyes wide, searching for any glimpse of him, for a sign that he could be hiding in the shadows playing round the interior; but seeing only the glitter of the witch-ball on a low chest — a small primitive stove and table, and a wooden chair pushed under it. On the chest were plates and a bowl. A gilt painted clock ticked on the table.

I pushed one leg out of the bed and discovered I was wearing a soft woollen garment — probably hand-knitted, that had been put on to replace my own. I touched the ground with a foot, and almost immediately a figure pushed through the gap. She was carrying a bowl; something warm steamed from it.

'Ah, dordi,' she said. 'Better are thee?' Her voice was harsh, yet kind, and familiar somehow. I rubbed my eyes, and as I did so felt the bandage tied round my forehead. 'Drink this—' the voice continued. 'Good broth. Bebee's best. Thy man — or mebbe he's not thy man, the wild one — is already revived. Enquiring for thee he was—'

I was too stunned by her words at first to answer. Then as I'd taken the bowl I began to shake. 'What man? And where is he? Don't let him near me. He's a beast — a — a—'

The woman shook her head slowly. 'Ah, lady, have no fear. The evil-eye has left the poor sick rai, and round thy neck is a sacred charm of my people, a charm of Develski, the divine earth-mother. From the breast-bone of the rainbow-feathered one it came, the Kingfisher bird, dordi—'

'Where is he?' I cried, feeling the charm at my throat. 'Where's Manfred?'

'Gone, daughter. Gone. We gave him soup, and as the bengh — the madness — died in him, he took off down the hill and was met by his man—'

'Another man? Who?' I cried, thinking in alarm of Garth.

She shrugged. 'His servant surely. Dark in the moonlight he looked, with the cloth round his head. There was a woman below. Together they took him to the big house.'

'How do you know?'

'Ah, rackli, my own man is swift as the panther, and cunning as the fox. His eyes are the cat's eyes. He saw, dordi. He saw.'

I was silent until she said in more remote tones. 'Take the broth now, and Saul shall see thee away. It would be bad should the gavvers find thee here.'

'Saul?'

'My man. He has a sturdy stout donkey and thine injuries are slight. A scratch or two — a cut, no more. And the chavi still thrives within thy womb—'

For a moment I was startled, forgetting her former prediction.

'You know,' I said rather stupidly.

The white teeth gleamed.

'Yes. Yutha knows.'

There was a pause.

'And now I'm leaving thee,' she continued rather abruptly. 'My man shall fetch the donkey; thine own clothes are dry, and cleaned up, and before the first dawn lights the sky you must be away.'

A little later, wearing my own night shift with a coloured blanket over my shoulders, I was seated on Saul's donkey, being led down the stony moor to Carnbrooke.

It was a silent uncommunicative journey.

Saul, a lean dark-haired, dark-skinned, man, replied only in a monosyllable to my one attempt at conversation. Very gradually the darkness was lifting to an edge of grey over the horizon. I glanced up once from under the blanket, and on the opposite side of the valley caught a brief glimpse of the towering Granite King emerging bleak and black over the low-lying mist. All around me boulders and tumps of rough furze-covered earth loomed like slumbering beasts about to come to life. The air was tangy and chill, but in an hour or two I knew, would be steaming from summer's breath.

As we neared the back of Carnbrooke, Saul halted the donkey, and put out a hand.

'Here we stop,' he said. 'And see thou says nought of this or of my people.'

For a moment his lean hand gripped my wrist. I jumped down, pulled myself together after threatened giddiness, thanked him, and handed him the blanket; then, shivering slightly from the cool air, I turned and hurried to the house.

I looked back once. He had already disappeared into the deep grey wilderness of the moor.

I hurried on. At the bend of the track joining the path, figures were gathered. A lantern glimmered to the left; in its warm glow I recognised Adam. Forms appeared from every direction, like magpies chattering.

A strange feeling of unreality filled me again — a sense of wandering through some hinterland of fact and fiction. I realised they were searching for me. Manfred's form moment-arily reappeared; a tall, bent figure with his man beside him. An instant later they turned again to Tharne. Manfred went quietly, as though bereft of will, like a great bird with broken wings. The scene could have been one in a macabre play, yet everything that happened on that terrible night was deliber-ately hushed up — either through bribery or fear — from any official investigation. Secretly tongues may have wagged — they must have done. But outward comment was repressed.

Even Mrs Crabbe refused to discuss things except to remark condemningly, 'I knew there'd be trouble for 'ee one day. Lord knows what the dear doctor'd say.' Her eyes blazed with indig-nation. But when I tried to explain her expression became sullen and blank.

'I know nuthen,' she told me. 'Neither do I want to.'

I guessed then that someone had already intimidated her, and that the one most likely was Miss Ruana.

That didn't worry me. My only concern was what Garth would think when he heard. I knew he would receive the full impact of the incident from his stiff-backed cousin, and that my story would inevitably sound rather thin. The confrontation in the conservatory would discredit me from the start. One card I held though to count in my favour — oh surely it must — that I was to have his child.

I never dreamed how Garth would receive the news. If I had my whole future might have been different; I would probably have packed a valise and left Cornwall for good.

13

I did not go out that day, but stayed mostly in my room resting. Mrs Crabbe brought the mid-day meal up on a tray. She was puffing, and looked heavy-eyed from the anxiety of the night's events. I tried to make amends by apologising and thanking her. She would not be mollified. 'It's beyond me,' she said. 'Doan' go on 'bout 'et. What's done's done — more's the pity.'

Towards tea-time I went downstairs. The sky was grey outside, and there was no sign of activity from the lane by Tharne. A few crows wheeled over the tips of the trees, and gulls dipped towards the sea beyond. The air was close; I flung a parlour window open, but Mrs Crabbe disapproved. 'There'll be fog later,' she said. 'Bad for curtains and furniture, and my rheumatics too.' She closed the sash with a rattle, and went out, grumbling under her breath.

I went to the table where daffodils were fading in a vase. I took them impatiently to the kitchen, emptied the water down the sink, flung the withered things into a bucket and taking a pair of scizzors from a hook went through to the front garden. There was a lilac bush near the door. Heavy purple blooms were massed in shiny heart-shaped leaves, filling the air with rich sweetness.

The tree was old now — my father had planted it, but every year it seemed to blossom more profusely, and I remembered with nostalgia how my father had said, 'Lilac will only flower where it chooses. Slow to start, but once it's got a true hold there's no stopping it. If we knew a quarter about nature that we do of human bodies, the world would look a pleasanter place. Care, Caroline. That's what flowering things need. And maybe happiness.'

I had listened to him then, a little surprised, because in spite of his medical skill — perhaps because of it — he rarely indulged in fantasies.

'Yes, Papa,' I'd said, reaching up and drawing a bloom to my lips. 'There — I've kissed it. It'll go on now, won't it, for ever and ever?'

His smile had died a little. 'There's no for ever and ever, my dear,' he'd said with faint sadness. 'Everything has its time. We must accept that; it's one of life's lessons.'

I'd only been a child then, but a sense of awe had momentarily silenced me. It was as though he had been preparing me for something.

The next year he had died.

As I cut the blossoms to replace the half dead daffodils, memory flooded me with acute pain and longing. I held the fragrant bunch to my cheek for a moment, reliving with aching nostalgia the days and years spent in his comforting presence. Even Garth was temporarily forgotten. I wanted to cry and laugh, and be held temporarily against a fatherly breast — to be innocent again, with all responsibility swept away.

I wanted comfort, and above all — understanding.

Perhaps such emotions were the result of pregnancy — perhaps all women felt as I did at such times. But I doubted it, most women surely did not have to face such conflicting circumstances — there were friends to discuss matters with, other women to gossip with and confide in over the daily discomforts and excitements for the future.

I had no one.

When I went into the kitchen Mrs Crabbe was preparing vegetables for the evening meal. A tart remark from her dispelled my self-pity shaking me smartly to the present.

'Adam's coming to fix a bolt on that door,' she said sharply. 'Doan' suppose you've found the key, have 'ee?'

'No, I haven't,' I answered shortly, resenting her air of authority. 'And I didn't know you'd spoken to Adam.'

'Hm! Someone had to. An seein' you'd a mind to shut yourself away I had to be the one it seemed.'

This was the first reference she'd made to my terrible experience on the moor. Her unnatural stubborn reticence about such abnormal happenings had even made me wonder at odd moments if I'd exaggerated things, or if I could have had some frightful nightmare in my sleep that had driven me from the house and sent me blundering towards Manfred in the dark.

The suggestion was terrifying because if true it would mean I was unbalanced. Such wild thoughts were quickly dispelled. I had never been neurotic. All that had happened had been real. If necessary I could prove most of it. The gipsies who had rescued and taken me in knew, Adam could verify certain things. A furtive sidelong look in his eyes indicated he was quite aware of Manfred's sinister behaviour.

The full truth, though, was known to me alone.

The bruises on my body, and scratched face sickened me every time I noticed, reviving a horrified vision of lusting twisted lips and grasping hands — the feel of them clawing my breasts and tearing at my shirt as I escaped from the bedroom. I tried always to deaden memory at this point, but the recollection of running — running — always running — of the bleak hill and slipping shadows — of darkness and light, then darkness again, stubbornly persisted. My heart would quicken for a time then settle into an uneasy quiet beat as the anti-climax of the event registered: a brief glimpse of Manfred being taken unresistingly away, and the strange manner in which my bedraggled presence had been almost disregarded.

Just an 'Are 'ee all right, lady?' from some local; puzzled faces turned to me for an instant, then suddenly diverted in curiosity upon Manfred. There had been a few questions that I'd answered mechanically; but my clearest impression was of smug hostility — hostility, doubt, and blame.

Oh yes. My sex, my past, my broken marriage to Horace and involvement with Garth made adequate framework in their eyes for a very wicked woman indeed. Mrs Crabbe had acted that night — or rather early morning — as warder of some criminal rather than an old retainer, bringing hot water to me silently, bathing my scratches and torn hands with set face and fierce eyes. There had been little kindness in her, only outrage.

No wonder then that the rift between us was still there.

A week passed before Garth returned. Mercifully it was late evening and a dark one, sultry with mist and lowering clouds when the sound of cab wheels and hooves stopped outside the gate. I was upstairs and my heart bounded. I rushed to the window and watched his strong form emerge to pay the jarvy, then turn and walk smartly up the path to the door. The limp he'd had when he'd first returned to Tharne had almost gone now. The bone and muscle injuries received in the Indian conflict had healed far more quickly than had been thought possible at the time. Hardly a scar remained. I was grateful for his sake, but occasionally selfishly wondered if he'd ever be tempted to rejoin the Army and be taken from me perhaps for months at a time.

As I moved from the window to the mirror, anxiety of a different kind gnawed me — the problem of how best to explain the tortuous incident with Manfred, my rash visit to Tharne in Ruana's absence, her violent reaction which had resulted in my leaving my reticule and key behind. He would be upset of course, but hearing facts from my own lips before anyone else contorted the story, would help. Once again I was thankful for the dreary damp light. On a normal summer evening he could so easily have been recognised, or stopped the cab for a chat with an acquaintance or local farmer. As it was, I could be pretty certain he had not yet heard any damaging news concerning my escapade.

So in a flurry of expectation and desire, mingled with relief that things were so soon to be in the open, I hurriedly pulled on a flimsy pink wrap, loosened my lightish tawny hair on the brow, and dabbed rice powder on my burning cheeks. The scratches, under subtle make-up, were hardly visible, and not at all in flickering candlelight. I had never believed myself to be really beautiful, but just for a second or two, with excitement lighting my eyes to rare brilliance, and the shadows playing fitfully round high cheekbones, the reflection told me I was. A temporary illusion perhaps, or the effect of such extreme passionate longing. It didn't matter. What loveliness I had was revitalised for Garth.

As his footsteps quickened up the stairs, I could hardly breathe. My breasts rose and fell tumultuously. I turned towards the door, both arms involuntarily half raised to receive him, hardly able to believe he was really back. It was all I could do not to rush forward in undignified abandon, unheeding that Mrs Crabbe was probably in the hall watching. But I restrained myself; and when Garth entered the bedroom I was still standing, trembling with joy by the dressing table.

He took four strides towards me, and I was in his arms. His lips were on my mouth, my cheek my temples and shoulders, then back again on my lips.

'Oh, Garth, oh, darling—' I said breathlessly, 'it's been so lonely—'

He held me by the shoulders, his brilliant blue eyes darkening with the tumult, the overwhelming utter need we had of each other. Then he released me, and took my hand. I saw then that he was trembling too.

'Glad you've missed me,' he remarked, with his glance searching first my face, then travelling over my whole body from head to feet, as though noting anew each contour and curve, assessing with fresh and mounting desire all I had to give. I was so thankful then I was wearing the pink chiffon thing. Pink — the colour of love, soft, silky-thin and glowing.

I smiled; it was a secret smile, warm and rich with triumph, with the glowing knowledge of what he soon would know — that I was to have his baby.

I half opened my lips to begin. But words died under the heady sweetness of his mouth again on mine, drawing the life from me until he lifted me up and I lay half-swooning in his arms.

I could feel his hand sweeping the hair from my forehead, there was a moment of complete silence, a pause as he held me close against him. Then we were lying together on the bed. His touch was gentle, reverent almost at first, until in an abandon of mutual passion the thrust of love was strong and fierce, uniting flesh with flesh, dark with the thunderous knowledge of ages past, brilliant with force of life to come, a wild and sweeping tide that took us both at last to a dazed and dream-like peace.

For a time we lay side by side, saying nothing, because there was nothing to say. My head rested lightly on his shoulder. One hand of his rested on my stomach, and presently crept upward to a breast.

Gradually thought registered. I was about to speak when he moved abruptly sprang out of bed, and said with a whimsical twist to his lips, 'What a one you are for befuddling a man, Caroline.'

'Befuddling? Not very complimentary, I must say.'

I sat up, pulling the pink wrap round my body. 'You haven't any sentiment in you,' I continued with mock petulance.

'Caroline, my sweet'—' his lips touched my cheek. 'Don't tempt me. You just wait, my girl. Later I'll show you—' he was straightening his clothes and smoothing his hair into a semblance of dignity. I watched him, slightly jealous that men — any man — even Garth — could so easily switch from the heights of passion to practical mundane matters once culmination was over.

'Where are you going?' I asked although I guessed. 'Anyway — can't it wait?'

He shook his head. 'Afraid it can't. It will only be for a few moments. I'll soon be back. Why don't you put something warmer on, and when I return we'll celebrate—'

'It's Tharne, I suppose?' I said, trying not to sound catty.

'Yes, Tharne. Naturally. I've got to see what's been going on.'

'I can tell you,' I thought, 'I must — I've got to say something before you get the wrong story from Ruana—'

I did try. I struggled desperately to find the right words — somehow to keep him by me while I explained as sensibly and coolly as possible what had happened concerning myself and Manfred.

But I did not get far.

'Oh Garth—' I said haltingly, getting up and running towards him, 'please not yet. Just stay; I've got something to tell you — several things. It's important. You see — please—'

He merely laughed and went to the door.

'Later,' he said. 'I'm sure half an hour won't make any difference.'

I sighed.

'It could make all the difference. Garth, I—'

He ignored me suddenly. His voice was more stern when he emphasised, 'I've told you. Later.'

The lock snapped to. He had gone.

For a moment I stood quite still, staring bleakly at the door. Anxiety drained elation from me into sudden tiredness. My nerves were still quivering from our passionate reunion but tension increased. I played with the idea of dressing properly and going downstairs; but the thought of Mrs Crabbe's primped up mouth and curious stare discouraged me. If everything was all right, I thought, if Garth wasn't too upset, and listened to my explanation without prejudice, we could celebrate in the parlour together later. I would wear my prettiest dress perhaps — a delicately shaded blueish-green silk, trimmed with cream lace, and we would toast the future after I'd told him my own news. However hard Ruana tried to set him against me I had something to offer him more precious than wealth or family name, stronger than jealousy or hatred; something to wipe all the troubles past away. A child. This one thing must bind us close I told myself, must eradicate resentment of Horace forever from his mind.

Gradually my optimism returned. But restlessness increased as the seconds and minutes ticked by. I walked backwards and forwards between door and window, pausing at moments to re-arrange my hair or pin a stray curl in place, touching my lips with salve, and spraying perfume intermittently behind my ears and where the nervous perspiration gathered. I was seated on the bed when Mrs Crabbe knocked and poked her head round the door. 'Sumthen for 'ee,' she said, thrusting a hand out. Normally I might have chided her for the abrupt uncivil inter-ruption. But the white envelope she held shocked me as though someone was threatening me with a sword.

I took it mechanically.

'Who brought it?'

'No one. It was under the mat. God pushed there I s'pose. This girl we have doan' do her job. Slip-shod that's what she is.' There was a pause until the old voice continued sharply, 'Well?'

I tore my eyes from the envelope and stared at her coldly.

'Thank you, Mrs Crabbe. You can go.'

She muttered something and grudgingly went out, closing the door behind her.

Determined not to be disturbed again until Garth got back I was careful to turn the key in the lock. Then, very deliberately, with fingers gone cold and stiff I wrenched the envelope open.

As before the lettering was large, in block capitals.

'GET OUT,' it said. 'WHORE.'

Just for a second or two I felt faint, and sat down again, with my head in my hands. When my head had cleared I went to the drawer where remnants of the other notes lay, and pushed the offensive paper inside. I stared blankly into the mirror. My face looked deathly pale. For a few seconds it seemed that time had added years to my age. I touched my cheeks with rouge from a small pot that had belonged to Aunt Adela, piled my hair higher on my head, and went to the small chest containing bottles of lotions and cures of medicinal value. There was a small bottle of brandy on a shelf. Without bothering about a glass I took a gulp of the stinging liquid and almost immediately felt better, filled with fresh confidence, even a touch of bravado.

Shortly afterwards I heard Garth's footsteps mounting the stairs. I stiffened my back, lifted my head proudly and stood quite still, waiting. There was a rattle, followed by a sharp knock and kick on the door.

'Open it.' The command was curt and angry.

I rushed to turn the key. 'Oh, Garth, I'm so sorry,' I said, 'I forgot to unlock it. It was Mrs Crabbe you see — she brought — she brought—' the rush of words broke off incoherently as he wrenched the key from my hand, pushed me violently back into the room, and then relocked the door.

He stood there for moments, breathing heavily, mouth hard, blue eyes cold and relentless, jaws set. Then he thrust something out at me. My reticule. A hand went automatically to my lips. I had temporarily forgotten it.

'Yours, I believe, Madam,' he said.

I stared. This was not the Garth I thought I knew. This was a stranger — a furious condemning stranger without mercy or understanding; pitiless. A man beyond the pleas or wiles of any woman, even a wife.

Thinking he might strike me, I involuntarily backed towards the bed.

He followed; I crouched against the pillows. He flung the gold bag on to the quilt.

Then he gripped me by the shoulders. 'You do well to cringe,' he said. 'Any man but a fool would teach you a lesson in the only way your kind of woman understands. Thank your stars I'm what I am with a degree of civilization in me—'

I struggled, and tried to speak. He slapped my face.

'Shut up, or I'll forget my gentlemanly upbringing and give you the beating you deserve. Now just listen, damn you. I've heard what's been going on — your lusting little game with my brother. Your cheap conniving, and leaving your reticule behind. The keys! Your own and the conservatory's — so conveniently placed by you in the bag for Manfred to see. But it wasn't quite so bright of you after all, was it? The likelihood of my cousin returning before time didn't occur to you. You slipped up there, darling—'

A few desperate words broke from me then.

'I didn't plan anything, Garth. It was a mistake. Ruana was so rude. She—'

'She was furious. Naturally she was — finding you'd sneaked in behind her back at the first opportunity, and against my express command—'

'Your command! *Your* command — it's always you — what *you* say—'

'And why not? Where Tharne's concerned, yes. My family *is* my affair—'

'And what am I?'

'My chattel.' The two words were cold as steel. His eyes were blazing. 'My woman. I paid enough for you didn't I? You have your precious Carnbrooke and finery to flaunt before the locals — you have your paint and powder and perfume to seduce Manfred just as you seduced me—'

My hand whirled. His words sickened me, made me want to vomit. My legs were trembling so violently I almost fell. He pushed me on to the bed. 'Now don't you dare to move,' he continued, 'before I've finished, or you'll regret it. Just listen to what I have to say and when I've said it you can scream, and storm and plead and pretend to your heart's content, but I won't be here to listen. Understand?'

The bitter condemnation of his stare, the threat of his tones kept me silent. After a pause, when he continued, his voice was quieter. But the wry twist to his lips, the rigid stance remained.

'I brought my brother from the hell of India for peace and quiet. He's sick and suffering from things you'll never understand. He has a wife and child needing care and sanctuary. I've tried to give it. But *you* — at the first chance fling your airs and graces at him — taunting his manhood — draining away every ounce of self-respect and dignity for the mere gratification of making another conquest. You ensnared him as you ensnared your precious Horace, and then — God help us — myself.'

At that point I sprang up. Garth swung me round and seemed about to strike me when I screamed, 'Don't, you mustn't. Listen, Garth — listen — I'm having a child — a *child*!'

He released me quickly. I fell back on to the quilt. He didn't speak. All colour, suddenly, had left his face; even his lips were pale — hard and thin as though etched in granite.

'It's true,' I insisted. 'I'm not lying—'

'No? How truly remarkable. And how very convenient — for you.' I winced.

'Don't you care?' I muttered dully. 'Doesn't it matter to you — at all?'

'Why should it?' The blue gaze was a mere cold flame now between narrowed lids. 'Whose is it, may I ask? Horace's? No. A little late for that. Mine? Perhaps. Or Manfred's? Possibly. Some women, I believe, soon know when conception has occurred.' He laughed, hatefully.

'How dare you?' I exclaimed. '*Manfred!*'

'Oh I wouldn't put it beyond him. But there are several gallants about the neighbourhood who doubtless would have no hesitation in obliging — Venn for one.'

'That's disgusting.'

He turned and walked to the door. 'Yes,' he agreed looking back at me. 'It was. I apologise for sinking my own standards to those of this extremely distasteful occasion. However, I'm sure you'll recover.'

His hand turned on the knob.

'Garth—'

'Yes?'

'I — please don't — can't we—?'

'Kiss and make up? No my dear, we can't. I've lost the appetite for gymnastic amours. Until tonight I wanted and loved you as much — more — than I'd thought it possible for any man to love a woman; so when Ruana disclosed your trickery I could have wrung your pretty little neck. Now all I feel is contempt — for you, myself, and the whole miserable situation. We shall get by, I suppose, with the maximum of facade and pretence. And you need have no fears that you and your future — offspring — will not be adequately provided for.' He paused, while I struggled miserably to regain composure. Then he continued in practical offhand tones, 'Tonight I shall sleep at Tharne. My brother may need me. In the meantime perhaps you'll arrange to have another room prepared for me here—'

'And what will Mrs Crabbe think?' I interrupted.

'She can think what she likes. But if she's wise she'll hold her tongue or she'll have no roof over her head at Carnbrooke.'

'You mean—'

'I mean what I've said, which shouldn't be too much for your bright brain to take in. Good night.'

The door slammed.

He was gone.

At first I couldn't make the effort to move. Then, as the truth gradually registered, I went dully to the window and stared out at the darkening landscape. The mist had already deepened into thickening rain from the lowering clouds. The grey sweep of it took rocks and bushes into sullen uniformity.

I went to the dressing table, lit two candles, and stared at the reflection through the mirror hardly recognising my own identity. The wan, flickering flames emphasised every hollow, line, and contour, giving the semblance of a ghost — some haunted creature — rather than reality. So I would look when I was very old perhaps — all beauty gone, leaving a shell of emptiness, a mockery of what once had been.

A shell.

That was what I felt as I climbed a little later into bed; a thing without purpose or energy to go on living. I slept for an hour or two, the utter sleep of exhaustion. And when I woke and remembered, apathy miraculously turned to a quickening rebellious anger.

I would show him, I thought, I would show Garth de Verries that I was not the tame creature he imagined — a woman of milk-and-water content to conform to his beastly bullying. He'd said he'd bought me, but he hadn't. I was no Eastern slave to be purchased with gold from some foreign far-off market place where women were cheap. Neither was he in a position to hurl insults at me, when he himself had been the first offender. I recalled the day on the moor near Castle Cromme when he'd so ruthlessly taken me by physical force. I'd fought him and yet he'd persisted.

'Quits,' he'd said afterwards.

Well, there was still more of the game to be played. If he wished to think of me as a whore, I would live-up to the image. I would flaunt my airs and graces in his face, dress with abandon, and spend his money rashly and extravagantly on outrageous clothes. Lady de Verries should make an impact on the district, and prove an embarrassment to Garth and his household.

Mrs Crabbe?

'Oh to hell with her,' I said aloud. 'To hell with all of them.' After that I felt better. I even took a glass of brandy on my own, which made me feel better still.

Inevitably when morning came a good deal of my defiance had died into a calmer mood. Misgivings threatened depression, but I fought them off. However difficult the immediate future was going to be, a hard core of stubbornness in me persisted. Some day — somehow, I would get Garth back. Not by any theatrical display or facade alone — but by patience, and planning, and waiting. Ruana's lies, her devious treachery couldn't win forever.

One day she would be bound to slip up, and Garth would know the truth.

I was careful to hang on to the thought. But it meant a constant emotional effort. Whenever I relaxed, sadness lurked very near. It was then I remembered the baby, and tenderness for a few brief moments dispelled bitterness and a feeling for revenge.

If only time could be swept away, and the next few months magically bridged like those in some fairy-tale fantasy. If I could awake suddenly from a dark dream to find the child in my arms and Garth standing by with understanding in his heart, oh if only it were possible.

But of course reality was not like that. Real life meant facing circumstance and moulding it with every weapon one had.

So I did what I'd determined I would during my fiery reaction following the quarrel. Without seeing Garth that first morning I got Adam to drive me to Falmouth, and there purchased the gaudiest, and richest, most exotic clothes from the town's most exclusive costumier's. My reticule contained not only most of my own month's allowance, but of the housekeeping sum as well. And what I could not pay for, I had credited to Garth's account.

He did not return to Carnbrooke for the evening meal.

I deferred my own, making some explanation to Mrs Crabbe that Sir Garth would be late owing to a business visitor at Tharne. 'Keep it hot,' I told her. 'I'll wait till he arrives.'

I don't think she believed my excuse for one moment. She eyed me suspiciously for a second before going to the kitchen, grumbling. Her expression had been startled — more than that, shocked — when she'd seen me. I didn't wonder. I was wearing a new cerise silk gown, cut low at the breast with huge bouffant sleeves. The neckline was so wide, my shoulders were exposed enticingly I hoped, though perhaps not entirely in good taste. My hair was fluffed out at the sides and taken up on top with an osprey feather curled from a centre parting to the back.

For a time I wandered restlessly from parlour to hall, then to the dining room, ostensibly to re-arrange flowers and flick a duster over the furniture. I felt wicked, and outrageous; but triumph gradually faded into gnawing disappointment and unhappiness when Garth didn't appear.

At last I said, 'Perhaps I'd better have my meal, Mrs Crabbe. Possibly my husband is having to eat with his — his visitor. I believe he was very important — someone to do with mining—' My voice trailed off vaguely.

I turned away to avoid seeing the expression on her face. She muttered something about good cooking being spoiled and withdrew, snapping the door to sharply behind her.

Although the meal was tastefully prepared, and despite the hollow feeling of my inside, I ate only a little; to save Mrs Crabbe's feelings I contrived to secrete a portion away for the dog and cat, and afterwards went up to my room.

It was ten o'clock before Garth returned. I hovered about the landing despondently, determined he should notice me. But when he came upstairs, almost immediately, he gave me a short cursory look that told me nothing. Pausing in front of me he said, 'Pardon me! I've had a busy day. My room, Mrs Crabbe told me, is at the end of the landing.'

'I believe so.'

He went on without a word, leaving me humiliated, furiously angry, but above all, desolate. He had not even noted my defiant finery or attempt at bravado — I was something merely to be ignored and despised. A shadow to be brushed aside — nothing.

For a time I hated him, refusing to accept that beneath the hate, something else still lingered — something too strong to die which like the Granite King, would endure in the face of the wildest storms and disruptions. Not love exactly; how could anything so relentless and fierce be termed 'love'? Love held gentleness and sweetness. But 'belonging' was different; and I knew whatever Garth and I did to each other, nothing, ever, could entirely dispel it. We were bound by a tie as ruthless and indomitable as the wild land itself to the cruel Atlantic. In my flesh his seed thrived and flourished – a sturdy dark root that would one day flower to winter and spring, to the fairest morning and the blackest night. A boy, fierce-eyed and strong like Garth himself, or a girl warm-hearted and free-spirited who would not be frustrated as I had been, but learn early to face the truth of her heart, and so escape the bitter aftermath of her own mistakes.

So much I planned for my child in those moments of longing for Garth. But always the ache returned.

Meanwhile the days passed, and we lived almost as complete strangers, eating together occasionally, but always under a veneer of indifference, speaking little, and then only of trivialities. My peacock attire roused no comment at first, until he said one day, 'I've had further bills. From now on I shall pay no more of your debts. So unless you keep within your allowance I shall insert a notice in the press disclaiming any responsibility for credit falsely claimed by Lady de Verries.'

I stared at him blankly.

He laughed: a contemptuous sound.

'Do you know how ridiculous you look?' he continued. 'Surely you're aware of the spectacle you're making of yourself? Or don't you? Is your brandy bottle so effective you can't distinguish between a freak and a duchess?'

The hot blood flamed in my cheeks. Tears thickened in my throat.

'You're horrible, Garth de Verries,' I said.

'And you're a cheat.'

Seconds later he had gone.

I rushed up to my room and gazed at myself, as I'd done so often, through the mirror.

But this time it was different. No grand lady confronted me – merely an over-painted over-dressed creature who could have been on the music halls.

I tore off the gaudy dress I was wearing, the lacy underwear and constricting stays, and flung myself on the bed. There, half naked, I lay on my face, sobbing heavily into the pillow. If Garth had appeared then I'd have accepted and even appreciated a beating, as a child could, when it knew itself to be in the wrong. But he did not come.

Presently, I sat up, and with a swift gesture swept the brandy bottle to the floor. It caught the leg of a table as it smashed, and I was glad.

I had never really liked the stuff. It had given me ballast, that was all, and consequently made a fool of me.

From that day I became — superficially — my old self again, the self my father would have recognised. It wasn't easy at first, because nothing any more was left to divert me. The spending spree was over; the glamour of it gone.

Only thought for the baby remained, and the deep, half-acknowledged hope that something must happen eventually to change things between Garth and myself.

What did happen was something I'd never expected, or could have foretold, and by then, September was already turning the gold and green of moors to bronze and brown, enriching the trees with orange leaves. My body was becoming heavy with child, but the fashions of the times enabled the fact to pass almost unobserved.

On a day in the middle of the month Garth had to go to Plymouth where he was to spend the night, and it was on the following afternoon that dramatic events were resolved into their terrible climax.

14

The heavy heat of August began to tire me. For most of the month no real rain fell. Mornings brought only a silvered thin line of mist which quickly disappeared under the rising sun. I gave up riding, but occasionally climbed to Castle Cromme where I stared across the valley to the stark silhouette of the Granite King looming proudly over the landscape. Below, to my left, Tharne stood clearly etched in the brilliant light. Details of gables and turrets were intensified; the enclosed paddock and gardens appeared like pictures in a children's book, dwarfed to miniature size against the vast panorama of moor and sea. I resented then that I could not be wafted magically to my favourite haunt, where late bluebells would not yet have faded from the shadowing clumps of gorse and heather, and the fox-gloves would stand thick and tall − as tall as myself in places, untrodden or plucked by human hand.

I should have been free to wander there, I thought fiercely many times, free to relax and dream against the cool enclosing arms of the Granite King, so my child could sense through my breath and longing, something of the earth's magic and inde-pendence, its strength and secret ancient knowledge. But there was no way, now. Garth had debarred it, leaving only the far bleak precipice to climb − the daunting terrifying boundary of jagged spikes above the sea.

'Never mind,' I would whisper to the unborn. 'When I can really hold you close against me, somehow we'll be there − *somehow*; together.'

Perhaps I was slightly mad; many people might have thought so. Certainly, on the few occasions when Mrs Crabbe heard me talking to myself, she eyed me furtively with a touch of fear.

'Why do you go forever wandrin' from room to room or up that theer hill?' she asked. 'Can't you bide still a bit an' get on with sumthen' useful? What's got into 'ee? There's clo'es still needed for the baby, edn't there? Another thing − you doan' dress as you used to—'

'Surely you don't want me to use paint and powder again?' I said curtly. 'Did you approve of all that flashy finery, as you called it, after all? Cheap gew gaws, I remember you saying—'

'Now you know what I do mean,' she replied, thrusting her old chin at me fiercely. 'One time it was all fine airs an' high an' mighty ways, an flautin' yerself like a − like a—'

'You needn't say it. A king's whore,' I interrupted sharply.

'Doan' you dare never say such a thing again,' she told me, her voice rough and rasping, 'As if I'd spik so to any chile of the dear doctor's—'

'You thought it,' I said coldly, 'which is just as bad, worse.'

'An what if I did? Aren't you behavin' that way? Isn't it clear to anyone with eyes in their head that there's sumthen wrong? That husband of yours! I'm not sayin' I was all for the marriage, not when you'd had one already. But marry him you did. An' since that day nuthen's bin right. All you've done's bin to defy an' taunt him. Spendin' his money right an left—'

'That's my affair.'

'Then suddenly lookin' as you do—' she continued relentlessly, 'wanton, half-wild, with your hair anyhow, an' your skirt forever gittin' torn from them brambles. Et was a good dress once, that grey. But you doan' seem to care 'bout 'et. Not 'bout anythin'.'

'Don't I look nice in the evenings?' I asked coolly, with false demureness. 'I'm tidy then for my husband. I wear the green silk and take my hair back; does it matter if I please myself in the daytime when he's never here, and probably wouldn't notice if he was?'

She seemed nonplussed at first, then she continued glumly, 'Most men notice more'n they say. You shud be aiming to please him now the baby's on the way. Tedn' natural the way you do carry on.' She paused a moment then added, 'Wek up my dear. Whatever's the matter between you two, do act as husband and wife should at such times.'

I did try.

But it was no use.

Whenever we spoke, whatever contact we had, he was formal and coldly polite; no more.

Once I said to him, 'Are we forever to go on like this, Garth?'

We had just finished our evening meal. I was standing aimlessly by the window, and knew he was about to leave for Tharne.

'Like what?'

I turned and smiled bitterly.

'Surely you don't have to ask.'

'No.'

'Then why—'

The bright blue eyes stared at me for a moment, and for that split second I thought something glimmered there, warm and desirous, that I had not seen for a long time. Then it died.

'Why don't we cohabit and pretend, and live a lie?' he said.

'I wouldn't want that; neither would you. Oh yes — if you must know, it would be the easiest thing in the world to ravish you, even as you are, my love. But hardly in good taste. And I wouldn't demean myself — or you, for that matter.'

'After we've had the child—' I began again desperately, '—when the baby's born—'

'You'll have something to concentrate on and care for, far more rewarding than me,' he remarked. 'And you'll do it well, I hope. Otherwise you won't even have that.'

Temper stirred in me.

'Don't threaten me. It will be *my* child—' My pulses were racing, my cheeks burned.

'Yes, of that there's no question, at least,' he said with hateful insinuation.

I was suddenly desolate.

'There was no need to say that.'

'No. Forget it. Our kind of situation doesn't make for good manners. I'm sorry.'

But I could not forget.

After he'd gone his words still taunted and hurt me. I told myself he hadn't really believed the barbed remark, but the fact he'd even spoken it showed the doubts in his mind; it was as though he hated me.

Presently I went to a side window and watched his tall form move out of the gate and cut down the lane towards Tharne. I wanted to call him back, scream, throw myself against him and pummel his chest, forgetting all codes of behaviour and my own wounded dignity, do anything to break the icy barrier between us. But his remoteness and cold contempt — so much worse than hot temper — made any contact impossible. How long could it go on, I wondered? Human beings could not forever live under the same roof in such mutual antipathy. If Garth found it possible, I would not. And when the baby came it would need warmth and love. Perhaps after all, Garth and I would be better apart, so the child should be spared any shadow of our own unhappiness. The thought always depressed me, and there were times when I half wished it had never been conceived. Garth came first and always would. I wasn't, primarily, the maternal type. All young things appealed to me; but deep down my strongest need was for the passion of the man I most desired in the world.

At this point I somehow managed to switch my mind to other things. Normally, in the past, when a problem got too much for me, I'd have ridden Flash to the Granite King. Activity was the only answer to despair. So I decided on the spur of the moment to have a stroll round the moor at the back of the house.

I put on a loose shawl, and slipped out by the side door in order to avoid any argument with Mrs Crabbe. In spite of my size under the full skirts, I was physically fit, and knew a reasonable climb would do me no harm. So I cut upwards to the left for a hundred yards or so, where the track led to the gipsy encampment.

The sun was already streaking low over the western ridge, sending violet shadows down the slope; soon twilight would encompass everything with its blue veil, but at the moment the rocks and undergrowth were clear, just tipped with gold from the dying rays. My first glance at the gipsy site told me the gipsies had left. There was no sign any more of a van or tent, just pale brown patches where their carts and vehicles had been. I felt a curious loss — of life having irrationally departed, leaving the moor bereft and chill. I shivered, although the air was still summer-warm, and turned sharply to walk back to the house.

When I reached the garden gate, the sun dipped behind the hills suddenly, leaving only a greenish shadowed sky touched with a few orange streaks; at the same instance I saw a dark shape move from the side of the house into the trees massing by the lane. It was quite indistinguishable. There was no way of knowing who it was. But the form had been purposeful somehow — eerily so, wearing what appeared to be a black cape and wide-brimmed hat. A man's? A sombrero?

I stood still for a moment, wondering if it would reappear. When it didn't I guessed whoever it was had reached the lane.

Deciding to ask Mrs Crabbe if anyone had called, I went in by the side-door intending to hurry to the kitchen. But I was diverted by something square and white lying on the flagstones.

An envelope.

I picked it up, with a queer feeling of Nemesis deadening all feeling in me. Before I tore the thing open I knew what it contained.

This time only one word was printed on the slip of paper. And there was no stamp on the envelope.

'SLUT.'

That was all.

Mrs Crabbe must have heard my return. She appeared at the corner of the passage, head thrust forward enquiringly under her lace edged cap, one hand holding a rolling pin. A smell of baking came from the kitchen.

'So 'tes you,' she said. 'Thought I heard sumthen'. Must be a wind comin' up. A few minutes ago I could've sworn I heard footsteps. Why—' she broke off abruptly seeing the note in my hand. 'Well — that's funny to be sure. What 'es et?'

'Oh—' I acted automatically, stuffing the offensive paper into my pocket. 'Just an advertisement or something — nothing important—'

'Advertisement? What about?'

'I've not looked yet. Jewellery, or—'

'Hm! you do go leavin' doors unlocked too much,' Mrs Crabbe said disapprovingly. 'There no knowin' who'll come sneakin' round with them gipsies roamin' the moors.'

'They've gone,' I told her quickly, seizing the excuse to divert the conversation.

'An who says so? You? Mean to say you've bin' to see, in your condition?'

'Exactly.'

'You should — you shud—' she broke off, lost for words, then continued after the pause, 'well if they've really taken off that's sumthen to be grateful for 's'pose. The fairs o' course. The big fairs is startin' now, Redruth an' Truro way.'

'I expect that explains it,' I heard myself saying mechanically. I didn't really care where they'd gone or why, at that moment. My head was beginning to spin in a queer way; the exertion of the walking and shock of returning to what awaited me, had exhausted me more than I'd realised at first. My stomach lurched in a wave of sickness, as Mrs Crabbe's face swam before my eyes in contorted quivering shapes. I steadied myself against the hall table. I must have gone pale because the old woman said suddenly with a change of voice, 'What's the matter? Are 'ee al' right?' A hand came out to me. I waved it away impatiently. 'Oh don't fuss, Mrs Crabbe. Just a little tired, that's all.'

I managed to pull myself together, lifted my head higher

walked to the stairs, and in a pretence of energy, but with one hand on the banister rail forced myself up, longing only for the solitary peace of my room where I could relax on the bed. I went more quickly than I should through anxiety to be rid of Mrs Crabbe's probing eyes. Each stair appeared uncertain, swaying like some strange mechanical device under my feet, or the waves of some darkening sea. A tight knot of pain was tensing my body, and I was suddenly frightened. 'I must get there,' I thought, 'must get there — get there.'

One foot plunged before the other recklessly. The dizziness had already blocked out everything but the emptiness and yawning void of swaying lines. I quite forgot a loose rod near the top of the flight, and when the toe of my right shoe caught it, I stumbled, and fell. There was a high pitched sound from somewhere as I rolled down, bumping my ribs and stomach against every stair — Mrs Crabbe's scream perhaps, or my own.

When I reached the ground I lay helpless, unable to move except for the heavy breaths tearing my body through searing stabs of increasing agony. Mrs Crabbe's face registered briefly between spasms. She held something hot and stinging to my lips that trickled down my throat and over my chin. What she was muttering all the time I never knew — was conscious only of a tremendous pushing and thrusting, of wetness and warmth, and of a force greater than any of my own body craving expulsion and life. My body arched violently. Then release came. There was a final shudder followed by a thin high wail. I tried to ease myself up, but two old hard hands pushed me back. Before I lost consciousness I had a vague glance of something small and squirming moving fitfully against a thigh like some puny animal, — something that was of me, but no longer a part. I reached out, and feeling the stickiness, heard myself moan.

Then mercifully, all was darkness and quiet, and when I came to myself I was in my own bed at Carnbrooke, with the doctor's face staring down on me.

The baby, Heather de Verries, though premature, withered-looking and monkeyish for the first weeks of her life, survived; and by October had developed into a healthy child, putting on weight day by day. Her wrinkled small face had changed into that of an intriguing imp's under a tuft of dark hair. I could see from the first that she resembled Garth more than me, and hoped the likeness would please him, although I guessed he'd have preferred a boy.

Garth was kind and thoughtful to me during the exhausted days following the birth, engaging a nanny to take charge of the child, and insisting upon me resting. But he showed little personal interest in either of us. His observations were clinical rather than emotional. Slight amusement lit his blue eyes when he occasionally let a tiny hand grip one of his fingers; but it was clear to me that he could not properly adjust to the situation or to Heather. Although I should have become resigned to our estrangement, I was hurt, comparing his lack of interest in myself and the baby, to his deepening involvement at Tharne. This fact rebounded even on my attitude to my own daughter.

It would have been so easy to love her passionately if the love could have been shared with Garth. But Garth's remoteness cast a shadow over everything. He'd left the naming, even, entirely to me.

'You must have your own ideas what to call a girl,' he'd said when I'd questioned him. 'I'm no authority on such matters.'

He didn't want to be, I'd thought bitterly. It was as though he didn't entirely accept her as his.

'Very well,' I'd said on the spur of the moment, 'Heather. The heather's so lovely this year.' And my thoughts had turned to the Granite King looming above his territory of crimson-bell filled bushes and flaming gorse.

So often then, I thought of that great carn as male — a living entity. A replacement for my lack, probably, my need of Garth.

Once, the nanny — a young woman of twenty-four with a determined jaw, fair hair, firm, fully developed bosom, and an authoritative air — caught me staring from the night nursery window across the valley to the opposite hill.

Heather was lying in her cot, just waiting to be fed. When I turned, the girl eyed me curiously. 'A wild view isn't it, my lady?' she said. 'It must be very lonely over there.'

'Yes, but I like it.'

She laughed brightly. 'Well I shouldn't. I prefer a little company myself.'

'Do you think you'll be happy here?' I enquired, rather hoping she'd say 'no'. I didn't care for her very much.

She shrugged her shoulders.

'I don't see why not. Already the baby seems to know me, and Sir Garth is very generous. The salary's good, and I shall have plenty to occupy me.'

For the first time I realised that I had no clue what Garth was paying, and that I'd had little say over the question of employing a nanny at all. While refusing to give anything of his heart he'd taken everything of responsibility away from me — except of course, concerning the child's name.

Perhaps if I'd been left in full control of the little girl I could have felt warmer towards her. As things were I sensed an alien quality that frequently made me feel an onlooker rather than a mother.

It was natural therefore that in late November I took to riding again, sensing more close companionship with the mare than with my own offspring.

'Is it wise to exert yourself so soon?' Garth asked one afternoon as he passed me on my way to the stable. I was wearing my habit and felt defiant.

'If I don't do something I shall go quite mad,' I answered, sweeping past him without looking at his face. He said nothing. All I heard was the click of my own footsteps on the cobbles. At the turn of the path I looked back and saw him striding savagely towards the lane. I knew he was angry, by the very erect posture of his shoulders — the way he swung an arm as though he'd like to strike something.

I was secretely gratified. Perhaps he was really beginning to notice me again.

So the days passed in a vacuum of misunderstanding holding uneasy undertones; rare moments of expectancy that quickly died into unfulfilment — occasional biting fits of temper fading into sullen silences followed by Garth's polite indifference. It seemed to me, as the late November days closed in, that the deadlock would never end.

The trees were mostly bare and brown now under yellowish grey cloud. The morning mists were cold, sometimes glittering with frost when the light lifted. Intermittent gales swept the moors and coast, dashing the sea's fury against the cliffs. I went out as much as possible, to avoid Mrs Crabbe's unspoken criticism, and the domineering attitude of the nanny whose patronising, faintly amused manner frequently annoyed and frustrated me. She was never impolite — I would not have allowed it — but obviously she felt me ill-equipped to deal with a child. Her name was Sarah Cullen, and I called her 'Sarah' on purpose to reduce her status to that of the daily girl's, rather than admitting superiority. But she *was* superior. There was really no denying it. She was so completely competent, and always so smugly cheerful. I knew Garth was impressed.

'You're very cool with Nanny,' he said on one occasion. 'Why? Isn't her work satisfactory?'

'Oh extremely,' I said with emphasis. 'She's a paragon of virtue and quite dedicated to her duties.'

Knowing I'd betrayed myself I looked away. But the discerning stare of his blue eyes seemed to follow me and burn into the back of my neck.

'Then I think you should show a little friendliness,' I heard him say in aloof non-committal tones.

'I'm not unfriendly. I never argue with her. She just doesn't interest me.'

'You could perhaps make some slight display of gratitude.'

I swirled round. My skirts rustled with the sudden movement.

'Why? She's an employee, isn't she? She gets well paid — perhaps overpaid for all she does?'

My cheeks were hot. I guessed my eyes were blazing.

He laughed.

'Are you jealous, Caroline?' he said, with a touch of wry amusement.

'Don't be ridiculous. Of what?'

'Of an attractive conscientious young woman who seems so willing to shoulder all the dull domestic tasks that you obviously resent.'

I was outraged by the unfairness.

'It was you who engaged the girl. Not me. I didn't ask for a nanny, as you call her. She was forced on me.'

He took a step towards me. Just for a moment I thought he'd touch me, end the stupid emotional duel by a single gesture of desire — contact of hand on my arm, of lips suddenly on my mouth, of his breath warm against my cheek, slipping — sliding sensuously from there to my shoulder and arms and breast. My sight was blurred as though tears filmed my eyes. My whole body was an ache of longing — for him to sweep me up and hold me close.

I waited.

Then his form stiffened and he said, 'I had the foresight to assess the practical situation, that's all. If you could sometimes see things in proper perspective — more objectively, life would be a good deal easier for you, and for all of us.'

He walked past me without another look and went out. The heat from the parlour fire seemed suddenly smothering. There was a heady suffocating smell in the air — my own perfume partly, that I'd liberally applied that afternoon as a boost to my femininity, and the scent of hot-house lilies and carnations. I had never really liked the flowers. Garth had brought them from the conservatory at Tharne. As a gesture, I supposed. But their heavy odour reminded me somehow of the past: of Aunt Adela's funeral, and my father's. I didn't like remembering. So sad, somehow, and symbolic of how everything eventually faded. On impulse I lifted the larger bowl from the chest and carried it out into the hall; then I replaced the slender crystal lily vase, with a pot of heather I'd planted earlier that day.

Mrs Crabbe watched me do it.

'Why?' she said. 'Why that common bushy stuff when you do have such lovely flowers brought specially by your husband?'

I gave her a brittle smile.

'I hate forced hot-house things. Heather's lovely — the tang of it, the kind of wild earthy smell—' I hardly noticed her sniff of disapproval. I was thinking of the Granite King, and my rides there on Flash. Thinking, and despairing and longing.

I was brought back to the present abruptly.

'Well?' Her sharp voice was rasping. 'What am I going to do with them, eh?'

'Put them in Sarah's, "Nanny's", room,' I answered tartly. 'I'm sure she'll appreciate them. Or the baby's—'

'Miss Cullen won't have 'em theer. Unhealthy she says.'

'Oh stuff!'

The remark was childish; I knew it a moment later, and was annoyed with myself; but it was very difficult to be logical in such unhappy and unrewarding circumstances.

In early December something happened that was to bring the uneasy tempo of life to shattering drama. The morning started calmly enough with overcast skies hugging the earth and sea into dull and uniform greyness. The air was sultry for the time of year; in the fields the cattle gathered close to the stone walls and hedges as though sensing storm ahead. I felt it too — a gathering apprehension beneath the calm, something Aunt Adela used to call my sixth sense, and which curiously enough, had seldom been wrong.

Garth appeared not to notice, and set off about eleven o'clock for Truro, telling me he had business to attend to. What 'business' he meant I didn't know, and had stopped enquiring. Sometimes I'd wondered jealously if another woman was tucked away somewhere. But with an effort I'd induced myself not to ponder about it. Whether I cared or not made no difference since he was obviously not interested in my feelings one way or another.

'I shan't be back until tonight,' he said casually before setting off. 'Dinner probably. If I'm later tell Mrs Crabbe not to bother about keeping anything hot. I can eat at Tharne.'

He didn't kiss me when he went out — not even a peck on the cheek which had been an occasional habit until recently. Secretly I'd been grateful when the dutiful facade had ceased. I didn't want to be a 'duty' to Garth, a pretence. If I couldn't have him properly as a husband, then it was better we should have no contact at all. This is what I'd told myself time after time — trying hard to believe it. But sometimes, after he'd left the house I'd gone up to my room and cried and cried. No-one knew. Not even Mrs Crabbe. And following such weakness my bravado and defiance had increased.

That particular morning though, it was different. My feelings for Garth were lulled by the restless oppressions that seemed to infuse the whole atmosphere. It was as though all nature waited.

For what?

By afternoon the threat of thunder seemed to have abated. A wind was rising, bringing a freshening of air that drove the clouds westward, leaving the moors harshly clear above the glassy sea. Suddenly I wanted to be away from the confines of four walls, riding Flash in a gallop over the hills. But first of all impelled by some strange instinct, I went upstairs to the very top of the house where a small boxroom had a view of the surrounding terrain.

I stared out.

The wind now was quite strong. Against the walls of Tharne the huddled trees of the copse were bent in a swaying mass. The paddock beyond stretched yellowish green in the clear winter light. Everything was vividly sharp, with that newly-washed look heralding approaching rain. Except for the movement of black branches and an occasional dead leaf driven past the window, the scene held the quality of an etching, or a detailed painting by an architect's hand. The effect was dramatic, giving me the feeling of staring into another dimension.

And then it happened.

Suddenly from the side of Tharne, the area allotted to the stables, a horse and rider appeared and started circling the paddock; in a canter at first, then gradually gaining speed until the stallion was given free rein for a gallop.

Yes. I knew the mount was a stallion — just as I knew the man who rode it was Manfred. With a shock I saw something else, something I was sure Garth wouldn't have allowed. The gates leading to the moor were wide and open allowing free access to the hill. Manfred at first did not appear to notice it. He sat fiercely astride, shoulders thrust aggressively forward, forcing the animal to its utmost pace, then suddenly leaning back, head to the sky, one arm raised in the motion of waving a sword or whip. There was something abandoned and unleashed about the scene that both exhilarated and terrified me. Why was he riding like that? Why? *Why?* Although I had no way of glimpsing his expression, or detecting details, I could sense, even from such a distance the tension, the frenzy driving man and beast, could imagine unleashed laughter through the wind, almost hear the thud of hooves and impact on the air.

Round and round the confined space they went; while I waited rigidly for some disastrous impact — of a dark figure flung upwards and down; of the great animal tumbling on top of it and rolling and rolling, until all was still.

But things did not happen that way. Suddenly a small form darted from the shadows of the house and trees, and rushed with both tiny arms out towards the centre of the paddock.

At that point I think I screamed. It seemed certain the little girl must be tramelled and killed. Just for an instant, the man reined abruptly. The horse reared, pounding the air; the child was caught up and swept by a single grasping arm on to the stallion's back before the rider.

Then they were off again, round and round and round, until quite unexpectedly a third figure, black hair streaming behind her ran from the thicket towards them.

From that point the scene was a nightmare — a dramatic terrible episode that could have been enacted by macabre puppets. Kara — I knew it could be no one else — flung herself at the approaching trio, hands raised desperately in an attempt to intercede. I could not hear her despairing cry, but could imagine it, as she fell backwards under the thundering hooves. The rider appeared not to notice, just plunged on, taking a swift line through the open space to the moor. The bleak light shone cold on the dark dot of the woman's form left lying on the pale brownish earth.

In the distance, heading towards the Granite King — but to its dangerous sea-side, where the precipice waited — Manfred and the child on the great charger grew gradually smaller and smaller, until they were only a tiny dot disappearing into the vacuum of darkening sky where cliffs met sea.

15

I waited only a minute before pulling on my heavy cape and rushing over to Tharne. I ran past the far side of the house and took the path nearest the stables and paddock. Just outside the back door a motionless figure was standing, her face a pale mask above the black dress. Miss Ruana. I turned and ran back towards her.

'Did you see what's happened?' I demanded. My voice must have sounded hysterical. I was gasping for breath. 'Manfred and the child. They were riding and went out to the moor. They—'

The coldness of her dull stare appalled me.

'They broke through. Of course; I know. The man and boy are out there—'

'But Kara,' I interrupted. 'She was trampled on, and there was no breaking through. The paddock gate was open—'

'How do you know?'

'I saw. From our top window — the box room.'

'Sight can get confused,' she said, 'especially from so much prying.'

Anger temporarily overcame my revulsion. 'Aren't you going to do anything?'

'Do you expect me to carry the woman in myself? The men are doing that? And I've already sent for the doctor.'

I stared bewildered and shocked by her coolness, then hearing the tramp of approaching footsteps turned towards the drive. Manfred's servant and the boy were carrying the recumbent figure of Kara. She was lying on a kind of constructed stretcher. A rug lay over her. Her black hair was loose and almost swept the ground. As they drew closer I saw that her head was twisted grotesquely to one side, and the bright stain of blood coursing from a temple down her face and from her parted lips. Her eyes were open — glazed and staring. I rushed forward. Ruana's vice-like grip pulled me back.

'Don't interfere,' she said. 'Go home. You can do nothing here.'

Memory seered me like a knife. 'No I won't go back. What about the others? Manfred? The little girl? They're in danger. They were riding towards the precipice! Someone should go after them—'

'You, I suppose. You can't forget him for one moment, can you — men — always men!'

Somewhere in my mind a shutter clicked open letting the light through, although at first I didn't completely realise its significance — only that Ruana hated me, hated me so much there was nothing she wouldn't do to see me away from Tharne forever.

I gave her one hard stare, saying nothing, then started to run — pushing her aside as she went forward to meet the macabre trio.

When I reached the stables there was no one about. The two remaining horses were whinnying in their stalls. One, a smallish mare, neighed as I approached. I soothed her in the only way I knew, as I soothed Flash, and with trembling hands somehow managed to saddle her. Time was precious. To have wasted minutes rushing to Carnbrooke for my own mare, might have made, I knew, all the difference between life and death. The horse responded well, and in seconds we were cantering across the paddock through the gate, breaking into a gallop when we reached open ground.

The wind was still increasing, blowing gusts of salty foam from the sea. Knowing the route so well, and keeping clear of danger spots — inky pools of lurking bog, and a hidden derelict mine-shaft over-grown by tangled bramble and weeds, I drove the horse to the left and onwards, almost level and not far from the coastline. Wherever possible the wall had been completed above the rocks; but there were gaps where narrow precipitous ravines dropped sheer to the water, cutting yards inland, and thrusting gigantic jagged fingers upwards towards the moor.

'On — on—' I urged, as the wild air blew against me, stinging my face and sweeping my hair behind. My own voice had a puny sound, and seemed only a faint echo through the shrill crying of disturbed gulls, thud of horse's hooves and thunder of breaking waves. I kept my eyes screwed against the elements, alert to any sign of human or animal. But there was none. The Granite King loomed dark and impregnable ahead. I reined as we drew close to its formidable promontory of up-thrust dark rock, and, leading the mare by its bridle, walked as near as I dared to the sheer drop below. The water, blackish and glassy one moment, thundered the next with terrifying force against the great boulders of the cliffs' base. Mountainous waves of foam were flung into the air, then swallowed as the tide eddied, taken back only to roll forward once more with renewed energy, like a monstrous elemental army bent on destruction.

I shuddered, and stepped back. As I examined the ground, I realised my wild ride had been in vain. A little to my left stones and earth had been torn away from the rough surface leaving only a jagged cut in a yawning space dipping cruelly to the swirling sea.

Looking more closely I found distinct signs of where they'd gone over. Undergrowth was broken and trampled. In one place bare dark earth showed unmistakable imprints of hooves.

I called and called, leaving the mare free for a moment as I cradled my mouth with my hands. There was no reply of course; there couldn't be. No one could have survived such a terrible leap.

I stood for a minute trying to gain composure, trying not to envisage the terror of those two human beings in the seconds that took them flying, over the edge. But the image persisted — the picture of the stallion galloping through the air like Pegasus for a moment, before falling — falling into the abyss waiting beneath, with the man and child thrown mercilessly as stones or small pebbles to the hungry waves.

In a futile shudder of despair a hand went to my eyes, and then, suddenly, I heard a shrill neighing I looked round sharply and saw the mare I'd ridden galloping through furze and bracken, mane and tail flying, back towards the paddock.

I called twice, but there was no response. The horse didn't know me of course; there wouldn't be.

I forced myself to move, even to take another look over the cliffs. Then instinctively I made my way inland to the right and continued up the remembered route to the great carn.

Once there I slumped down resting against its cold granite back, with my arms over the enclosing slabs of rock. Screaming sea birds flew above. Towering round, the elemental protective presence of the Granite King seemed everywhere. As my breath eased, I felt cold. But exhaustion — emotional rather than physical — was overwhelming, and for a brief time I simply sat there, numbed into static immobility. When at last I got up, I took the turn leading eventually downhill to Braggas. There was a possibility — though hardly probably — that the strong current could have swept the bodies round the terrifying cliffs overhanging a corner of the small harbour, and flung them against the granite spikes. If not — if there was no sign of them, or of any rescue attempt being made by fishermen from that end of the headland, I would simply pick my way down carefully to the village and report the terrible incident. There would be time for a rest and recovery before returning to Tharne.

The very idea of going back there at all had by now become terrifying. Ruana's hatred! — Garth's inevitable reaction when he heard the news — all the questioning and probing, and Kara! poor Kara! Without knowing it, I was certain she was dead.

Everything about that old mansion grew more menacing as memory registered. So I made a further great effort to shut it away altogether, quickening my pace, plunging round the Braggas side of the moor, becoming careless of unseen stones lurking beneath the undergrowth, and the twisted branches of heather and gorse grasping at ankles and skirts.

Suddenly a toe caught something and I fell. There was a wrench of my foot, a seering pain as my temple caught a rock, lights darting across my eyes for a few seconds blinding me, and then darkness.

When I recovered consciousness, twilight had already faded into night. The wind had died a little or perhaps it was just that I lay in a sheltered spot.

I was cold, and dazed. My ankle ached, but I managed to drag myself upright. I touched my face and found my fingers sticky with half-dried blood. I tried to remember what had happened, but I couldn't. My mind was a complete blank. This was the most frightening thing of all. Dimly I was conscious that I had been running. But from what? Where to?

I started trembling, and for minutes was shaking so violently I had to lean against a stone. Nausea threatened, but the feeling passed, and I moved on automatically, feeling the way cautiously downwards, clutching at rocks and obstructing branches for support, pausing, lifting the strained foot for brief rest, then continuing until I reached a small clearing.

Lighted windows glimmered fitfully from below, throwing the dangerous black silhouette of the cliffs into momentary clarity. A watery moon was already rising behind the clouds – eerie and wan, like a pale disc-face in a nightmare.

A face? Whose? From the back of my mind an image lurched and a name registered. Horace. Horace Coutts. Of course. But why? I couldn't at first place him at all, beyond a deepening conviction that he was of some significance and might help me. Might? But how? How?

The terror began to mount again. My heart was racing. I must find him I thought. I had to find Horace Coutts, because I was – his wife or his sister perhaps? Yes. I must be. That was it; then why had I been wandering about by the Granite King all alone at night with a strained ankle and cut face? One after another the questions danced and jigged in my brain like a procession of macabre figures whirling through some monstrous nightmare.

The Granite King made sense of course — it was my own place. My father had taken me there so often when I was a little girl.

My father? I touched my shoulders and tried to bend to see if I still wore socks. But naturally I didn't. My father wasn't here any more; he had died a long time ago.

I felt the dampness streaming down my face again. But this time it was tears, not blood.

When at last I reached the village lane, I looked for someone anyone — to direct me to Penzance. Horace lived in Penzance. If I got there he would be able to help me. I had to concentrate on Horace because it was from something to do with him that the unremembered pattern of my life stemmed. At the same time dread rose too. Dread of the future — even of facing him, though I knew I had to.

I searched the deserted village main street through blurred eyes. There was no sign of anyone except the shrouded shape of a man at the bottom of the hill. A fisherman probably, if he was real at all. But was he? Was anything or anyone real of that ghostly moon-washed scene? Perhaps I'd died and was wandering through some half-world of lost forgotten things.

I went on automatically, climbing and limping up the slope, on leaden legs that were so heavy and cold they had no tangible feeling of being limbs at all, meeting no one.

When I reached a cross-roads I went straight ahead. How long the aimless wandering without purpose or direction continued, I never knew. But at one point I heard hooves and wheels approaching down a side lane. I stopped, and stared blankly as the vehicle halted and a rough kindly voice said, 'Can I do anythin', ma'am? Lost are 'ee? Or wantin' help mebbe? Can I give a lift?'

I guessed he was a farmer. The cart had an earthy vegetable scent.

'I'm Mrs Horace Coutts,' I said, speaking quite clearly. 'I come from Penzance, and have had an accident.'

My voice did not sound weak to my own ears, but firm and strong. The man after peering at me curiously through the watery light offered a hand. 'I'm goin' there meself,' he said. 'Not an elegant cart — this. But you just get in lady. There's room at the front for two.'

I obeyed him automatically and the next moment we were off.

As the journey continued a strange kind of half-sleep enveloped me. The jolting and continuous monotony of the horses' hooves brought a curious kind of dazed contentment. Rocks and trees waving in the thin wind provided an endless kaleidoscope, of half-formed dream-like entities disappearing into mist as we passed. I must unconsciously have given Horace's address to the driver, because shortly after reaching Penzance he stopped the cart in the middle of a side-street. Curtained windows, like eyes, seemed to watch furtively when he got down and went to a door. It opened, and he returned almost immediately.

The next thing I knew was being ushered into a hall that seemed somehow familiar.

And then, with a terrible shock, I saw a face staring down — a tight-lipped, pale, grim, condemning face, that wavered uncertainly under a lamp swaying in the draught of chill air.

The face of Horace Coutts.

I stared at him as figments of memory registered.

Then I fainted.

16

I was in hospital for over a month, during which time Christmas came and went with a show of festivity I could not share.

I had a private room, and was visited by Garth each day. At first he appeared tired and worried, but as memory returned and facts one by one registered, forming the pattern leading to my distraught appearance at Horace Coutts', his manner became more reticent and a certain coldness lit his blue eyes. I learned that I'd had a certain amount of concussion but that it should have no permanent consequences, that Ruana had been doing her best to take charge of things at Carnbrooke, which, he pointed out, was 'fairly decent' of her under the circumstances.

The circumstances, of course, being the tragedy of Kara's death, Manfred's and the little girl's. There had already been an inquest where a verdict of death by misadventure had been delivered on the former, and 'presumed drowned' concerning the other two. I shuddered inwardly when Garth told me the mutilated body of the stallion had been recovered, but except for pieces of torn clothing nothing had been found of his brother or niece.

'So there's no need for you to think of it any more,' he told me in unnaturally remote emotionless tones, 'It's all over and done with.'

My eyes which had been closed briefly, opened suddenly. I could hardly believe my ears. No need to think of it — but I should always think of it from time to time. How could I ever forget? How could he speak so casually and apparently without feeling?

I stared at him, speechless. He touched my hand.

'What's the matter now?' He asked.

I didn't reply at once, then I asked, more for something to say than anything else, 'You say Ruana's taken charge at — at Carnbrooke. Did Mrs Crabbe agree?'

'Naturally she agreed,' Garth answered. 'It was her business to.'

'Why? She's managed to look after the house quite well before. I should have thought—'

'There was no baby before,' came the abrupt reminder.

The baby! I'd almost forgotten.

'How is Heather?' I enquired quickly.

'Quite well. She's at Tharne now.'

I sat up abruptly. 'Why? Why is she there?'

'Because it's simpler and easier for my cousin. However capable that old retainer of yours may think she is, her knowledge and capacity for helping with a young child are limited. Besides — I wanted my daughter on my own premises.'

'But—'

His voice was quiet but firm when he continued, 'There's no point in discussing details yet. When you're stronger we can plan the future practically and as objectively as possible.'

A niggle of resentment seethed in me.

'What is there to plan? And why can't we talk now? You've hardly told me anything really — how Horace reacted—'

Garth's glance hardened. 'Neither have I burdened you with
my own shock of losing a family so tragically. Is Coutts so
important? As far as I know he simply took your sudden appearance as an unexplainable wild gesture because you were ill, and
got a message to me through the police.'

'Oh.'

'Why can't you relax and leave the past alone? It would be far
better — for both of us.'

'Because—' I hesitated. 'Because there are things not right.'

'What do you mean?'

'Things I want to know. Why the gate was open — the gate to
the paddock—'

Garth sighed, 'It isn't your problem, Caroline—'

'It is, it is,' I interrupted. 'You don't know everything. Lots of
unpleasant incidents have been happening that you've no idea
of. Letters — I've been having sordid threatening notes put
under the door. Words printed, calling me slut and whore, and
threatening me—'

Garth's expression changed. Although I had a headache starting, I noticed a small muscle jerking in his cheek, saw his brows
converge in a frown. I knew he didn't believe me. There was
doubt in his voice when he asked, 'Why didn't you tell me before?'

'I didn't think you'd believe me.'

'I'm not sure I do.'

'Of course not,' I agreed dully, as the old familiar pain began
to nag my temple. 'But I can prove it. I've kept them.'

'Where?'

'At home in a drawer. Bits and pieces. Oh—' a sudden
thought struck me. '—There's one in my cape pocket. It came
just before — before I went out. It's here. It must be; I was
wearing it.'

'I'm afraid not,' Garth said. 'Your cape went back to Carnbrooke. I took it myself. Ruana wanted to have it cleaned.'

'Ruana? Why should she bother?'

'Because she's thoughtful and competent, I suppose,' Garth
said stiffly. 'She's been attending to things, as I said. Seeing you
had the necessary change of underwear needed in hospital — all
the small etceteras I wouldn't know about—'

'Fiddling in my dressing table and chest-of-drawers — that's
it, isn't it? Searching through my clothes?'

'Oh, Caroline!' A helpless note merged with rising irritation in his voice. 'Try and pull yourself together. You've been having nightmares. You're all mixed up. Ruana's trying to help. Get that into your head once and for all. Please—' his mouth softened. 'For your own sake.' He bent closer. I turned away.

'No, Garth. Don't treat me as though I'm − I'm off my head. Everything's quite clear. What happened, I mean.'

'You may think it did. And no one's suggesting you're off your head. But concussion can do odd things to the memory.'

'I'm glad you admit that,' I said, staring at him again suddenly. 'Because it explains about Horace, doesn't it? Why I went there − the other things happened first, before I fell.'

He straightened up abruptly. 'Stop talking about Horace, if you don't mind. Obviously some lurking instinct, stronger than any need of me, drove you to his apartment.' His face appeared as bitter as the underlying contempt of his words. 'And don't argue,' he continued quickly. 'Anyway—' he took his watch out of his breast pocket scrutinised it for a second, before concluding, 'I've overstayed my time. I must go now for both our sakes. At the end of the week I understand you should be discharged. We'll have a few days at Carnbrooke for any necessary discussion before moving to Tharne.'

'Tharne!' I interrupted. 'No. You're not wanting me to live there − not that place, after − after—' a wave of fear drenched me in perspiration. Garth opened his mouth to speak, but was interrupted by the white uniformed figure of a nurse entering.

Garth put on a facade of cheerful politeness, kissed me politely on the cheek, and a few moments later was gone.

As predicted I left hospital the following Saturday, accompanied by Garth who had driven over in the chaise to fetch me.

It was a cold clear day with cottonwool clouds blowing across a paper-pale sky. The brown moors were spinkled light green where young bracken thrived thrusting sturdy curled fronds through last year's decay. There would be snowdrops and primroses also, I thought, with a stab of nostalgia. Soon, in the weeks and months ahead, the speared points of young bluebells would be pushing to the sunlight. Already the gorse blossomed bright gold in places. Hedges foamed with blackthorn, and in bleaker spots 'old man's beard' trailed indiscriminately between elder and pussy willow.

At intervals the flash of a stream glinted silver beyond the shadowed undergrowth. In spite of Garth's silence, his veneer of disapproval, I felt a flood of gratitude at being back in my own surroundings, and warmth stirred me when I contemplated once more riding Flash again.

'Are you feeling all right?' Garth asked more than once during the cross-country journey.

I answered in the affirmative; once it was on the tip of my tongue to add, 'Only it would be nicer if we could talk.' However, I kept silent.

His profile was set and rigid. For the first time, the strain he had undergone starkly registered, adding years to his age. I realised quite suddenly how reticent he had been about the tragedy, brushing aside any reference to the funerals almost as though they were everyday occurrences. And Manfred was his brother, the child his niece! Yet Garth had managed to hide emotion from me as though both were comparative strangers. Hadn't he cared for them much? But he must have done, or he would not have been so protective and obsessive about no one worrying them at Tharne. Even me. His wife.

Why hadn't he spoken of Manfred to me when we were first married. If he'd been open about things I'd have understood; — or, would I? I had no first-hand knowledge of life in India — knew nothing except what he'd told me, and what I myself had read or heard from my father. Perhaps something more sinister than the trouble and bloodshed there, had darkened his life — something perhaps that he thought might harm me if I knew. A faint tinge of sympathy stirred me until I recalled his earlier doubts and accusations — his attitude and unpleasant references to Horace Coutts — never believing me, never listening.

Always Tharne.

Tharne and its occupants.

His heritage.

Well — I doubted that I could be a part of it. But I was too mentally wearied still to form any clear possible picture of the future. So as we neared Carnbrooke I managed to bring my thoughts to more immediate matters; excitement stirred me when at last the chaise drew up at the gate and the familiar house and garden came clearly into view. I hastily smoothed a strand of curl under my bonnet, adjusted the neck of my cape, and took a whiff of smelling-salts from the bottle in my reticule. It had been Aunt Adela's, and was gold-topped, with silver ribbon tied round the neck.

The heady aroma invigorated me. I forgot the slight weakness of my knees, and as the vehicle drew up, confidence returned. Garth stepped down and opened the door for me before the man could get there. My taffeta dress rustled under the cloak as I got up and allowed him to take my hand.

Feeling, for those brief moments assured and determined I walked ahead of my husband up the path to the front door, followed by the man carrying the valise.

Mrs Crabbe was waiting in the hall to receive us, and Ruana in severe black, stood at the entrance of the large parlour. Everyone suddenly seemed anxious to help. The girl came scurrying from the kitchen, and as I was divested of my outdoor clothes I heard Ruana saying in her clear, but rather harsh, voice, 'Coffee is already waiting. Naturally you will want to rest before you go upstairs.'

'Thank you,' I said automatically, at the same time intensely disliking to find her there — so confidently installed in my father's house.

The rest of the day passed as a weary kind of anticlimax. After a mid-day meal Garth insisted I went upstairs to bed. It was not until Ruana left in the early evening that I had sufficient energy to start a search of all the drawers in my dressing table and chest.

I went through each one meticulously, turning what underwear had been left there inside-out, even lifting the paper lining to see if a sign of the threatening notes remained.

There was nothing.

Garth presently left for Tharne. I watched his tall figure moving through the gate into the shadows of the lane, noting vaguely that his half-limp had returned, then I rang for Mrs Crabbe.

She came up as quickly as possible, breathing heavily. 'Yes, Miss Caroline — yes, m'lady — what is et? Feelin' bad?'

I shook my head. 'No, I'm all right. So glad to be back. And it's nice to see you again—'

She sniffed emotionally.

'An' so'm I,' she said after a quick look round, obviously to make sure no one was listening. 'Et's not so easy for a body of my age to be told this an' that, and ordered about by any stiff-backed madam I can tell you, even if et's Miss Ruana herself.'

'I'm sure it isn't, it must have been very difficult for you.' There was a pause. Then, in casual tones I enquired if anyone had been upstairs looking through my clothes.

'Tidying up perhaps?' I suggested.

The old woman shook her head.

'Not that I've heard. Certainly not. You know me better than that I hope. An' the girl wouldn' dare. Not she. O' course Miss de Verries now — she wus always fussin' 'bout. An I could'n say "you jus' leave Miss Caroline's things alone now," could I?'

'Of course not,' I agreed.

'And Sir Garth, he was never here at all hardly. Kept away from your room, I'd say. Unnatural, it did seem to me. No. I doan think he looked at anythin'.'

Neither did I. If he'd found the notes I was sure he would have admitted it.

'Why, Miss?' I heard Mrs Crabbe continuing curiously, 'has anythin' gone?'

'Oh — just a few papers,' I told her ambiguously. 'Perhaps I put them away myself and have forgotten.'

But I knew it was more than that. Knew without any doubt, that Ruana had confiscated the letters for some devious malicious purpose of her own — to discredit me in Garth's eyes probably.

So the days of adjustment and complete recuperation began, and I steeled myself to face the inevitable removal from Carnbrooke to Tharne. Ruana, Garth insisted, would remain there — it was her home — but in her own premises — a suite of rooms that had already been adequate converted, and she would have her own maid to attend her.

'*Why?*' I demanded, many times before we left. 'Why has everything to be so different? Ruana won't like it. She'd be happier on her own, with us staying at Carnbrooke.' His answer then, was curt and cold.

'She's already agreed to my suggestion. And very often she can have meals with us.'

'Yes. That's what I thought.'

'Do you object? Are you too selfish to allow a little sharing? Especially after all she's been through?'

The condemning tones infuriated me. I was standing staring through the window of the lounge; but no longer able to contain myself, I swirled round to face him.

'What about me? What *I've* been through?'

'You, Caroline?'

'Yes. You surely don't think it's been easy, living so long with this — with this mystery between us, you keeping everything so secret, your brother—'

'My half-brother actually.'

The flat statement temporarily silenced me.

'Oh.'

He waited. 'Go on.'

'The terrible time on the moor with Manfred—'

'Which was all due to your own actions,' he interrupted relentlessly.

I ignored the remark. 'And then seeing Kara killed. That ride to the Granite King — it wasn't obstinacy, you know—' my voice rose shrilly. 'I was trying to save them.'

'Yes, I'm sure you were.' He sounded suddenly gentler; tired. 'I know you did your best there. But in the end — eventually, you found yourself back with your old love.'

I was shocked at first beyond words. Then I remarked in a bitter half-whisper. 'That's a dreadful thing to say.'

'But true.'

'No. And you know it; he was never my love — and I didn't plan to go there. If I hadn't—'

'You wouldn't have fainted. Of course not; by nature you're not the fainting kind. But this time it was an exceedingly convenient swoon, — or so it would appear to most people.'

I went towards him, trembling with anger more than weakness, gripping the table, before I said:

'If you believe such insinuations, there's no point in my moving to Tharne, Garth. Life would be quite impossible. I don't want to go. I'd rather stay here with Mrs Crabbe.'

'Without your daughter?'

Heather. I'd almost forgotten.

'She's my child,' I told him steadily. 'She'd live here with me. It's my right.'

'You have no rights in the matter at all,' Garth said, with his temper rising. 'Tharne is my home, and as such yours. If you choose to make obstacles that's your own affair. But you'll regret it. And in the end you'll be in your rightful place even if I have to drag you by the hair of your head.'

He turned sharply on his heels and left the room.

He returned minutes later.

'Caroline,' he said. 'I don't mean to flare up. I'm sorry,' He put a hand to his head. 'What got into me I don't know. In your state you should be resting.'

'It doesn't matter,' I told him, lifelessly. 'It's all right.'

But it wasn't of course. My brain felt numbed. There seemed no point at all over which Garth and I could agree − even the baby. I'd wanted Heather back immediately following my return, but Ruana had insisted pointedly, backed up by my husband, that it was bad for a tiny child to be removed here and there for no legitimate reason. Nanny, too, had grown accustomed to Tharne. And the doctor had recommended I should have peace and quiet for a period.

I hadn't really minded at first. My own daughter had scowled, cried, and turned away from me when she was brought over, obviously preferring the efficient young woman who'd so cunningly taken my place from the first moment of her entrance at Carnbrooke.

Perhaps cunning was too hard a word. Perhaps I had become oversensitive and suspicious, but I couldn't help feeling that some bond or pact existed between Ruana and the girl. Indifference in me at first had gradually changed to resentment as the days passed.

If − or rather when I moved to Tharne, and that, now, appeared inevitable − I would see somehow that my own authority was recognised. It would be more possible, I told myself, with us all under one roof.

Perhaps after all Garth was right. Disasteful as the idea was of leaving Carnbrooke − I should see more of him, and I would be able to pop in to my old home whenever I chose. Mrs Crabbe was remaining there as 'caretaker-housekeeper'. On that point I had been insistent, and my husband had not objected.

'The house is in your name,' he'd said. 'It holds memories for you, and Mrs C's an old retainer I suppose. So long as she can take care of it properly I wouldn't want her moved. We're not poor. I can afford the upkeep − even pay Adam a bit extra if necessary.'

So Wheal Daisy's still doing well?'

'Thanks to Joe Harry, yes. An excellent manager. If things had been left to the old man we'd have had a white elephant on our hands long ago. I was delving into the books a week or two back and discovered there was a time when things were pretty shaky; something to do with striking an underground stream. Money, quite a lot of it, had to be spent in diversion — new levels struck that petered out at first, then a fresh shaft sunk. All extremely risky. But Harry refused to give in, and managed to convince most of the men — tut workers and adventurous alike — that a wealth of copper remained further inland. He's a born engineer of course, and diplomatic in his down-to-earth way. Dedicated.'

He'd paused thoughtfully then added, 'That's the trouble with Venn. No real interest in mining, and certainly no judge of men. The earth doesn't matter to him — fundamentally. All that counts is what his acres yield with the minimum of effort. Riches to add to riches for his own pocket. The failure of Wheal Crane was probably inevitable when it came to a test. No manager worth his salt was prepared to sacrifice his guts and livelihood for a lost cause. And I wouldn't blame him. Without confidence and encouragement from the top, initiative was bound to die. It's my conviction that's what happened — just a gradual death and decay.'

'And for the Breames too.'

'Yes, and all the rest.'

'I didn't realise you'd thought so deeply about — about mining,' I'd said, rather tactlessly. 'I mean it isn't as though you'd lived here for very long—'

'My dear Caroline, life in India hasn't completely warped my Cornish roots. At least I hope not; and since destiny and a groggy leg intend any future I have to be spent at Tharne it's common-sense to get involved as quickly and firmly as possible.'

'Yes. I see.' I'd waited a moment then rashly asked, 'Did you expect — Manfred — to feel the same?'

'Manfred?' The bitterness, the pain in his voice had not escaped me.

'I'm sorry. I shouldn't have mentioned him — after what's happened. It was because of Tharne; of moving there. Do you really think it's wise? You'll be reminded all the time.'

'Of what?'

'Why—' I'd felt nonplussed, taken aback. 'The accident of course. Every time you walk past the paddock you'll wonder—'

'I shall wonder nothing.' His sharp tones had silenced me. 'Brooding's no use. Life is very much a practical business. What's gone is gone. No one knows what the next day will bring. We have to do what we think best at the time and hope it will work out. And that's the way for us, Caroline — to accept the mistakes we've made and try and carve out some sort of future. Without dreams or expectations.'

I'd shivered inwardly.

'How cold you sound. To have no dreams — rather sterile.'

'Practical though.' His blue eyes had bored hard into mine for a second. Then he'd looked away, saying, 'Take my advice and set your own feet on the ground for a change. Despite the quite clever little business streak lurking beneath your feminine exterior, you can be surprisingly naive over some things. For instance, those imaginary poison-pen notes—'

'They weren't imaginary. And someone took them. I told you—'

He'd sighed.

'Oh well, we won't go into that again. But don't expect me to believe your fairy-tales, Caroline. And don't go on looking yourself.'

Not knowing what his last remark implied, I'd let the matter rest there.

Some day — oh surely a way would be found to convince him of the truth — to prove I had not been lying. This thought buoyed me up during the rest of the time before moving, and thankfully, the last few hours at Carnbrooke became so crammed with practical matters I had very little chance to brood. There was personal possessions to be packed; clothes, the photograph of my father, small mementos of Aunt Adela, and books I had cherished from childhood.

Mrs Crabbe became quite disturbed in the end.

'Actin' just as though you were leavin' for another country you are,' she complained. 'Wantin' to take this an' that away an' then, jus' as I'm thinkin' all's done, you remember sumthen's else. It's only a matter of a hundred yards down the lane, edn' et? Yet you mek it jus' as though you want to mek a break with everythin' an everyone. A kind of funeral, et seems to me.' She dabbed her eye emotionally.

I took her hand.

'Don't be morbid, Mrs Crabbe. You've always wanted peace and quiet. Well – now you'll get it. And I shall probably be in every day to see you're all right. Most days anyway. And the girl will be with you, for the mornings; Adam will be close at hand. And you'll have Rufus as a guard.'

'An' how am I to deal with that dog? I can't go nipping round with him on a lead like you do, or racing up hills like a wild one.'

'That's all arranged,' I said firmly. 'Adam's going to exercise him when I can't. His bones and food will be delivered just the same. Oh goodness!—' I broke off, feeling suddenly sad and more aware of the coming change and the inevitable threat to personal contacts. 'Please—' I began again, 'don't dwell on the miserable side. Do you think I'm looking forward to spending evenings at that great place with Miss Ruana probably sitting staring at me disapprovingly over her tapestry? Don't you understand I'd much rather be here, with Rufus lying close and dropping hairs over the rug?' I smiled slightly. 'You always disagreed when I had him in the lounge. I should have thought you'd be pleased to have him chewing bones in the kitchen or at Adam's place. Just think how comfy it will be for you in your own small parlour.' I paused. 'Actually, Mrs Crabbe, I do think Garth – my husband – has been quite generous—'

'Yes, yes.' She nodded grudgingly. 'Not that it's all for nuthen' – that generosity of his. The property will be looked after well. You needn' think I'll be wastin' my time idlin' 'bout twiddin' my thumbs.'

I laughed. 'Don't be silly. You're a worker. You always have been. We all know that.'

A wistful half-frightened look crossed her face for a moment.

'That's as maybe, Miss Caroline. But a day comes when an old body can't be doin' what it wants. An' it'll fret me then.'

'Nonsense. If you're ever in need of being looked after you know very well I shall see you have every care. That's a promise. It's what my father would have wanted, and Aunt Adela too.'

'Ah yes. The doctor.' Her voice had softened and sounded suddenly very tired.

I touched the shelf over the parlour fireplace. Then pressed a palm against the wall. The paper was slightly faded, but still firm, and somehow comforting to touch. it was a pale brownish shade, patterned with tiny orange and gold leaves and flowers. So familiar. So reminiscent of childhood. Mrs Crabbe did not know it, but countless times I'd gone through the whole house making renewed contact with each room, each wall, banister and article of furniture, lightly feeling every one of them with my finger tips, as though to press identity upon the varying surfaces, with an inner voice whispering, 'Dear home, dear room. This is where Caroline Dorric lived and grew up. Me, myself. And part of me is here for ever and ever—'

When the mood had passed I'd chided myself determinedly for being childish. But occasionally, during the last two days it seemed to me that childish thoughts might have greater value than adult passions and longings.

Yes, deep down I knew that leaving Carnbrooke this time marked a complete change in existence − the dividing line between the past and the future; between youth and maturity. Horace, though still a menace in my mind whenever I remembered, had been an incident merely; a blunder of adolescence.

But ahead − ahead lay reality, which somehow had to be moulded with all the commonsense and strength possible.

The trouble was I had never really been a commonsensical kind of person. How my father would have smiled if he could have known my admission. Once − such a short time ago it seemed, when I looked back − he'd said, with the quiet amusement, the friendly logic that were so much of him, 'Being sensible isn't so important, in the end, child, as having a warm heart. Commonsense can make millionaires, but kindness can feed the human spirit − something that wealth can't buy.'

I'd tried to think what he meant. I'd been very young at the time and fretting over the death of a pet cat, Tip-Toes. Mrs Crabbe had told me to be sensible. 'You can get another cat,' she'd told me, which was quite true. What she hadn't understood was that I could never get another Tip-Toes. So her advice hadn't comforted me at all, but my father had, taking me to another sphere altogether, − a world quite beyond small personal issues.

Memories! so many of them.

What a crowd of them flooded the moments of sorting, and packing, and wrapping up.

But at last the day for removing to Tharne arrived. Garth went ahead, leaving me to ride in Adam's cab sitting with my own special possessions packed round me.

I was tensed up when I entered the hall of the house that had been so long denied to me. The front door was already ajar. A thin beam of spring sunshine sprinkled the floor, striking the face of the man servant who appeared from the back premises to assist with my boxes and valise. I had never seen him before. Garth had already told me Manfred's Indian attendant had left; he was returning to India. Except for Ruana's maid the small house-staff had been replaced. This man was chubby, pink complexioned, and had a benign, rather patronising air about him. I wondered how much he knew or had gleaned, about Tharne's past history. At the foot of the stairs he paused and called 'Alice' in a sharp, high voice. I was surprised; the tones somehow didn't match his portly exterior. A pale faced prim looking girl wearing a high-necked black dress and white apron with a frilled cap appeared almost instantly. She gave a little bob and said, 'Whilst the luggage is taken up m'lady, madam, Miss Ruana said for you to see her in the conservatory—'

'Oh,' I answered abruptly. 'And where's my husband?'

'Sir Garth, at the moment is at the stables, my lady,' the man said pompously. 'I will see he is informed that you are here.'

'Thank you.'

I turned, in some bewilderment, and made my way to the parlour which led immediately into the conservatory. Why did Ruana wish to meet me there, I wondered, of all places? An unpleasant reminder to both of us of what had occurred before. And why hadn't she been near the door to welcome me? Or at least put on a show of welcome?

Still, she was probably just as resentful at having to share her home with Doctor Dorric's daughter as I was to be there. So pretending indifference I pushed the parlour door open and went in. I didn't have to go to the conservatory after all. Ruana was standing by the table, looking very erect, condemning, and regal, in purple silk, with a lace-cap at the back of her severely dressed black hair. Although the fashion was out-of-date, the fact did not detract from her air of authority which was rather frightening. Her expression was hard and cold, her voice thin as cracking ice when she said with a wave of a mittened hand, 'Sit down, if you wish. Although what I have to say is brief—'

'No, thank you. I'd rather stand,' I told her.

'Very well.' She went to the window, turned, and came back again. Then she said in deadly precise tones, 'You will be reigning here from tomorrow, I understand—'

'Reigning? It's not—'

'Stop. Hold your tongue and let me finish. The wife of the master of Tharne will naturally put herself in that position. It is traditional.' She paused; there was something in the hard concentrated glitter of her eyes that unnerved me. 'However,' she continued after a moment, 'tradition occasionally errs. Morally this house is mine. The best years of my life were given to its maintenance, straining and striving to keep expenses down and the inheritance intact. When my only brother − the rightful heir − died, fifteen years ago, I still went on, caring for my father, a selfish old man who drained me emotionally by his insatiable eccentricities and demands. His death left me free for the first time in my life − or so I thought. Then Garth appeared. The legal owner of Tharne!' Her voice was contemptuous. 'And with him a dissolute half-caste family. Can you imagine my feelings?' She drew a deep breath. 'Still − I made no word of complaint. I just went on, doing my duty, catering to their needs putting up with heathen habits and heathen servants, and all the time − morally, spiritually, Tharne was mine − *mine*. Do you understand?'

'Yes, oh yes I do,' I said, trying to stop the flow of bitterness. 'But it will be different now—'

She smiled grimly. Or rather the thin lips twisted upwards in the travesty of a smile.

'Of course it will,' she said flatly. 'They've gone, haven't they? All of them − except *you!*'

The last word came out as a hiss. I winced, and involuntarily stepped backwards.

'But you wouldn't go, would you? Whatever I did, however hard I tried − you just stayed there smugly at Carnbrooke waiting for a chance to steal and possess − *you!* a divorced woman, no better than a slut − a *whore!*' Her breathing had become violent.

A dark flush stained her sallow face. And in that moment the truth registered.

'Those letters,' I cried, 'those terrible words; the dreadful things pushed under the door — you wrote them—'

'Of course,' she agreed calmly, with smug satisfaction, 'I wanted you out. It was my right. With Garth alone, I knew I could have existed filling my rightful place once his parasites had gone. But you were stubborn. Thick-skinned, a typical little plebeian climber—'

Shock left me temporarily speechless. There was a long pause until I managed to ask, 'And the reticule — the bag I left behind that day — with my key in it and that other? You put it there deliberately, didn't you? The conservatory one, so Manfred could find it. But why? What for?'

She shook her head. 'No, I wasn't responsible for the key. My — *half*-cousin—' again the derision, the contempt '—did it himself. I watched him. He was a very sensuous character, you know. Something in the blood. In that you were quite two of a kind. I saw the lusting look on your face, and in his eyes when you fluttered your lashes at him — oh it was all clear. I guessed what would happen.'

'Then why didn't you stop him?'

'Why should I have done? Let life make its own pattern, I thought.'

'He could have killed me.'

'Yes.'

I shivered.

'And the gate? Did you open it? The gate from the paddock to the moor?'

'Not personally. But I didn't forbid it. You see, Miss Dorric, and — that is all you are really, to me — just *Miss Dorric* — I had grown tired of looking after mad invalids and foreign usurpers. Tharne was well rid of them. The difficulty is that you remain. However—' she drew herself up, adding inches to her height '—it is not such a great difficulty after all. During these last two days I've discovered that although I still remain moral owner of the ancestral home, I no longer want it. It's a decadent place built on thwarted hopes and dark genes. If I could say I wish you well of it, I would. But I do not wish you well. I hope every bad echo, every insane laugh, every grasping thought and every malicious note, played on that old violin by Manfred's child, haunt you for ever.'

Wave after wave of icy cold swept over me.

The truth had shattered me like the thrust of a sharp barbed sword; yet for the moment all feeling seemed to have deserted me. Then I heard myself saying almost in a whisper, 'You mean you're leaving?'

She bowed her head in affirmation.

'This evening Adam will drive me to a hotel in Penzance. Rooms are already booked. Later I may move to Torquay. I have quite a comfortable personal allowance which will enable me a few of the pleasures of life, instead of suffering the degrading conditions of living beside a — *slut*.'

At that moment the parlour door which was not latched, opened quietly, and Garth came in. Once glance at his expression told me that he had been in the hall and overheard; how much I didn't know then, but sufficient for him to say in controlled, hard tones, 'I advise you leave immediately, Ruana, just as soon as the man can have the chaise ready and the horses harnessed. Needless to say that after what I've just learned, I have no wish to see or hear of you again. For your own good, it is better not. Do you understand? Collect your clothes immediately, and — get out.'

Ruana's lips formed an ugly scar-like shape on the sneering mask of her face.

'Certainly,' she said, adding insultingly, 'I never liked you, Garth. As a small child even you were always an uncouth and undisciplined character. I'm sure you're well suited to your second-hand spouse.'

For a brief few seconds they stood face to face, neither flinching from the other's gaze. I thought at first he might strike her. Then, with an exaggerated lift of the head, she swept past him, long skirts held up by both hands and forming a train behind her.

When the door had closed, Garth put his arm round my shoulders and eased me into a chair.

'Oh, Caroline,' he said, 'I'm so sorry. I didn't know.'

'Perhaps even now you don't,' I told him. 'Not everything.'

'Neither do you. That's been the trouble.'

'Yes.'

Later that evening when Ruana had gone, he told me.

I shall never forget the sight of the tall, rigid, black-clad figure walking stiffly down the steps, and across the drive to the waiting chaise. Garth and I were standing hand in hand at an upstairs window watching. It was as though, before the whole story was unfolded both of us had to be quite certain that the last episode of the nightmare was over.

When at last the rattle of wheels and clip-clop of horses' hooves had died round the corner of the moorland lane, we left the room and went downstairs to the library. The interior, lined with books, reminiscent somehow of so much past history and secrets yet unfolded, seemed more conducive to shared confidences than the archaic reception rooms or parlours where Ruana had wielded such stiff-backed authority.

There was an alcove at the far-end. Logs spluttered in the vast fireplace, throwing fitful light and shade to mingle with the warm glow of hanging oil lamps on either side. The binding of ancient calf-bound books was mellowed into yellow-brown uniformity. The heavy brown velvet curtains shielding the windows, though old, seemed friendly and somehow comforting, shutting out the tragedy of recent days. An atmosphere of timelessness brooded there, as though countless voices whispered, 'All things pass. Sadness eventually dies, leaving only the best to remember — the early dreams and aspirations — the deeds each one has contemplated but somehow never achieved. The failures that overcame us because of our mortality. Yes — we are old — these volumes are old, but because of age are forever young, as you are young. No word spoken or recorded here is without reason, or was written without cause. Through parchment and pen we live. We are your heritage—'

It was odd I should be caught up in such retrospection. For a short while, before Garth began to speak, I think he too shared that almost mystical experience. He placed cushions against the back of an ancient settle facing the fire and when I was comfortable he took the seat opposite, so we could see each other, yet not touch. The time for touch and renewed emotional contact was in abeyance — it had to be, until faith and confidence in each other had been truly cemented.

Then, at last, he spoke.

'You had to know some time of course,' he began. 'I knew it in my bones; but loyalty's an odd virtue — maybe it's not a virtue at all in certain circumstances, but a damned encumbrance—' His voice wavered, his blue eyes had a gold glint as they stared at me reflectively over the smoky orange coils of wood-flame.

'Go on,' I said.

'You've already discovered that Manfred was my brother — or I should say, my half-brother. We had the same father. But our mothers were — different.'

I waited, thinking I was to learn Manfred was half Asian. So I was surprised when Garth continued: 'Except for a brief spell at Harrow, most of my life was lived in India. My mother died when I was eight years old, and I was left in the charge of an Ayah. I won't begin to describe the conflicting standards — racial emotions and ideologies — the hypocrisies, and bitter undercurrents of power-struggles between European and Indian communities, with wealth and greed wielding the sword. Even in early youth I was aware of unfairness somewhere. But my father's colourful character held me completely fascinated. That he was fighting for a good and glorious cause I never doubted. When he told me a young brother was to be brought into our home I was at first a little jealous and resentful, until Julian, my father, managed to convince me that I would always be first in his esteem and affections, and that it was 'up to me' as a future officer and gentleman — oh yes he was quite determined my destiny lay with the Army — to teach proper values and a decent code of behaviour to my less fortunate brother. It was only when I enquired about Manfred's own mother that Julian became angry.

'"She's nothing to either of us any more," he said. "Forget her. When you're older you'll know more of such things. She just happened." His voice was so stern I'd kept silent. For a time though, I'd brooded, because I'd never imagined my father, the noble handsome Captain de Verries, having more than one woman. What Indians did was their own affair. It had always been impressed on me that although those of great riches and power might be cultivated, within certain limits of course, the majority — the pariahs and "untouchables" of lower caste — were little more than heathens, with standards of morals and living in every way discreditable. Still—' his lips had a wry twist, 'I came to accept the situation, and feeling rather superior in my childish snob way, took Manfred under my wing. In those early days it wasn't difficult to love him. He was sensitive, warm hearted and intelligent; far too intelligent for those bloody days—'

Garth's breathing had quickened. His eyes, briefly upon me, wavered and stared ahead as though gazing upon another scene in another world. After a minute I said, 'Please go on.'

He brought himself back to the present, commencing again in more practical tones; speaking abruptly and rather quickly, obviously wanting to get his painful story off his chest.

'Manfred's mother,' he said, 'had been a beautiful selfish creature — the wife of one of Julian's fellow officers. My own mother at that period was already ailing—' he paused as though to prepare me for a shock, yet one needing a shred of compassion and understanding. 'She had been of little use as a wife—' his voice shook, '—for a considerable time. So they became lovers.'

'Your father and—'

'Lena Thornton, yes. Now I'm not sitting in moral judgement on either of them. Such liaisons out there were not unusual during those days, in such an unstable and frequently corrupt society. But Lena Thornton was not only a complete nympho-maniac — she was mad. Hereditary, I believe, though when Jim Thornton married her he couldn't have known. When she became pregnant she had already left her husband. This was shortly before my mother's death and she clearly meant to com-pletely capture my father. As Jim had been killed, the future appeared, for her, assured. But by then my father had a shrewd assessment of Lena's character and made it quite clear he had no intention of making her his wife, though accepting the child would be his.

'The upshort of the sorry affair was that she ran off with some minor civil servant — to save her face, as they say, lived with him until the baby was born, and when he — her latest conquest — deserted her, she drowned herself.'

There was a long pause. I made no such trite remark as 'how terrible,' or 'how sad,' although I thought it; and presently, with a shrug, Garth said, 'So that was it. Julian, feeling responsible, took the baby, and Manfred in every way shared with me until I was old enough to join the Regiment.

'My father was killed soon after that, and from that day on, through circumstances, the duty of seeing to Manfred's welfare was mine. Because of this I suppose we came closer to each other than many brothers are. In youth, though ultra sensitive he showed no sign of inheriting any of his mother's warped traits.

'He joined the Army when he was old enough, and I managed to have him under my command so I could keep an eye on him. But certain events, later, proved too much for him. The continual upheavals and tragedies, the killings, treachery and hypocrisy, the bloody awfulness of it all, got his nerves so tensed he turned to other things; women mostly — to keep him sane. Ironic, wasn't it? It was women in the end that were his undoing — sex, the insatiable appetite that triggered off the tainted streak inherited from his maternal blood. At first, through influence and constant watchfulness, I managed somehow to keep a certain control, camouflaging his affairs, and bringing him to heel. For a time he'd be reasonable and repentant, and pull himself together; superficially anyhow. Then, some act of violence — a chance conversation perhaps, or argument — quite a minor thing would start him off again. Twice I only just managed to save him from a court-martial. In his dark lapses he had no respect for himself or anyone else — not even race or colour. Inevitably he had to resign his commission, and shortly after that he assaulted an Indian woman. She was not even beautiful. The husband made an attempt to assassinate him, was found guilty and later executed, poor devil.'

Garth sighed.

'*That* was my brother!'

I didn't know what to say. The effort of divulging such an unsavoury portion of family history had obviously put him under great strain. Through the firelight beads of moisture glittered on his upper lip. His eyes had narrowed, the lines of jaw were tensed.

Instinctively my right hand went out to him. He did not take it, but lifted his own, waving it as though to dispel past shadows. Then, speaking in even tones he began again.

'That's the story in brief. There may be small errors in my telling of it — faulty sequences of time and dates. But the overall picture is true. Except for one thing.'

'Yes?'

'Manfred was not evil. The bad genes in him were only a part, and not of his making. At heart, when he could see straight, he was kind and compassionate. Too much so.' There was a pause. 'I loved him. He needed me, and need breeds affection. Also I gulled myself into believing that under the proper circumstances, with peace and quiet, he could be cured. Kara too. She was a good wife. Whether he'd have married her if he hadn't already got her with child, I don't know. But there was never any question of her devotion and fidelity. Unfortunately my little niece was abnormal. On one hand, wild and ungovernable – a genius on the other. I suppose you could have called her a child prodigy. From very earliest years her passion for music was outstanding. She could handle a violin earlier than she could properly talk. But in other ways she was extremely backward; her tempers and rages were at times beyond control.'

I remembered the sighing trees and the wailing music of Tharne – the gyrating shape of thin legs and arms outspread against the high windows.

'I'm sorry,' I said.

He appeared not to notice, but continued quietly, reflectively, 'So when I got this damned wound, when it was obvious my Army days had met their Waterloo – I knew England was the answer. You could say my Uncle's death was opportune. Looking back to Tharne in childhood days I visualised a castle, an iron retreat where the family would be safe from intrusion and prying eyes, from warfare and massacre and above all – from bloody memories.'

'That's why you had the wall built?' I said. 'To shut the world away.'

'To keep them safe. Manfred above all; safe from himself and his insatiable woman-hunger. Then—' he looked at me with a sudden return of the old ardour in his blue eyes '—then I had to fall in love with you.'

'Oh, Garth!' words just then seemed futile, and quite inadequate for the confusing emotional torment – sympathy, desire, above all, regret for my own blundering – that had caused such rift between us. And yet, I thought the next moment as I had before, Garth was also to blame. If he'd loved me with his heart and mind as much as his body, he would have had confidence in me, given trust instead of doubt. Only

Ruana's outburst had forced the truth from him, not I. There was still a great deal we had to get straight between us.

He got up at that point and came over to where I was still seated. Taking both my hands and heaving me to my feet, he said, 'Well, Caroline, that's enough for the time being. Time for other things, don't you think?'

I nodded mutely, and together we went to our room for the inevitable reconciliation. We made love, but beneath the passion a shadow remained. There was still much to be explained; but I was too tired to formulate exactly what, and the reason for my lingering discomforture.

Sleep soon came; any dreams I had were vague and intermittent, confused with a distorted image of Ruana's gaunt face and figure looming from a shadowed black sky.

Why had she hated me so?

The question was still in my mind when I woke. Garth had already got up and gone. I had a second's panic. The large bedroom and empty space beside me were suddenly frightening. I felt bereft and lonely, deserted in a house of memories and tragedy that promised little comfort ahead. Though summer was on the way, the atmosphere was chill. It was as though the very walls of the place retained resentment at my presence.

It was not until I was fully awake and standing at the window overlooking the moors, that I managed to dispel the dark mood. The early sunlight was already filtering over the landscape. A froth of white blossom foamed by the lane above the drive. There came the mooing of a cow from a nearby field, followed from Nanny's quarters by the faint tinkle of a pan and a young child's voice.

Heather. My little girl.

I pulled on a wrap and made my way to the night nursery.

Sarah was polite and obliging in allowing me to interrupt her domestic ritual with the baby. At the same time I felt rebuffed and annoyed. She made me feel I was a stranger, which was quite ridiculous. In future, I decided, I would insist day by day in taking further responsibility.

Whether she sensed my thoughts or not I couldn't tell, but there was a smug look on her face when I left the room, and in one straight glance at each other I noticed how clear, hard, and cold her eyes were. Light grey under arched dark brows which contrasted strangely with her fair hair.

Cruel.

Yes, they were cruel eyes. But not to Heather; Heather obviously was already deeply attached.

I walked along the landing disconsolately, chiding myself for imagining things.

When I reached the bedroom I found the maid had left a breakfast tray for me.

Garth came in as I was pouring tea.

He bent down and kissed me. 'Glad you had a good sleep,' he said. 'I rather laid it on last night, didn't I? The family saga, all that?'

'I'm glad you told me,' I said, thinking how commonplace we both sounded after what had occurred. 'I understand now. About Manfred, I mean.'

'And Ruana, I hope. She must have led a hell of a life with that awkward old man.'

'Yes.' I could have added, 'And what about me? Has it occurred to you what a hell I've been through? Those letters? The insults? The deliberate lying and scheming?' But I kept silent.

Garth must have sensed something. His hand enclosed a shoulder then slipped to my wrist. After a pause he said, 'We'll get over all this in time. Anyway you've nothing to worry about any more.'

But I had of course, I decided irrationally.

Danger of something — or someone — still lurked in the very air, heralding — what?

My 'sixth sense', I thought, recalling Aunt Adela's forecasts of the past. It was my sixth sense stirring again; or perhaps it was just fear. Fear could do funny things to the mind. Horace for instance! how Horace had frightened me that evening following my fall. But Horace now, was out of my life for good. Or would be when Garth managed to accept the truth. It occurred to me rather sadly that despite his own revelation the previous night, he'd never once said he believed me — but to the contrary had steered conversation away from any vital personal issues.

I loved Garth. Loved him passionately. But without trust I knew a quality would be missing from our union. And I wanted

the whole of him, just as I wanted to give the whole of myself.
Utterly.

In my bones, I knew another hurdle had to be faced before
his complete commitment.

Mrs Crabbe would have said I was imagining things. But I
wasn't; as later events proved.

17

I did my utmost during the following weeks to assert my
authority at Tharne. But Sarah Cullen's influence, especially
with Heather, insidiously increased.

With the return of my own health resentment in me
deepened. Garth seemed so completely satisfied with the girl's
presence; and when he was there she appeared in all ways
respectful to me. But during the short periods he was away —
sometimes for two days at a time in Truro, Plymouth, or Bristol
where he had business meetings concerning shipping or mining
— her glances at me were occasionally hostile, accompanied by
an air of contemptuous servility.

On an evening at the end of June shortly after his return following a day's absence, I told him bluntly I thought it better
that Nanny left.

We had already finished dinner, and had gone through the
conservatory to the garden. The air was warm, almost sultry;
heavy with the sweetness of flowers and blossoming growth. I
had removed the lace shawl I generally wore, so any faint breeze
could fan my shoulders, which were bare above the gold
coloured silk of my gown. My hair was taken simply back, resting in coils on my neck, and starred at the side by a simple
cream rose, similar to the posy pinned at my breast. The leaves
of trees and undergrowth stirred very faintly and my skirts
rustled with each step. A sensuous evening, an evening of
unspoken communication with nature, between the deepest
needs of one individual for another; yet words had to be said.

Awareness was not sufficient. Soon that hour of half-light and mystery would be over. Dreams would recede into fact when we entered the house again. Sarah Cullen would be there, competent and sturdy; unpleasantly reminiscent of Ruana's formidable shadow.

'Garth,' I said presently, as we turned by a trellis of roses.

The pressure of his arm tightened round my body. My senses leaped with the joy of a flower about to burst from its sheath.

'Yes?' The touch of his lips was soft on my hair, just brushing the top of my head.

'I can ask you something, can't I? Something that might annoy you, but I hope won't.'

He laughed, but not in amusement. It was a low sound, suggesting desire and incomprehension that anything in the world at that moment could break the harmony between us. Possibly gratification was there too. It was so very seldom I begged anything from him.

'Ask on,' he said.

'I'd like Nanny to leave,' I told him quietly.

He stood quite still for a moment, with a twilit shadow of a branch half masking his face. There was the rustle of leaves as a bird flew suddenly upwards from a bush. Then his arm fell away from my waist. He took my chin in his hand, as the other enclosed a shoulder firmly.

'Why?' he asked. His head was bent down to my face. Even through the half-light the frown above his eyes was obvious.

'I don't like her. I know she's qualified and looks after Heather well — in one way.'

'In one way? What do you mean? Why the reservation?' He freed me automatically. I took a step forward and we walked on as I tried to put my point of view.

'I'm better now, but I've very little contact with my own child. Sometimes we — I think we should be together more; you and I, and Heather.'

'Is that all?'

No. No — it wasn't. There was so much more I couldn't properly explain because I didn't clearly understand myself.

'It's just a feeling — a sense of being shut out,' I persisted.

'Of your own home?' His tones were incredulous.

'Yes. It hasn't been my home for long, after all. Sarah and Heather were here first. Actually, Garth——'

Garth's footsteps quickened. I could sense his stance, the set of chin and mouth — his manner, attitude, — the whole of him — had become rigid with opposition.

'I think you're being rather silly,' he said. 'Is it — surely you're not jealous?'

'Oh don't be ridiculous.' I turned with a flutter and rustle of skirts, at the same time pulling the lace shawl round my shoulders. Garth shrugged and accompanied me back to the house. Before we reached the door, he said, 'Please don't bring the question of Nanny's leaving again, Caroline. She has the highest recommendations, and is extremely capable. To dismiss her without good cause — which you certainly haven't given me — would be most unfair. Not only that — inconvenient. I shall be busy during the next week or two. I have business meetings ahead in Plymouth, and have to go to Bristol probably. I shall feel far more satisfied knowing you have company and that the baby is being properly cared for, than if you were on your own——'

'I shouldn't be,' I interrupted. 'There are the servants——'

'Just three of them, except for the boy; and all new.'

'There's Mrs Crabbe at Carnbrooke. I can always run over and have a chat.'

'I don't want you getting too involved with Carnbrooke again.'

'Why not?' I could hear the old rebellious note rising in my own voice.

He waited a moment before answering. Then he said, 'This is supposed to be a new beginning. Ours. No ghosts from the past. Please, Caroline.'

Ghosts? I felt suddenly derisive. He meant what he said, I knew. But didn't he realise, that for me, Tharne was full of ghosts? No. He didn't, of course. The ghosts he referred to were any memories of my former life, from the days when I knew Horace. It didn't occur to him there were far worse ones — the ghosts of a demented child and a sick maniac who had once placed a flower in my hair, in the conservatory; of a woman with long black hair called Kara who had been trampled to death before my eyes; and of a woman's hatred — Ruana's — who had conceived such a vile way of frightening me.

Those notes; her lies. And now Sarah Cullen who somehow seemed to echo Ruana's resentment. This was not imagination; I wasn't ill or neurotic. But Garth was just blind over some matters — unless he secretly wanted Sarah there because he held more than a respectful admiration for her.

The idea came to me as a shock. I couldn't grasp it at first, and when I did, I staunchly set it aside.

Garth loved me. And only me.

But desire was different. Desire could be an evil thing.

I shivered. The beauty of the evening had disintegrated as quickly as though blasted by a gust of icy cold air. All bird-song had ceased. The flowering glory of the greenhouse appeared faded and yellowing from the pale flare of candles in the room beyond.

Tharne!

As I entered the shadowing wide hall and went up the broad stairway to the bedroom, I hated it. The sombre portraits of bygone ancestors seemed to taunt and sneer at me from their heavy frames when I passed. Some of the lamps were already lit, casting eerie shapes across the vast landings. Faint mist pressed against the tall Gothic-style windows, streaming in blurred blueish light over the cold floors. A semblance of movement seemed to stir amid the grotesque elongated forms of swords and ancient armour placed in shadowy alcoves and by the corner where a narrower flight of steps cut up from the main corridor to a second floor. I had never been up there. It was dark and forbidding, and led eventually to a tower containing two rooms where old Sir Garth had worked at his research or whatever it was — and hoarded his personal books and relics. At that point, I always quickened my pace. And I did so now. The night nursery led off from the main landing.

As I went by, the murmur of Nanny's voice was audible. Little Heather must have woken and been restless. The idea of Nanny comforting and lulling her to sleep again was distasteful to me. I had the quick impulse to join them, and insist on saying good night to my own child; on holding her in my arms, and telling some amusing tale that would bring the delightful chuckle and smile to her round baby face.

But of course she was too young yet to understand. Yet Sarah Cullen managed it. By a single gesture, a lift of the finger, a 'shush' at her lips, or conspiratorial wink of an eye, she could hold the baby's attention and bring her to complacency and quiet. Only on very rare occasions had I seen Heather rebel or turn away. The knowledge of such influence was intensely hurtful to me, and when Garth appeared in our bedroom a little later I was still seething with indignation.

He appeared not to notice. I knew he wanted me, but he was so cocksure. So sensitive over a matter that was of utmost importance to me, that I found it impossible to respond. For the first time, as his hands sought to caress, and to subdue in passion any lingering chill between us, I drew away.

'Please, no,' I told him, freeing myself from the sensuous touch on breast and thigh, 'I'm tired, Garth. The weather perhaps. I've a slight headache too—'

He jerked himself upright immediately.

'So sorry,' he said stiffly.

I knew he was scowling, could feel it, and could sense his frustration also. It was untrue that I had a headache, but the tiredness was genuine. Yet it was a long time before I slept that night, or came to terms with Garth's obtuseness. When I did, it was only through the instinctive recognition that most — perhaps all men were the same at heart — assuming it was the male prerogative to soothe all arguments into negation by subtle sexual prowess.

Man the possessor.

Woman the possessed.

I sighed as the lids pricked and fell heavily over my eyes.

Tomorrow was another day, I thought dreamily. Tomorrow something might happen to change things.

From a nearby tree outside an owl hooted. A familiar sound recollected from the far-off days of childhood. As I drifted into sleep I was riding Flash up the sweep of moor to the Granite King. Gulls were flying overhead, and the air was speckled silver and white in the sunlight from flying foam. The smell of heather mingled with brine was in the air, and as I reined, the magic of 'place' encompassed me. I climbed up between the great boulders, and the great stone arms were waiting to receive me. When I looked up the wild rugged face towered over me; the earth seemed to quiver and move just a little, becoming one with the clouds and glittering distant sea. Then there was distortion and a darkness that seemed like death. I lifted my arms to the air, and when the light lifted, the moor and the stones had disintegrated. I woke suddenly, reached out, and in semi-consciousness found my fingers tracing the contours of a face.

Garth's!

I eased myself up. A full moon had risen and was striking through a chink in the curtains across the bed.

Garth's features were relaxed and at peace. In sleep he looked so much younger. My heart warmed, and at that moment his eyes opened.

'Caroline—' he murmured.

My arm touched his chest and lay there. The next instant he was breathing deeply and rhythmically again. I felt strangely the elder just then.

After all, the one thing I'd ever wanted — to be Garth's wife, had happened. Other things were small in comparison, and eventually could be ironed out.

And so the night passed. And when I woke up it was past nine thirty, and Garth was no longer by my side.

18

Time passed. In the woods and verdant ditches of the lanes, the glint of bluebells gradually merged and died into the thrusting deep crimson of fox-gloves below the sun-splashed moors. Gorse flamed brilliantly that year in sudden clumps of brightest gold among the heather. By the old stones of Castle Cromme broom flowered gently, as it had blossomed perhaps, thousands of years ago, when the small dark men — the early Britons — planned their village and lived there, farming and working at their simple crafts, and worshipping their ancient gods.

Sometimes I walked that way, trying to recapture the old magic of childhood. But the atmosphere was shadowed — not by imaginings of those far-off settlers — but by the recent memory of my frightening experience with Manfred.

I kept away from the Granite King, not wishing to relive my last recent ride there when I'd made such a vain and useless effort to intercept the tragedy of those three doomed human beings. I would frequently stare out of a side window though, and when the light was clear the massive silhouetted form of the carn would appear very clear — a fortress of strength against which human actions and weaknesses appeared mere incidents played against the vast backcloth of Nature's own drama.

Once or twice, at that period, Garth wishing to please me, suggested we rode there together. Each time it either rained or there was mist. In the past I wouldn't have cared. But it was hard to pull myself from the increasing sense of depression and unease induced by Sarah Cullen's presence.

One afternoon in early September, Garth had a business appointment in Truro. He set off before the mid-day meal, which I ate alone in the breakfast room.

Soon afterwards, the servants who had been given the after-noon off, left for Redruth where there was a fair. Nanny didn't go of course, although I'd told her I would quite like to look after Heather for a change. My idea was to take the baby over to Carnbrooke for tea with Mrs Crabbe.

But Sarah pooh-poohed the idea. 'Oh I wouldn't dream of giving you so much trouble, Lady de Verries,' she said. 'She's quite a handful now, you know — beginning to crawl about the place; these early days are very important and formative of a child's character. Routine is necessary.'

'I don't want my baby's life entirely ruled by routine,' I said sharply.

She frowned slightly, then gave me a faint smile. 'Of course not. I understand that. But really—' Her tones were most reasoning. 'I'd much rather have my *usual* half-day out. I don't care for fairs, and I've already arranged to go to Penzance on Thursday; Miss Ruana has asked me to tea.'

Ruana! I'd realised that she and Sarah had become friendly during their time together at Tharne, and had suspected they occasionally met. But the blunt statement annoyed me. It was somehow as though Nanny had flung it out as a challenge.

'I see,' I said coldly, adding almost immediately, 'is my husband aware that you're on such intimate terms?'

'Oh I wouldn't say we were intimate,' Sarah answered blandly.

'And I don't tell Sir Garth what I do or where I go in my spare time.' There was a pause. 'I don't think he'd dream of asking; it's my own affair.'

So she stayed that day at Tharne, leaving me angry and irritated with myself for not putting my foot down. I realised I should have asserted my authority. I could have insisted on taking Heather to see Mrs Crabbe. But Nanny obviously would have made it her business to come too. She always had a quick excuse and reason for doing anything she'd set her mind on, and it was clear to me that she was determined not to leave Heather that afternoon.

So I busied myself with small unnecessary tasks, and gathering chrysanthemums from the garden for the house. I cut some early autumn leaves too. Sycamore and beech; they looked colourful arranged with the gold and bronze flowers, and brought a refreshing heady earth-scent into the parlour.

As I was placing them on the table a shape passed the small window which overlooked the path leading from the drive. There was something very familiar about her, and the way she walked with her head and shoulders upright, shawl and hair blowing behind her, a basket over one arm. In a second I knew.

Yutha. The gipsy.

I ran out of the room and called her before she reached the side door. She turned. The late sunlight touched her face to rich mahogany. 'Yutha!' I exclaimed.

'Dordi!' she said, 'Greetings to thee and thine.'

I smiled, and stretched out my hand. She enclosed it for a second in her lean rough palm. There were sprigs of heather in her basket. I touched one lightly. 'I'd like one.' She handed it to me. 'Take it, lady, with my blessing.'

'Oh, but I must — if you wait a moment—'

She waved her hand in negation.

'No. No. No silver from thee, — just a word in thine ear though — it is for that I'm here.'

I glanced round cautiously, wondering if Nanny was about. There was no sign of her.

'Will you come in?'

She shook her head. 'No, dordi, no. This is no place for our kind. It's written by thy gate.'

'Written? How?'

Again that strange enigmatic smile. 'Our secret, lady. Not for thee.'

'Then—'

She bent towards me and continued almost in a whisper, 'Have a care. Be watchful. The Mochardi o Bengh threatens thee. Evil, daughter. Watch the pale one—'

'But—'

'Enough – enough—' she said, with her eyes narrowing as the faint tread of a footstep came from the direction of the stairs. 'I must go, lady. Good luck to thee and thine.'

She turned quickly, and sped back the way she had come towards the drive. I closed the door as quietly as possible, and went down the hall. Sarah must have heard. She appeared at the foot of the stairs almost soundlessly, and stood there staring, reminding me somehow of some watchful feline creature with her pale hair and tawny cold eyes.

I went towards her. 'I didn't know you were here, Sarah—' it was a stupid thing to say, giving her a chance, in words, to outwit me.

'I wasn't, Lady de Verries.' Her tones were normal, quiet and polite. 'I happened to see that woman – that tinker – coming down the drive. I was at the window. As you were alone, I thought you might need me.'

'Why should I?' I said sharply.

She shrugged.

'They can be difficult sometimes, these people. Once a fortune-teller sets foot in a door she can be very hard to get rid of. Besides—' her manner became that of an adult speaking down to a child, which intensely annoyed me. 'It's wisest not to encourage vagabonds when there are young children like Heather about. It's been known for babies to be stolen, you know.'

Anger rose in me, mingled with a surge of fear – not of Yutha – but because of the subtle threat underlying the suggestion. Nanny was obviously trying to frighten and put me in the wrong.

'I think I'm a fair judge of people,' I told her coldly.

'Are you?' The remark held contempt.

'I've known Yutha for years,' I said. 'She'd certainly harm no one of mine. Neither is she a vagabond.'

'I see.' The short remark held contempt.

I forced myself to stare her out, and was gratified that for once I won.

'If you're on your way to the kitchens,' I said, 'I'll have a few minutes with my little girl. Do you mind allowing me to pass?'

She paused only a moment before moving on. I swept past her, not looking at her face, but sensing an atmosphere of extreme hostility.

When I reached the nursery the baby was in her cot with one tiny arm round a teddy bear. Her dark eyes — so like Garth's — opened wide. I bent down to cuddle her, but she pulled away, with a thin wail of resentment. Not wishing Sarah to hear I got up, shrugged helplessly, thinking bitterly how effectively Nanny had alienated me from my own child.

As I left the room a few minutes later, Nanny appeared at the corner of the landing where the back stairs cut up from the kitchens. From there the smaller corridor divided, taking the steep turn up to the short flight leading to the tower where old Sir Bruce had studied.

I walked quickly in the opposite direction to the main staircase. I had never liked the vicinity of the back stairs, perhaps because of the shadowed recesses and odd twists and turns of higgledy-piggledy passages containing closets and dark cupboards that gave an impression of haunted unease — an impression heightened that afternoon by the vague glimpse of Sarah Cullen's white clad form emerging so quietly in her soft-soled shoes.

Except for her size she could have been some condemning wraith from the past.

When I was downstairs again I laughed at my odd fancies. Nanny! a wraith. What a ridiculous idea. I wished I was back at Carnbrooke. My nerves seemed to grow more tensed every day. If only we could have a little more company, I thought. Even a dinner party including some of the de Verries' dull pompous friends would be preferable to being confined for so many hours of the day, within the vast precincts of Tharne.

As though sensing my mood, Garth suddenly told me the next day that he was expecting a business acquaintance and his wife from Truro the following week — something to do with investments concerning railways in which Garth had interests.

'Are they nice?' I queried naively, when he informed me of the forthcoming visit. 'Shall I like them?'

Garth glanced at me with a hint of amusement in his eyes.

'He's a very astute man. Principled, religious, elderly; a leading Methodist of the county.'

'Oh.' My hopes for a touch of colour and excitement were completely dashed.

Then Garth laughed.

'Don't worry. I'm sure you'll find Jane Boaze very amusing.'

'Why? Is she old too?'

'Middle-aged, stout, effervescent, with good humour, rather over-dressed, but very very rich, which is why, I suppose, Joseph Boaze—'

'Married her,' I interrupted.

'Mostly,' Garth agreed. 'Although it may have been the other way round. She's quite a persuasive lady in her ebullient fashion.'

My thoughts wandered briefly; then I enquired, 'Isn't it rather surprising that anyone so − religious − as your friend, or rather your acquaintance − agrees to visit us?'

'Why?' The word was sharp, slightly irritated.

'Well, you and I. Me being such a wicked creature—'

I shouldn't, of course have referred to the disreputable happenings of the past. I was only speaking from mild amusement.

Garth frowned.

'As far as anyone else is concerned, you're my wife. Lady de Verries. Probably Boaze may not have heard anything of your earlier little matrimonial gymnastics. If he has he'll have the good sense to keep his mouth shut.'

'Yes, of course.'

I tried to look and sound demure.

Garth's mood suddenly changed. He swept me up into his arms.

'You're a very naughty girl,' he said into my ear. 'A tease, as I said before. I ought to put you over my knee. But the making up process would be so − titillating − it would inevitably lead to other things − and frankly my love—' he glanced at his watch, '—I haven't the time to indulge in amours at the moment.'

I pouted childishly, shrugged, went to the mirror, and asked, 'When exactly is this important event? And how do you want me to dress? Modestly? Or alluringly, to outvie Mrs Boaze?'

Through the glass, I saw Garth's eyes watching me from behind. Their blue was intensified in a beam of light cast from the window.

'Subtly,' he said, 'becomingly of course, but not sufficiently to deflate Madam Boaze's ego, or disturb her spouse's aplomb. Religious he may be, but human for all that; it wouldn't please her at all to catch his eye wandering.'

'I see. A quiet and attentive hostess content to preside, but only in your shadow, as a background for Boaze enterprise—'

Garth laughed shortly.

'Hardly that. And you don't know what you're talking about, Caroline. There's no enterprise where Joe's concerned. He's nearing the very top rung of the business ladder — Railway business. It's just a matter of whether or not I decide to take up shares in his company. The next century's going to be the one of the Railway — I haven't a doubt of that. And although I'm in no need of finance it's necessary to look ahead. To be a part of the future as well as the present — it's a challenge.'

'But why?' I couldn't help asking. 'If we've enough in the bank as it is, why do you want more wealth, Garth, and for an age we probably won't see?'

Garth waited before replying.

'I can't just stay at Tharne twiddling my thumbs. I've got to have action of some sort — something to fight for with my brains, even if my leg's let me down—'

Inwardly I winced. 'But you've got so much. Wheal Daisy, the estate — and our life together. Or don't you find that rewarding enough?'

'There's Heather to think of, and more children ahead I hope. Another thing — the Breames; the unemployed natives you're so concerned about. I'm not intending to be a mean-fisted miser; there are many important issues to be faced round here, Caroline, and I'd have thought you'd be the first to encourage me.'

'Of course,' I said, bewildered by his sudden enthusiasms for Railways and business affairs. 'It's just that you've never mentioned that kind of thing before. It's always been shipping and the wall, and—' I broke off, realising I was once more blundering. But he appeared not to be upset.

'Ah well, the wall's no longer so important any more,' he remarked, 'as you well know.'

'Yes.' To change the subject quickly, I continued, 'you didn't tell me what day these important people are arriving.'

'Thursday,' Garth said. 'For dinner. That will give you a clear three days to get your menu arranged, and your wardrobe in order. And by the way, Caroline—'

'Yes?'

The blue eyes twinkled. 'Don't think this business is a one-sided affair. A side issue — but a very important one — is to get our friend Boaze interested in speculating in the Venn project. So you should feel gratified.'

I was.

More than that, quite bemused. Obviously I had vastly under-rated my husband's latent business acumen. It was surprising and somehow odd to think that only a few years ago his whole life apart from the trouble with Manfred, had been concerned with the army in India, with war and tragedy far removed from Cornwall and mining.

Now here he was embroiled in big finance, and also with philanthropic notions in his head.

I made some trite remark, adding, 'I'll do my best not to let you down in front of the Boazes, Garth, and I won't appear at all spectacular. I'll wear the dove-grey I think, with the cameo brooch that was Aunt Adela's. Then, if you think the dress is too low on the shoulders for Mr Holy-Joe-Boaze — I can pin the chiffon closer for respectability's sake.'

Garth smiled in the slow speculative way that always excited me.

'It's extremely difficult for me to think of you as a bosom friend of respectability, wife dear. However, life sometimes provides very agreeable surprises, and I'm not at all worried about you coming up to scratch on this occasion.'

He looked so young and cheerful when he left me, my heart lifted. It really did seem, then, that the cloud between us was fading, and that if it hadn't been for my instinctive mistrust of Nanny, life at Tharne might eventually become normal; not only bearable, but the background to the new beginning I so longed for.

On Wednesday evening, as planned, I greeted Mr and Mrs Boaze wearing the dove grey silk as I'd promised Garth I would. It had been made by a dressmaker in Penzance, copied from a style by the famous designer Worth who had become a leader of fashion in London and Paris. Miss Lake, who'd had a magazine with a drawing of the dress in it, had agreed to modifications. The dropped shoulder-line had been lifted, the suggestion of a train dispensed with, and a froth of tulle added to the neckline. The crinoline effect had been contrived simply by voluminous frilled skirts and petticoats beneath the silk − I would have found a frame extremely irritating and confining. The original design had been taken from one worn by the Empress Elizabeth of Austria, but in the altered version looked far less impressive. Still, I was quite aware of its discreetly fashionable effect. I wore my hair gathered from the sides into a bunch of curls on top, held by a tortoise-shell comb and a wisp of ribbon.

Garth stared as he came into the drawing room shortly before the arrival of his visitors.

'Good Heavens!' he exclaimed. 'You look—'

I whirled round, with a rustle of skirts, waving my fan in the air.

'What?'

'Quite regal,' he said, grasping me by the shoulders.

I sobered down instantly, pushing a stray lock of hair away, and re-arranging my bodice. 'Not too much, do I? I mean I won't affront Mrs Boaze?'

'You'll just make her green with envy,' Garth said. He moved to caress me again, but I managed to avoid him.

'Please—' I begged. 'Not at this moment. You've no idea what a business it was getting my hair to lie flat from the parting. I even had to—'

He waited.

'Spit on it,' I added laughing. 'Aunt Adela's lotion didn't work at all. It seems to have lost all its sticking power.'

'Well, don't tell Mrs Boaze that,' Garth said. 'Ladies don't spit, or—'

'—Prance, or show off—' I interrupted.

'Exactly. Only wild-cats. Certainly not Lady de Verries.'

I sighed, drew a deep breath under the stays which were beginning to cramp me slightly. Cook, I knew, had prepared a three course dinner plus etceteras. But I doubted whether I'd be able to wade through it all, with my waist and stomach pinched to such small proportions.

However, when the time came there was so much conversation from the ebulliant Jane Boaze that I was able to take the minimum of each course.

She must have been quite twenty years her husband's junior, and as Garth had inferred, was stout, rosy-cheeked, with an abundance of black glossy hair intricately arranged. The bright purple shade of her velvet dress clashed somewhat with her rubicund complexion. Surplus flesh bulged slightly over the mittens, which I'd read were no longer in vogue. Jane Boaze I soon gathered, was a 'character' in her own way; a woman who only deferred to fashion if it suited her, or if she considered it did.

She was amiable, chatty, and had a fund of gossip to unfold, which I soon discovered, when we retired to the drawing room leaving the men to have whisky, and smoke cigars in the billiard room. Apart from the intrigues of London's Victorian Society, she seemed anxious to impress on me that she also had a 'mind', and purposefully I guessed, had made it her business to gather knowledge of the changing position of feminine role in the country − referring to Florence Nightingale, and Frances Mary Buss who had established the North London Collegiate School for Ladies in 1850.

'And then, look at Dorothea Beale,' she said, eyeing me shrewdly. 'They say she's a most progressive character − her school for clergymen's daughters is extremely go ahead. And—' she suddenly broke off, fanning her broad face vigorously.

'Do you know—' she continued after a pause, 'I don't believe you're interested in the new women for one minute. That's true, isn't it?'

I nodded. 'I'm afraid I'm not. Not the studious political kind. But there are things women should make men do − like looking after the poor—'

She smiled broadly, leaned forward, and tapped me on my shoulder with the gauzy sparkling fan.

'I agree with you. So much pleasanter to fit the role God intended for us, such as caring for our families and children.' She sighed. 'Alas, Mr Boaze and I married rather late in life. We have no family. But you have a little girl, haven't you?'

I told her as much as I could of Heather. Then the subject inevitably reverted to Queen Victoria and her children. Most of the time I listened, or appeared to, and by the time the men joined us I was already half asleep.

The outcome of Garth's conversation with Joe Boaze had evidently been successful. An aura of good-will emanated from both.

Later, when their chaise had driven away, Garth said, 'Thank you for being cooperative, Caroline. You were quite a hit with both of them.'

My cheeks warmed with pleasure.

'Mrs Boaze was easy,' I told him. 'It's hard to think of her being married to someone so − religious.'

Garth chuckled.

'Religion can be quite adaptive in the marriage-bed when circumstances demand it,' he said sceptically. 'Outwardly Boaze may appear something of a cold-blooded fish, but under the sheets it may be a different matter altogether.'

And I stupidly shivered, recalling Horace.

Time passed. Routine at Tharne appeared to have become established, and although I made up my mind every day almost, somehow to find an excuse to dismiss Nanny myself, saying nothing more to Garth until the deed was done, no legitimate opportunity seemed to arise. My life with my husband appeared to be on a more even keel; but underneath niggling doubts and reservations festered. Passionate interludes had become almost habitual. Desire was there, but the tragedies and unpleasantries of the past had left a mark. The fire and romance had somehow dulled under lingering misunderstanding.

However, there were occasions, as we went riding together, when happiness was mutual and I felt momentarily freed of responsibilities and doubts, and the hundred questions of 'ifs' and 'whys', of wondering about Heather, and how to tackle the Nanny situation. Sometimes we took the nearest route seawards riding a mile along the coast towards Penjust, then cutting down a sharp track leading through the Valley of the Rocks to the beach. The cliffs were precipitous above; further westward the abandoned Wheal Crane mine stood bleak and stark on the rim of moors and sky.

Garth told me part of the Venn estate was for sale, including a farm and the mine itself. 'So now you know why I wanted to cultivate Boaze—' he said. 'I intend to buy. It will be a mutual project.'

'Oh.' I was nonplussed for a moment, 'So it wasn't just Railways.'

'No.'

'I see — well, if you can open up there again you'll be able to take on men like young Tom Breames, won't you?'

'Of course. That's my intention.'

It was a lovely day. Clear and sharp holding the tang and excitement of autumn. Nostalgic somehow.

'Why didn't you tell me this before, Garth?' I questioned.

'Because mines are men's business,' he answered.

'Providing women can induce those with the wherewithal in their pockets to invest,' I reminded him sharply.

Garth's glance was ironic, but he said nothing, and presently we were on our way back to Tharne.

It was inevitable that with the new interest of the Venn property demanding attention, Garth was more away from the house than formerly. As the days grew shorter I frequently went over to Carnbrooke and occupied hours by wandering round my old home, re-arranging pictures, giving a vigorous polish here and there, or seeing that no woodworm was invading the ancient furniture, and that the curtains and carpets were in good repair. Mrs Crabbe did her best, but her old eyes were slowly failing, and except for very important matters she refused to wear her glasses, saying there was nothing wrong with her sight, why should she make herself into an old granny before her time?

Sometimes I spent an hour in the kitchen or small parlour with her, chatting, and praising her crochet work, which was still excellent despite her poor eyes. She made yards and yards of lace, and afterwards sewed it on to table-cloths and doyleys. For the hemming the odious glasses were brought out and perched upon her nose.

'But I doan' *have* to use them,' she was always saying then, 'et's just that I doan' like wastin' anythin', an they cost sumthen', these ugly things did.'

'Of course,' I agreed, feeling amused but slightly sad at the same time.

The weather was mild for that time of the year, veiled with

mists in early mornings and evenings which left the ditches damp with slippery fallen leaves. Sometimes the skies never completely cleared. The air then was dim and close about Tharne, hugging the trees of garden and copse into spectral shapes, yet beautifying the cobwebbed branches with diamond drops.

Grey damp light pressed against the windows creeping under doors with chilling persistence. I longed at such times for the crisp sharp days of winter, and the brittle crunch of frost under foot when I walked the moors. Sometimes I went to Braggas, or a farm for cream. Berries smelled rich and pungent from the hedges; there was seldom any wind to stir the crouched bracken or lingering yellow leaves of sycamore, thorn, and elder.

One afternoon when thin sunlight, for a change, penetrated the clouds, giving the landscape the furred radiance of an Impressionist painting, a note was delivered by hand for Garth. It came from Penzance, and was from Ruana. Garth frowned and read the letter a second time.

'Ruana's ill and confined to bed,' he told me. 'She urgently wishes to see me.'

Foreboding filled me.

'Why?'

'How do I know?'

'Are you going?'

My voice must have sounded cold. He flung me a shrewd searching glance and said, 'What do you think?'

I shrugged, annoyed that he should ask such a question after what had happened, yet not wanting to appear quite heartless by saying 'no'.

'That's for you to decide,' I told him. 'It will mean I shall be left alone in the house with Nanny and the baby again. It's the servants' half-day. But—'

'Is that so very distressing?'

I could hardly answer, 'Yes it is, I hate being shut up in this place with only Sarah Cullen for company — she dislikes me and makes me feel uncomfortable,' so I merely remarked, 'Distressing? No. Not exactly. But—'

'But what?'

'Oh, Garth, I don't know. You must do what you think fit. I said so, didn't I?'

His voice was a little softer when he replied.

'I'd like to think you meant it, Caroline. Ruana behaved very badly I know. But she is getting on, and she had a raw deal with her father—' His voice wavered. I knew he had made up his mind to go.

'Lots of people round here have had raw deals,' I snapped. 'Or had you forgotten?'

The familiar obvious thrust of his chin appeared.

'No, I'd forgotten nothing. Least of all your complete incapacity, it seems, to be charitable for once.'

'Charity! you talk of charity, when − when—' I struggled with rising indignation for a drawn-out moment, and ended by saying, 'All right, yes, of course you should go. If she's *really* ill, I mean—'

Glancing through the window to the drive where the messenger, a man, stood by his horse waiting, Garth said, curtly, 'Of course she's ill. This—' waving the note, 'comes straight from the hotel. The doctor apparently was there this morning.'

'Oh very well. Don't wait then. If you think it's urgent perhaps you should be off.'

Garth stuffed the letter into his pocket without letting me read it, turned his his heel and went to the door. I waited miserably for him to come and kiss me but he didn't.

'I shall change immediately and ride cross-country,' he told me curtly. 'It will be quicker than taking the gig through Braggas. Meanwhile I'll inform the man. Expect me when you see me.'

He slammed the door, and was gone.

Five minutes later I watched his figure astride his favourite gelding cantering down the drive, and finally disappearing beyond the lane leading to the moors.

I was annoyed with myself for not having handled the incident more tactfully; miserable that so many conversations with my husband ended in argument and cold misunderstanding; and lonely.

Never had Tharne felt so hostile or depressing. The fragile, fitful sunlight streaming from odd angles through windows and between curtains across the flagged floors, only seemed to accentuate the brooding, shadowed recesses and alcoves, giving intensity to the watchful portraits and archaic foreign relics cluttering the walls.

I was on my way to the nursery shortly after tea, when Nanny appeared unexpectedly at the end of the passage leading from the kitchens. Just as though she'd known I was about to visit my own daughter, I thought resentfully.

She put a finger to her lips and hurried towards me. Her soft slippers made no sound on the floor.

'If you were going up to see Heather,' she said, 'I wouldn't, just at the moment, Lady de Verries, she was a bit fretful earlier this afternoon and is sleeping now. Give her—' she glanced at the clock '—half an hour. She'll be ready for her feed then.'

'I shouldn't disturb her,' I said coldly.

Sarah smiled. 'Of course not, intentionally. I was only making a suggestion.'

Thinking I might perhaps have sounded unreasonable, and possibly was, I shrugged.

'Very well, if you think that best I'll go up later.'

The look of self-satisfaction on Nanny's face did not escape me. Her upright stance as she returned to the kitchen, her air of competence, were quite infuriating.

I went through the parlour to the conservatory and tried to busy myself snipping bits of old growth from potted plants on shelves. The geranium scent was heavy, and moisture trickled down the glass. I'd never really cared for the hot-house atmosphere, and as I wandered about, picking a few exotic blooms of a foreign plant, memories of my first meeting with Manfred rose suffocatingly, reviving a host of past fears.

I took the flowers into the parlour quickly, and laid them in a cool place on the table ready for arranging in a vase, once Sarah was safely out of the kitchen. I waited about until almost half an hour had passed.

Then I went upstairs.

As I went along the landing towards the baby's room everywhere and everything seemed very quiet. There was no sound of Nanny talking to the child, no slight indication of life, no murmur or tinkle of pots from downstairs.

I was suddenly apprehensive.

I hurried on, past the gloomy curve leading up the stairs to the high tower room, trying to dispel an absurd and quite irrational rising fear.

When I entered the nursery a dying beam of sunlight

temporarily dazzled me. I blinked, and glanced towards the crib. It was empty, half on its side, with the pink silk quilt and blanket on the floor. I rushed towards it, picked the quilt up automatically, staring helplessly round. There was no sign of Heather anywhere. My heart pounded.

'Nanny,' I called, 'Nanny — where are you, Sarah? Where's baby?'

There was no reply.

I started searching the room, then realising the futility, ran back along the landing, past the nursery to the stairs. I called again; there was still no answer. Running, almost jumping — with one hand brushing the banisters, I raced down to the hall and from there to the kitchens.

Nanny was standing by a stove heating some milk.

'Where's baby?' I gasped, with one hand feeling my throat which was so constricted I could hardly breath. 'Where's Heather?'

She turned, mouth half-open, eyes wide with astonishment and disbelief.

'Heather? What do you mean? In the nursery of course. I was just getting—'

'But she's not. She's not.'

Sarah's cool brow crinkled. 'She's not what, madam — my lady?' There was cold unspoken contempt in her voice.

'She's not there,' I almost screamed. 'The crib's overturned. The blankets and things are on the floor. But Heather's gone.'

Sarah took the pan off the light and came towards me. 'She can't have gone. I've only been down here a few minutes and she was cooing to herself when I left.'

'But she's not any more. There's no sign of her.'

Sarah put the pan aside, and rubbed her hands on a towel. 'We'll go and see, together,' she remarked steadily talking to me in the manner of a sane person to someone mad. 'When we get there I expect we shall find her sitting on the floor beaming like some innocent little cherub — naughty little thing.'

'How? She can't even walk.'

'She can crawl,' Nanny affirmed, 'she's probably taken it into her head to hide. Did you look under the table, Madam?'

'No. No — why should I? There was no sound — nothing. You can always tell if a baby's about.'

'Not always. Sometimes they can act like young animals. Look how a cat plays you up. You can call and call and it'll never appear until it thinks fit. Quiet and still as a mouse it can be—'

'Heather isn't a cat or a mouse,' I said shortly.

She didn't reply, just turned quickly and hurried ahead of me, taking the back stairs which were nearer to the baby's and her own quarters.

I followed.

When she opened the nursery door, the room looked just the same as when I'd left. The crib was in the same position, the curtains trembling slightly in a drift of wind from the slit of open window. I rushed forward and looked down. There was no sign of anything or anyone lying below. In any case a small baby could hardly push a sash open to climb through, and down the thick masses of ivy trailing and entangling the tall granite wall.

We searched almost soundlessly, but frenziedly – at least I did. Nanny appeared unconcerned.

'Heather will turn up,' she said, with deadly certainty. 'I'm sure of it. We'll go to my rooms now and look there. Then when we come back she'll probably have got tired of the game and be smiling, sweet as pie, or sitting with her thumb in her mouth, thoroughly pleased with herself.'

I didn't believe it, but as a last hope I accompanied Sarah into the adjoining room.

Heather was not there. After a few minutes, further intensive searth of the nurseries it was clear to me that the baby was missing.

'Now what have you to say?' I demanded. 'Have you any other ideas?' My voice sounded shrill in my ears.

'Yes.' Sarah stared me very straight in the eyes, her expression dead-pan, but somehow condemning. Then she spoke.

'What about those tinkers? The gipsies?'

My heart lurched.

'What do you mean?'

'They have a fancy for pretty babies,' Nanny remarked with chilling insinuation. 'They use them, for begging, and heaven knows what else. I did warn you, Lady de Verries, when you encouraged that wild-looking woman with the heather. But you said she was all right.'

I was aghast.

'Yutha, do you mean, but she was — she's a friend. I told you—'

'She's not the only one, is she? There are quite a number at the camp near Castle Cromme?'

'I don't believe it,' I protested. I was trembling. 'It couldn't happen. How could it?'

Sarah shrugged. 'Unfortunately Cook left the back door unlocked when she went out this afternoon. I only discovered it when I went down. Anyone could have crept in and hidden for a time. Then the window — those sly creatures are nimble as foxes and can climb like cats. A man or young boy could easily have opened it and got through. I wouldn't put anything past them.'

Part of what she was saying registered. But only part. At first I couldn't accept her outrageous statement. When the full implication at last penetrated my mind I knew there was only one thing to do. I must go up the moor myself to the camp. I stared at Sarah coldly.

'Stay here,' I said, in tones no longer hesitant, but as a command. 'Don't move from Tharne when I'm away. We'll soon see if the gipsies have anything to do with it.'

'Where are you going, Madam?'

'Where do you think?' I asked her coldly.

'Not up there surely. Sir Garth wouldn't approve at all.'

'Whether Sir Garth approves or not isn't my concern or yours. I'm going to find my child.'

I went mechanically to the door. Sarah opened it for me. At that moment it seemed to me a thin sound — either laughter — a child's laughter — or the beginning of a wail echoed from somewhere above, — somewhere in the vicinity of old Sir Bruce's study.

I stopped abruptly. 'What was that?'

'What?'

'Didn't you hear it? It sounded like a child—' I pushed past her and ran along the landing until I reached the recess and bend where the narrow stone steps led up to the higher tower room. Nanny followed.

I stood at the foot of the short flight, listening.

There was no further sound.

'You're imagining things, Lady de Verries,' I heard Sarah saying in flat unemotional tones. 'How could a baby be up there?'

'How could a baby disappear into thin air?'

'She has *not* disappeared into thin air?' Nanny stated flatly. 'She's either playing somewhere, or — well, I don't like to think of it, but those tinkers—'

'Don't call them tinkers.'

'I'm sorry, I'm sure. I'd forgotten they were your friends.'

In spite of my distress the sarcasm in her voice did not escape me. But I pretended not to notice.

'I'm going up,' I told her, taking the first few steps to the heavy door. The light was very poor. I tried the latch which had an iron drop-handle. It moved, but wouldn't open. I suddenly remembered there was a lock at the side which had a key hanging from a hook nearby. I had only noticed it once when I was exploring the house and had surmised that the old man had had it put there for his own use, and to ensure privacy when he wanted it. I looked, but the key was not there. A blueish light streamed through a window immediately facing the short passage from the landing, casting a thin beam across the floor. I glanced down. There was no sign of the key.

'Where is it?' I asked, with panic gathering again.

'What?'

'The key. You know what. I heard something — listen.' It seemed to be a furtive scratching scrambling sound came from above, then silence.

'Rats,' Sarah said contemptuously. 'Just rats. And I've no idea where the key is. No one goes to that place. Look, Lady de Verries—' she touched my shoulder placatingly, 'you're getting hysterical. How could Heather be up there? She may be able to crawl a little — but not up those steep steps. Now be reasonable. I really must get back to the nursery. Come along now, please; you're in no fit state to be on your own. We must have another search through the nurseries. I'm quite sure your baby's all right.'

Her hand tightened on my arm. I pulled myself free. 'Leave me alone. Where's that key? I must have it. And I'm not hysterical; do you understand?' I stared hard into her clear grey eyes. They were very cold, like glass. 'Every corner of this house

should be searched. And I believe — I believe you know something about all this—' There! it was out. I broke off breathlessly.

Nanny sighed. 'That's quite ridiculous, Lady de Verries, and
I advise you to get yourself under control before Sir Garth
returns. I'd give you the key if I had it or knew where it is. But I
don't. I'm sorry.'

She walked stiffly ahead of me towards the nursery quarters. I
stood for a moment or two watching, then ran ahead, hoping
against all hope that the baby would be back when I got there.

But she wasn't.

I made no further effort to argue with Sarah. Through my
distress the thought of Yutha and the gipsies penetrated.
Nanny's remark that Yutha was not the only one, was disturb-
ingly true. There were several vans at the camp; a number of
families. Any, out of the itinerant community might have
fostered a fancy for Heather, or been in need of a small baby for
begging purposes.

Heather might have been spotted lying in her pram by prying
eyes. Greed could have prompted a kidnap.

But I found it hard to believe. Difficult — yet possible, and I
knew I had to miss no clue, no chance of having her safely back
at Tharne.

Yutha might know something. The Romanies had signs. She,
herself, had mentioned secret writing by the gates of the house.

So I pulled on a pair of boots, slipped on a cape, and ran
downstairs through the hall, and out of the front door. I didn't
call at Carnbrooke, but from the drive cut down a farm track
that led eventually across the lane, and from there narrowed
into a sheep-path. It was narrow, winding along the base of the
moor. I walked quickly, occasionally running, pushing gradually upwards, past boulders and through furze, while the light
deepened, turning to a greenish glow above the brown hills.
There was a sudden protruding bump of the hill on my left,
looming like some gigantic immense prehistoric monster as I
approached. I hurried round, knowing that the gipsy site lay in
its dip a little beyond.

There was no sound though; no murmur of people talking,
no guiding light but that of a pale moon already climbing above
the distant horizon. And when I reached the spot where the

encampment should have been, I stared blankly. There was nothing but a few empty cans, and ridges where wheels had been, the indentures left by horses' hooves, and a broken pot lying by a stone.

They had gone. To a fair somewhere, I supposed, dully. The early autumn fairs were already in full swing through Cornwall; the gipsies never stayed in one place for long at that particular season.

I turned and made my way back to Tharne, filled with an eerie, hopeless desolation. If Heather had really been stolen would I ever see her again? And how would I explain to Garth? Sarah Cullen would be bound to emphasise that she'd warned me about Yutha.

Inevitably the blame would appear to be mine.

But it wasn't, I told myself stubbornly as I plunged back desperately into the house. Sarah Cullen knew something; I was sure of it. But why should she lie about a helpless baby?

I was exhausted and breathing heavily when I walked up the stairs to the nursery.

I opened the door and went in.

Then I had a shock.

Heather was propped up in her cot, holding her teddy bear, and gurgling happily. Nanny held a tray with the childishly decorated bowl and baby spoon ready for washing up.

Sarah turned, staring, when I entered with my skirts and cloak all muddied and my hair loose.

Relief, shock, and the anger of reaction blazed up in me. Speech was incoherent as I exclaimed, 'Why — What? — She's here. How—'

'I told you, Madam, didn't I?' Nanny said coolly, complacently. 'You were making a fuss and getting yourself all wound up just for nothing. Heather's all right, aren't you, love?'

'Where was she?' I demanded. 'Explain immediately. I've been worried to death.'

'She was in the cupboard,' Sarah answered, pointing to a low piece of furniture with doors where linen was generally kept. 'I did tell you she must be hiding, if you remember. Still — everything's all right now. And if I were you, Lady de Verries, I'd try and settle down so things appear normal when Sir Garth gets back. He wouldn't like to find you so distraught for nothing.'

Was there a threat underlying her words? I couldn't quite tell.

But of one thing I was certain.

Things were far from normal yet. A great deal of explaining still had to be done.

When I glanced round before leaving the nursery I saw one baby sock lying on the floor near the door. Nanny didn't notice as I bent down quickly and picked it up. She was too concerned in tying Heather's little jacket at the neck.

I pushed it unobtrusively into my pocket, not knowing quite why.

On reaching the bedroom I placed it in a chest where I kept odd items of clothing. Then I washed and changed hurriedly, in preparation for Garth's return.

I was only just in time.

I had flung myself on the bed for a brief rest when he came in. I got up quickly to greet him. But his expression chilled me into silence.

'What's this I hear?' he asked coldly, 'about you worrying Nanny with your hysterics and rushing away up the moor like a mad woman? Have you really taken leave of your senses or what? And remember this, Caroline — whatever stupid scenes you want to make in my absence I won't have Nanny upset by any false accusations, neither will I have you trailing after a bunch of tinkers. And that's final.'

I stared at him, too shocked and bewildered at first to speak.

Then I managed to say dully, 'As you never believe me, I won't try and explain now—'

'Perhaps that's as well. I would hardly be naive enough to accept your fairy tales.' He bent down and took me by my shoulders, staring into my eyes. I faced him defiantly thinking, 'If he's going to strike me, let him. I don't care any more. I don't care about anything. But one day I'll make him sorry for this.'

I waited.

He let me go abruptly, shrugged, picked my bedraggled cloak from the floor. 'You'd better get this cleaned, or else send it with my most sincere curses to any tinker lover you may have,' he retorted cruelly.

Then the door slammed.

My body suddenly crumpled. If he could think such a

thing! — but he didn't. The idea was preposterous — his last
bitter words merely a weapon to wound me. All the same, even
lies hurt. I felt weak and degraded, wondering how, or who —
had planted such a vile suggestion in his head.

Nanny.

But Sarah wouldn't have dared. Not openly. She was too
clever — just devious and calculating. I wondered what she'd
told him when he'd come in. Obviously the true facts had been
falsified to a highly colourful account of my own actions meant
to make him believe I was off my head — or very near to it.

Was that her intention? Was she scheming to get Garth for
herself?

As I sat slumped on the bed a rush of blazing anger filled me.
The wicked scheming creature! No wonder she'd been so
friendly with Ruana; they were two of a kind, only Nanny was
far worse, with no excuse for her behaviour.

I jumped up, remembering things I'd temporarily forgotten;
quite small things, that under the circumstances could be very
important indeed; — the faint movements and murmuring I'd
heard, or thought I'd heard from old Sir Bruce's quarters when
Sarah and I were searching for Heather; the disappearance of
the key to the tower, and Sarah's skilful manner of diverting me
from the subject! — in a flash it occurred to me again that the
baby had been up there all the time — that Nanny had known it
and had therefore put her there herself for some sly purpose of
her own.

To frighten me?

Could it be true? Was even she capable of going to such cruel
contrived means to put me in the wrong?

Yes, she was. I realised in that brief period of cold reasoning
there was very little she wouldn't do in order to discredit me in
my husband's eyes.

But how could I prove it?

I searched wildly for an answer. My head was reeling. All I
could think of was to get Garth and Nanny up to the Tower.
Some sign might remain of the child's presence if she'd been up
there — baby footprints in dust on the floor — a toy perhaps;
but no — Sarah would have noticed a toy when she fetched her
down again.

Then I remembered the tiny sock; the sock I'd picked up

224 *The Granite King*

in the nursery. Just one. Where was the other? The little girl could have pulled it off herself of course; it could be lying among the blankets. If it was, that idea was no use. Still, there could be something else — a piece of ribbon — signs of fur from the teddy bear — oh any number of give-away possibilities crowded one upon the other through my head. Everything at that point was deduction. But the conviction that Heather had been secreted somewhere in old Sir Bruce's rooms — bribed by a sweet or some new toy persisted. On the whole she was a contented little thing and Nanny would have seen she was completely settled before she went downstairs again on a pretence, for my benefit, of warming milk. She'd known I was intent on seeing the child and guessed I'd go to the nursery. If I didn't Sarah would have found some excuse to lure me there, or else have conveyed the news of her disappearance — her 'baby game', herself.

Everything suddenly seemed to be clear, to make a cunning pattern that would never have emerged if it had not been for those two important small memories — the echo of a child's faint cry, and a missing sock.

I went to the chest, lifted the lid, opened it, and seeing the sock was safe, covered it more effectively with a silk shawl, and then walked quickly along the landing towards Nanny's and Heather's domain.

I was almost there when Garth appeared from the nursery.

'I thought you were resting,' he said shortly.

'No. Why should I rest when there's this mystery of Heather to unravel?'

Garth shook his head slowly, unbelievingly. 'Do go and lie down,' he said. 'There's no mystery. The child is safe. Nanny has explained. You were imagining things. You're probably run down following the move, and the concussion you had from your fall. A kind of post reaction. In the morning we'll have the doctor to examine you.'

He sounded so reasonable that for a moment my confidence ebbed. Then I said loudly and clearly, 'I'm not sick, Garth, or mad, as Sarah's trying to make you think. I'm sure—' my voice wavered.

'Yes?'

'I'm *almost* sure,' I resumed, 'that Heather was in the tower room all the time, where Nanny put her.'

There: the accusation was out.

I waited, breathlessly, watching his frown slowly change to complete incomprehension. He was going to scold or else deride me, I thought miserably, put me in my place as though I was a foolish child playing some ridiculous trick. But he did neither.

For a long pause his eyes stared very directly into my own. The light from the lamp in the side-window caught their brilliance filming their blue with flashes of gold – of questions and unspoken moods that somehow brought us together briefly in communication.

'Do you know what you're suggesting, Caroline?' he asked presently. 'Do you realise your implications?'

'Yes, perfectly. I couldn't go up there, you see, at the time. The key wasn't there. I heard something, and I asked Sarah for it – for the key. But she said she'd no idea—'

I didn't finish explaining. Nanny appeared just at that moment from the nursery. She came close up, and stood looking down at me from her superior height. Her face was very calm. There was the suggestion of a smile on her lips.

'Were you talking about me, Lady de Verries?' she enquired coolly.

'Your name cropped up,' Garth replied. 'And I think perhaps—'

'Yes, Sir Garth?'

'Just to put my wife's mind at rest, it might be a good idea to have a look round for the attic key.'

Nanny's brows lifted.

'The key? But it's there, on its rail.' Her voice sounded incredulous.

I saw Garth's lips tighten. He glanced at me quickly, then said, 'Well, just to make sure we'll have a look, shall we?'

He turned and went to the door that shut the steps from the rest of the house, followed by Sarah Cullen and myself. Garth stopped, staring for a few seconds through the half-light. I didn't have to wonder what he saw; I saw it for myself – the gleam of the heavy key hanging on its usual hook, at the side. I felt, rather than heard, Nanny's complacent reaction – then the smug satisfaction in her voice when she said, 'You see, the key was always there, Sir Garth. It wasn't missing at all. Her ladyship was mistaken – distressed of course by Heather's little game—'

Suddenly her lies were too much for me.

'You cheat,' I cried, 'you liar. What are you trying to do to me?' I took a step forward. Garth grasped my arm. 'Stop it, both of you. I will not have two women quarrelling in my house.'

What Nanny's reaction was to his short command, I had no way of judging. She had lifted her head and turned away as though to go back to the nursery. Garth stopped her.

'Come along,' he said, 'both of you. As we're here, we may as well go up and have a glance round.'

Sarah said nothing. She stood perfectly calmly a little behind me, as Garth inserted the key.

We went inside.

Dim blueish light penetrated from the one high window throwing a misty radiance round the granite walls. It was almost dark outside; shadows patterned the musty interior. But it seemed a faint perfume mingled with the smell of wood, and the parchment of papers and books on the table. That was all.

My heart sank.

'Would you like me to fetch a lamp, Sir Garth?' I heard Nanny ask politely. 'If you want to look round properly a better light would help.'

'There's no need, thank you,' Garth replied curtly. He took two or three short strides towards the small fireplace which obviously had been added to the room not so many years ago — for Sir Bruce's benefit probably.

'When was there a fire last here?' he enquired looking very directly at Nanny. I glanced at her myself. Her face was a set blurred disc against the shadows.

'I can't tell you exactly,' she said. 'I know it's made ready and lit at least once a month to keep everything aired. The girl sees to that. But—'

'The once-a-month must have been very recently,' Garth said placing both hands to the gate. 'It's still warm. And no attempt has been made to clear the embers. But of course I suppose that's planned for tonight—'

'I don't know the servants' plans,' Nanny answered stiffly. 'My concern is with your daughter.'

'Yes, of course,' Garth's voice was so reasonable, so formal and cool, only someone who knew him well would have recognised its rising underlying tension.

I stood perfectly still, waiting.

For a few moments nothing happened, then Garth got up, rubbing his hands, and remarked pointedly, 'My uncle must have been a very careless eccentric, or he certainly wouldn't have bothered about having a fireguard.'

'A fireguard?' Nanny echoed.

Garth pointed to a wrought-iron shield affair lying on the stone floor where it had fallen.

'*That*, Nanny.'

Sarah laughed shortly. 'I suppose it was a safety precaution.'

'For what? Rugs? But there aren't any — except for that woolly one over there, by the inglenook.'

He pointed to a corner. My eyes followed.

I hadn't noticed the rug at first. Now, with my eyes becoming accustomed to the gloom I saw it — pale, furry, and half rolled up.

I pushed past, ran across the small interior, knelt down and straightened the soft material. A film of powder fell from it, and something else — a child's sock.

For quite a minute it seemed as though the scene had become petrified; a static impression depicting a stage-set. No one spoke or moved. All I was aware of was holding Heather's sock up, with my hand shaking slightly.

Then I said, 'Here it is; Heather's sock. The other one's in my own chest. I found it in the nursery after I got back. So she was here all the time.'

I was staring hard at Nanny's face. It looked blank, expressionless.

'Well?' Garth demanded, 'what about it Nanny? Can you explain? I very much hope so.'

Sarah gave a short dry laugh.

'I don't think I need to,' she said. 'No crime's been committed. Yes, the baby was here. But she was in no danger, I've always cared for her, and you can prove nothing against me. If you ask me—' she stared at me contemptuously '—I've done you a good turn, shaken a little of the complacency from your high-and-mighty lady wife — if you can call her that—'

'But why?' I gasped. '*Why?*'

'Why did I put her there? I'll tell you. You had everything. I'd had nothing. Since being a child — and an unwanted one — I've had to fight every inch of the way to get where I am. But you don't want my life story, do you? And I'm certainly not going to give it. You see you were always so smug about things, so condescending, and so obvious! Playing your own little games with any man of your choice, airing your looks and graces; taking everything and giving nothing. *Nothing.* Did you even care what Miss Ruana felt when you stole her place?'

'Ruana?' I was mystified.

'Yes. Miss Ruana de Verries, the rightful owner of this mausoleum. Oh, I don't envy her the house; in fact I envy her nothing. She's generous, you see. So generous it's a pleasure to join in any small game of hers if she wishes me to—'

'You mean Ruana was at the back of all this?' Garth's tones were harsh.

'I didn't say that,' Nanny said. 'And I'm saying nothing more about this — this ridiculous business except that if you try to harm me, take me to court or anything I'll deny everything flat. And you'll be the laughing stock of the district.' There was complete silence until Garth spoke. His tones, though quiet, were icily, dangerously cold.

'Don't threaten me, Miss Cullen, I've no intention of giving you the satisfaction of publicity, or of bringing the name of my cousin — Miss de Verries — into disgrace. As you must realise, she's become a sick woman mentally, and emotionally. I'm sorry for her. Without you she may have a chance of recovering her balance — in time. With you she certainly won't. So I'm prepared to make a deal. You'll take a cheque from me tomorrow for a month's salary in advance, with the proviso to the effect that you will never intentionally see or speak to her again.'

'I—'

'Wait. If you break your undertaking I'll have you behind bars in no time. And that's not a threat, it's a promise.'

'I'd planned—'

'I know what you'd planned. You'd planned to go to Torquay with her next week as her companion. She told me as much this afternoon when I visited her. But instead I shall provide you with a ticket to London. And I shall make sure you stay there for quite some time. I have the means of doing so, I can assure you.'

Nanny's face had gone very pale.

'You're exaggerating. You can't—'

'I can do anything I've a mind to, Miss Cullen, believe me.'

I glanced at Garth's face. It was perfectly still and set; so hard that Sarah's eyes flinched, and she hung her head. Garth never moved until she muttered something, went to the door and left, not even slamming it behind her.

Garth still stood for some seconds, resolute, immobile; I didn't speak, just stared at his strong profile outlined and reflected from the lamplight below, against the wall. The shadow − magnified through the distorted light, held, momentarily, the uncanny quality of the great carn itself − of the Granite King reigning supreme over its own territory.

I felt suddenly faint. It seemed that the force of an earthquake hit me. The floor swayed under my feet. The walls seemed to converge and enclose me. Then I found myself supported by Garth's arms, and heard him saying, 'It's all right, Caroline. It's over now.'

What was over? I wondered, dragging myself back to the present. Everything was so complicated and difficult − so hard to assess what was real and what false.

But when the light in his eyes registered, I knew. So clear it was − so bright and all consuming with desire, holding the radiant blue of summer skies and the wild brilliance of Cornish seas under a frosted moon.

Yet above and beyond all that − human, filled with warmth and passion for me − his wife.

I tried to speak, but he placed a finger on my lips.

'Not yet,' he said. 'There'll be time for words later.'

He caught me up in his arms and carried me from the Tower to our own room. The nightmare had turned into a fairy-tale after all.

For that short journey I really did feel like a character in a book from childhood. But the illusion was brief. After all, I was no child, and Garth no cardboard hero-figure. He was flesh-and-blood, strength and weakness, jealous, demanding, generous, adoring, selfish and above all − completely male. The one I'd been searching for, and knew to be mine at last.

My love.

18

The next morning, following the final settlement with Sarah, Garth drove her himself in the gig to Penzance, where he saw her safely with her few possessions, on to the steam train for her journey to London.

'I waited until the train was well away,' he told me when he returned, 'and I think we can safely assume now we've seen the last of Miss Cullen.'

'Did you call on Ruana?' I enquired.

'Just for a few minutes, on the way back.'

'How was she?'

'She seemed all right. Edgy, of course. That's natural.'

'Oh.' I didn't pretend to be sympathetic. 'So she'd recovered quickly from her — illness.'

'Don't be sarcastic, Caroline. It doesn't suit you.'

'I know, but—'

'Oh she behaved badly. We know that. But very childishly. It's far better for us to see the whole sordid little plot in such a light, don't you think—?'

'Not entirely,' I told him. 'The sordid little plot, as you call it, could have spoiled our lives if it had worked.'

'Nothing can spoil a life,' Garth retorted quickly, 'except the ones concerned. And I hardly think we'd have continued bickering for ever. We're far too — involved.'

'Yes.' I sighed. 'But to think of her deliberate pretence — feigning illness, and it was only that, wasn't it — just a trick to get you away so that wretched Cullen woman could torture me?'

He gave me a slow smile, 'Luckily you've a remarkable talent for recovery,' he said. 'And you've tortured me quite a bit in the past. Remember?'

He took my chin between a finger and thumb, and tilted my face up to meet his. I pulled myself away.

'Don't, Garth. It's no laughing matter.'

'Neither is it so terribly melodramatic as you're trying to make it. Look, my love, we've got to put the past behind us, and concentrate on the present from now on. I thought we'd decided to do that. Ruana's off to Torquay tomorrow, where she'll no doubt find some congenial acquaintance or companion to make up a bit for her miserable life with the old man. I'm not making excuses for what she did — she's a battle-axe of a character with a deeply rooted grudge that she had to work off somehow. Whether she's done it yet I don't know. But she's got a chance to, at last. Anyway—' his expression hardened, 'I'm going to hear no more recriminations, or have you fretting over what might-have-been. The worst didn't happen, and all things considered I think we're both quite lucky. We can go on from here—'

A sudden thought struck me.

'No, we can't, Garth. We can't. Not from this place.'

'What do you mean?'

'I don't want to live here,' I told him firmly. 'It's depressing — too large, and lonely, and filled with ghosts. If you try and make me it's no use. I just can't forget some things. Don't you understand? Won't you even try?'

Something in my eyes, my voice — where a knot of emotion was gathering — must have conveyed a little of the tumult, the distress — I was feeling. He took my hands in his, shaking his head slowly. Then he said:

'Maybe. In part anyway; as much as a man can, of a woman's unpredictability.'

'Well?' I queried after a pause.

He shrugged. 'I don't know. I'm not too keen on the house myself. But I have responsibilities. It's mine, my heritage, I suppose you'd call it. Ruana's gone now; I can't just throw up the estate, especially in view of the plans I have.'

'I wouldn't want you to,' I said eagerly. 'We could stay at Carnbrooke for a time, then find somewhere else in the district if you wanted. Tharne perhaps be converted into something, or—'

'Or what?'

'I don't know. But — but if you love me, Garth, please please don't make me stay here.'

We discussed the problem seriously after that, and eventually recognising how deeply I felt — perhaps sensing for the first time the extent of my aversion to Tharne, Garth, with some reluctance, gave in.

We moved back to Carnbrooke the following week.

I shall never forget the first night of our return.

It had been heavy and close all day — far too warm for the time of year. The cattle in the fields had been restless; the atmosphere was uneasy, with perfectly windless yellow skies hugging the brown earth. In the distance the Granite King was only a subdued dark shape towering over the grey Atlantic. It was as though all Nature waited for some approaching climax to shatter threatened disaster. Something was going to happen; I felt it in my bones, although Garth laughed when I told him.

'Of course it is,' he agreed. 'We're going to make love. I'm going to ride with you up to that old carn you've such a passion for, and have you there — all sweet and wild and newly-born — mine completely as you were meant to be from the very beginning.' His voice shook a little. I felt the warm blood suffuse my whole body, like flame. Passion stirred me with a hunger and magic I'd never thought to feel again.

'Oh, Garth.'

The half-smile on his lips died.

'Get your cape,' he said, 'and put something warm on your head. It may be cool up there—'

I glanced at the window. The light was already fading. 'It will soon be dark,' I said.

'You'd better hurry then.'

'Sometimes,' I said, before I moved to the door, 'I think you're a little crazy.'

'Sometimes, my darling, I have to be — with you,' he added after a short pause.

His blue eyes held mine for a moment, then I ran quickly from the room, and up the stairs for my cloak.

Five minutes later I was seated before Garth on his stallion, and we were cantering through the gates of the paddock up the slope of moor towards the Carn. A faint film of milky mist was steaming from the moist ground. The moon had not yet risen, but the Granite King rose darkly symbolic over the earth's veil.

I had tied a scarf over my head, but presently it loosened, and I let it fall, leaving my hair free in the tremulous wind.

The breath of heather and distant sea, of tumbled black-berries and all the pungent odours of the past season, mingled sensuously with the unseen forces of spring to come. My arms instinctively tightened round Garth's waist. A wild bird flew, screaming from the undergrowth. Our pace increased to a gallop. My heart sang, and my blood raced. It was as though through that evening of wanton desire and secret impulses, all Nature thirsted, and urged us to wild fulfilment. As we neared the standing stones, the ancient magic, born of countless centuries seemed to stir them to life, giving a semblance of movement, in obeyance to the old gods.

Garth reined, tethered the horse to a wind-blown tree, and opened his arms. I slipped into them, and he held me close, staring down into my face. I blinked. My spirit drowned, and was enmeshed by the brilliance of his eyes which even through the grey light were more blue and gold than the fire of lightning, stronger than the power of death, or the pangs of birth. Just for a second all knowledge was mine; − ages died, and mortality ceased. That one moment was in perfect unison with all mysteries. Beyond time or the enigma of existence. Itself complete and absolute.

Then Garth moved.

I could hear my own sigh as he turned, and holding me firmly against him, walked steadily upwards to the Granite King. There he lay me down below the giant shape, where I lay supine, as women must have lain with their lovers in primeval times, waiting either for death or the purging and plunge of passion.

I closed my eyes as he untied my cape, and disrobed me. My arms reached towards him blindly; his flesh was strong on mine − in me and of me, as bodies and spirit became submerged in a tumultuous wave of mounting desire.

The present, for an unknown period, died.

In that moment of culmination the earth and sky faded, taking me to a vortex of leaping darkness and utter fulfilment.

When at last sight registered, the first star hung jewel-like above. Mist was already lapping the feet of the Granite King; but the gaunt proud face was starkly clear and cold in the twilight.

Strength of movement returned at last. We both stood up. The air was suddenly colder. Garth wrapped clothes and cloak round me, and pulled on his cape. From the west a fleet of clouds rose, blurring the last dying light.

The tethered horse neighed. Somewhere far away an ominous clap of thunder rolled.

Garth took my hand, lifted and placed me on the animal's back, then swung himself into the saddle.

Neither of us spoke; there was no need.

We rode easily at first, then faster through the heightening wind. When we reached Tharne stables the horizon had deepened to encroaching black shot with zig-zagged forks of lightning flame.

We were in time to escape the rain. As we entered the doors of Carnbrooke only the first heavy drops were starting to fall.

Mrs Crabbe was waiting near the kitchens.

'It will be a wild storm, this one,' she predicted in sombre tones. 'The old cat knows. Never stirred from the fire he hasn' — all the time you wus out. An' the dog too, hunched on the rug he is, with his ears down, all sad an' frit lookin', I hadn' the heart to send him to the back, though et's my belief he had a roll in the dung somewhere this mornin'—' she looked at us questioningly, then continued, 'A fine night you've chosen to come back, an' no mistake. Mark my words, before dawn do come agen, there'll be a change in the land here'bouts. I remember in my granny's day how a whole mine was took — then there was that wreck of the *Lucy Girl*—' she went on muttering in a flood of retrospection that finally drew her back to the kitchen hearth.

Garth and I went upstairs. There was a fire in the large bedroom; everything looked freshly cleaned and polished; the air was fragrant with lavender and beeswax; a bowl of Christmas roses had been arranged on the dressing table. The girl and Mrs Crabbe had evidently been busy through the day. The silk quilt now, was already turned down, and the small French clock that had been Aunt Adela's was ticking away merrily on the mantelshelf. The curtains were drawn across the windows. Logs spitted, and Garth's favourite blend of Madeira with two glasses had been put ready on the small round rosewood table. In the small connecting room Heather was slumbering peacefully in her crib.

Already just a faint odour of cooking penetrated the atmosphere.

Mrs Crabbe must have opened the oven. I guessed she'd have a tasty evening meal prepared.

'Well,' Garth said, as I bounced on the bed contentedly, 'you've got what you want — me, Carnbrooke, your own place. Everything. How does it feel?'

'Good,' I answered. 'So very good — if you feel the same.'

He smiled; it was more of a grin.

'My feelings are neither here nor there any more,' he told me, 'unless of course — you take it into your pretty head to go trailing after some roaming gipsy lad.'

'Oh, Garth. How stupid. There was never any gipsy lad. It was only Yutha. She helped me when no one else did. And anyway — I don't suppose I'll ever seen her again.'

'When spring comes you will,' Garth predicted.

Spring. It was hard to imagine it at that moment. The lash of rain beat with increasing persistence at the windows, and as I went to the fire, with both hands extended towards the flames; menacing thunder growled from the hills. Lightning flared, and I hoped fervently no fishing craft had been caught by the angry tide. A little later the storm seemed to abate somewhat, and the rain died into a steady downpour. But during the night it revived and gathered force again.

Garth and I had gone to bed early — about a quarter to ten. Shortly after one o'clock I woke suddenly, and sat up, listening, shocked by the tremendous onslaught of the elements.

It was as though cannon-fire had split the earth. I dragged myself from Garth's protesting arms and ran to the window. Lightning streaked and zig-zagged down the slope from the Granite King, distorting the turrets and towers of Tharne into a semblance of swaying trembling shapes through the driven rain. Trees dipped defencessly to the sodden earth, swept on a whining hungry wind. For a brief few seconds fury faded to a creaking moan; and through that short recession it seemed to me that the sad wild ghosts of Tharne shuddered and cried through the wanton night — Kara's long black hair streamed with the clouds across the sky. The child's distorted form was a leaping shape behind the empty windows; Manfred's face and pale white hands were grasping, reaching, and thrust towards me.

I pulled the curtains close, turned suddenly and ran into the small adjoining room where Heather lay sleeping. Garth followed. The small rosy face was completely composed, her mouth crumpled like that of some budding flower; into a contented secret smile. I drew the soft blanket a little closer round her shoulders, and tip-toed with Garth back into our own room. Then with renewed fury the holocaust started up again.

There was no sleep for us after that. Even Mrs Crabbe was awake, and went down to the kitchen to make tea.

'I tole you, didn' I?' she said, as she handed us the tray. 'I said et wud be a wild one. On a night like this sumthen' or someone's always took. An you mark my words so t'will be — so t'will.'

Her prophecy was correct.

In the morning all was quiet again. But desolation was everywhere. Livestock had been drowned at adjoining farms — fowls and chickens mostly — windows broken, and trunks of trees lay across the lanes. Greens and winter crops of the small stone-walled fields had been massacred. Streams had over-flowed and flooded low-lying ground.

The tower of Tharne where old Sir Bruce had worked, had tumbled, and was now no more than a heap of fallen granite and timber strewn about the moor. Even the partially built wall of the estate on the sea-side, had great gaps in it. Down the lane to Braggas it was the same.

All that day Garth tramped about in his heavy cape and boots, assessing the damage as best he could.

I insisted on accompanying him during the morning, but when the horses had been found to be safe, I helped Adam and the boy remove them temporarily to our own smaller stables at Carnbrooke, and after that rejoined Mrs Crabbe.

'You do look fair done in,' she commented, as I went into the kitchen with my hair hanging wet and heavy over my forehead and shoulders, mud caking my boots and skirt. There was a great patch of dirt staining one cheek. 'Oh my dear luv! wherever've you bin? An whatever've you done to yourself?'

'I shall be all right,' I said, throwing myself on to a settle. 'If I can get these things off—' tugging at my boots, 'and have a good wash. And if you've got any of your nice hot broth—' I managed a smile. 'I'd like some.'

The old woman started busying herself at the stove, muttering in an undertone. When she had a pan and kettle in place she asked, 'An what's your good man going? The maister — Sir Garth I shud say.'

'He's gone to see if the mine's all right,' I told her. 'Part of Tharne's fallen. Did you know?'

'What? The old place?'

I nodded.

'The Tower, leaving a great hole where the staircase was.'

'Mercy me! what a miracle you wusn' there. You could've bin took — all of you.'

'Yes. And Heather. Is she still upstairs?'

'She's all right,' Mrs Crabbe assured me. 'What did you expect? With me in charge. I shud know how to look after little ones at my age. The girl's with her. Turned out better'n I thought — that one. Better'n that Nanny person. Didn' like her, for all her fine ways. Nosey. Cold — wouldn' have trusted her for all the tea in China—'

I let Mrs Crabbe ramble on until her flood of conversation was exhausted. Then, when the can of hot water was ready, I took it upstairs and had a thorough wash. After that I changed into a velvet day-dress. It was deep blue, not a crinoline, but full-skirted, bunched at the back, and trimmed with ribbon. When I'd bought it, I'd been in an extravagant mood, but I was grateful now for its softness and warmth. My body felt warm and glowing. And my hair, when dried and arranged loosely from a centre parting, shone from its wetting by soft rainwater.

I couldn't help being pleased by my reflection, and longed for Garth's return.

When he came in at last it was already past two o'clock. He hardly appeared to notice me, but just had a quick meal and then went out again, telling me he'd be 'back sometime,' when he'd taken a thorough further survey of the estate and lands. I felt — not piqued, but disappointed.

'Haven't you done enough for today?' I asked. 'You look tired.'

'I am; but so are many others. No one appears to be hurt — except for the livestock. But property's been badly hit. Not only Tharne itself; the farms.'

'What about the mine?'

'It's all right. A bit of flooding near the adit on the sea-side. All men safe though, thank God.'

'Then—'

Garth's face was stern, firmly set, when he gave me a very direct glance. For a moment his eyes softened. 'You look—' The ghost of a smile touched his mouth. He kissed me lightly on a cheek. His lips were very cold.' Beautiful,' he finished after the short pause. 'Keep your loveliness till I return.'

A second later, cape round his shoulders, head thrust forward under his stove hat, he was hurrying down the path to the lane. I could see that his leg was troubling him. The limp was again quite obvious; and I longed for the tempestuous months to be over and for next year's spring time, when surely we could be at peace, together.

The following day, because I insisted, Garth showed me round Tharne. 'It was struck,' Garth told me. 'A direct hit by a thunder-bolt. Adam found it this morning, early, amongst the rubble.'

I was shocked, but in a strange way also felt vindicated. The protruding corner of the north wing was gone, leaving no evidence whatever that a tower had once stood there – the domain of an eccentric recluse, and the scene of the monstrous trick played on me by Sarah. Shadows no longer haunted the musty interior – no fitful crying or wailing of violin strings mingled with the creakings of old wood or forgotten footsteps. Instead, above and beyond the scarred skeletal remains of the crumbled wall, brown far-flung boulders were visible on the open moors sloping to the sea. Gulls wheeled against the calm grey sky, and in the distance to the far right, the gaunt shape of the Granite King reigned indomitable. Supreme and invincible as it had been for countless centuries, over its own domain.

Later that afternoon Garth and I once more rode there. A lump of coast had been taken nearby, leaving a cleft that would no doubt become a future narrow ravine bordered by sea-plants and flowering thrift. I could imagine it providing the outlet for a clear stream flowing from the moor above. The earth had always been damp there.

But above – I turned my head slowly upwards. As I did so a pale quiver of sunlight pierced the sullen grey, throwing the great proud shape into sudden clarity.

And in its shadow Garth and I stood, hand in hand watching

and waiting while the ancient magnificence of Nature's handi-
work encompassed us. Did the monarch's head move slightly?
Did the outthrust chin turn towards us with a stone hand raised
in blessing? Or was it just the fading of light again behind the
cloud?

Whatever the answer — and there are some questions that
have none — it didn't matter.

My spirit felt free and relaxed as it had not done for many
many years.

And presently, as though following a benediction, Garth and
I returned to Carnbrooke.

There is little more to tell; only that during the following
months Garth decided to rebuilt the north wall of Tharne,
demolishing completely the back portion of the building.

His intention for the front of the house was to have it as a
museum, where the valuable historical relics stored away in the
attics and cellars by old Sir Bruce, could be viewed by interested
visitors.

'Old Adam might like the job of custodian — or curator —
for a bit of a salary,' he said. 'I'd no idea myself, even, that there
was so much valuable stuff hidden away. Books — yes; I knew
something of those. But the pottery — the armour, the swords
and shields and documents! For years that old miser had been
sitting on a fortune; and probably his own daughter had no
inkling of the extent of it. If she had, she kept mum. They were
both oddities — and I'm putting it that way because there's
been too much cruelty round here. Time's come for a little
charity, I think.'

'Will you contact Ruana?' I asked.

'Probably. Anything she wants — in reason, she can have.
But I think it's highly unlikely she'll ask, or condescend to
accept from me. I've heard — from quite a knowledgeable
source — that my repressed cousin is far from repressed any
more, but is titillating Devon society by her eccentric extrav-
aganzas and behaviour. Dressing like a duchess, I'm told, and
reigning like a queen over her court. She has her own suite of
rooms in some select hotel where she holds soirées, and gives
musical evenings.'

'But how can she afford it?'

Garth smiled.

'She was always quite rich, through some great aunt on her mother's side.' He shrugged, as the smile died into a wry twist of the lips. 'What a pity that a sense of duty could be so destructive. She wasn't bad-looking as a young woman. But completely cowed by obligations — as she thought — to tradition and her family. That wretched old man in particular.'

My hand gripped Garth's. 'I used to envy rich people so much. I'm quite glad now I never was. But if I had been, I don't think I'd have let duty spoil my life. I'm sure I wouldn't. I'm too — too—'

Garth didn't allow me to finish. In any case I was hardly certain myself what I was trying to say.

'My darling,' he interrupted, 'for both our sakes, don't try to rationalise your own qualities which are completely unpredictable.' He paused, then continued, with his blue eyes crinkling in his dark face, 'To me you'll never be anything but a pain-in-the-neck, and—' he drew me close '—my own sweet, wayward, wonderful love.'

I smiled secretly, with my head against his breast, because I knew he meant it, and whatever we had to face in the years ahead, we were together, and would be for the rest of our lives.